YOU DON'T KNOW ME

Lori A. Mathews

Audreana,
You are so strong and wonderful and
your family is so proud of you. You
will be the best at whatever you
choose to do.

Lori A. Mathews

You Don't Know Me
Published through Lulu Enterprises, Inc.

Interior Book Design and Layout by
www.integrativeink.com

ISBN: 978-0-6151-8116-5

To my sons wonderful sons Amaru and Samir; to my family and friends and to God. Without you all I am nothing.

CHAPTER 1

"They're all killers you know," Felipe Montez's voice trembled even as it rose over the pounding rendition of Benny Goodman's, Don't Be That Way. "I'll step out and one of them'll shoot me, blow my head all over this clean white kitchen then laugh about it; they're like that you know—killers. You think I'd lie to you, Jose?"

Jose Ulloa, his co-worker, shook his head as he went about collecting the loaded garbage bags.

"They'd think I was stealing instead of making an honest living here," Felipe straightened to his full five feet two inches and spat in the sink where he was removing dirty utensils from a plastic tub. "How does one of the best nights in the city turn out to be the worst night of my fucking life you tell me," he glared at Jose who passed by him with the bags.

"And you're no better wasting your night off doing a favor for Sam-the-Man; no way I'd done it; not tonight. I wouldn't be here now if Karas wasn't on my ass about taking too many days off. Can I help it my mother's sick and needs me? Man, if I could help it I wouldn't be fifty miles near this place," he jerked his head toward the kitchen door, "and los puercos."

He put a hand on his pot belly the other in the air closed his eyes and rolled his hips to the music coming from the ballroom, "I'd be out in the street listening to Celia and dancing with a caliente little mama who can't wait to get me home and naked."

"You're complaining as usual," Jose said and bumped open the kitchen's screened back door. "And dreaming as usual too," he added as he left.

He walked down the alley thinking that the music was so loud outside it seemed to bounce from wall to wall. He was feeling

1

good tonight and for once didn't mind hauling the trash down to the rat-infested dumpster. No one else had wanted to work this evening's shift and for two good reasons; reason number two, it was a warm and gorgeous night rarely seen in New York in late October, too beautiful to sacrifice to work. Reason number one, the most important, was because of who was attending the gala function in the main ballroom.

Sam the head busboy had begged to switch shifts with him. He'd come with his broad red face plastered with a grin as he asked the favor in bad Spanish and had even sweetened the deal with an extra thirty bucks for what he'd called 'Jose's trouble'.

Though he would never tell Sam this he would've taken his shift anyway and not because the man had practically gotten down on his knees and begged or for the extra cash but because he had no problem helping out a co-worker, even one like Sam-the-Man who called him a 'spic refugee' behind his back.

At the dumpster Jose tossed over the bags; one of them missed the opening and dropped to the other side. He stood deciding if he should just leave it there, but if he didn't retrieve it, rats by the truckload would tear it apart and he'd be left with a bigger mess to clean up.

He walked around back of the dumpster and screamed; a high pitched wail of terror that drowned out the thumping music and everything else except for the sight at his feet. A man and two women lay dead, obscene amounts of black blood pooled around their bodies, this was bad enough, what was worst were the rats; ten, more than ten and all the size of puppies slunk back and forth across the corpses sipping at the blood. As he watched frozen, one of them its whiskers heavy with dripping blackness took a nip out of the soft flesh underneath the dead man's chin, sat up on its haunches and stared at Jose as it chewed.

At this, Jose's nerve broke he ran screaming and throwing terrified glances over his shoulder as if he were being chased by a rat welding a torn off body part. He slammed face first into the backdoor and didn't feel it as he snatched the door open and almost fell into the room.

He collided with Felipe who dropped a tray of dirty glasses the breaking glass sounding like gunshots, "Policia, policia," Jose screamed and ran pass Felipe who stared after him.

Cursing, Felipe bent over the sea of broken glass at his feet. It took him a minute to register what Jose had yelled before he turned toward the fleeing man and yelled back, "Policia? Who needs a fucking cop? Ain't it bad enough the place is crawling with them."

CHAPTER 2

Detective First Grade Owen Story of the New York Police Department out of the 1-9 walked through the sea of police officers resplendent in their medal lined dress uniforms; having the time of their lives as they laughed and talked beside their designer gowned companions under the warm soft light from the luminous chandelier that wrapped the room in an aura of beauty and pleasure.

A sham, all of it and they don't realize it. Only he understood what was actually going on here and he knew because of the pain; it opened his eyes, made him aware and he blamed it for showing him the dark traitorous truth he hadn't wanted to see. He was sick to death of the pain it had been with him since the morning; he could feel it pulsing inside him a live thing in his belly that had taken control reminding him at each step what she'd done. How the hell could she? Why did she do it? He told himself over and over again it was done and he hadn't meant to do it but had reacted without thinking, reacted badly. He needed to get a handle on himself, wrestle for full control or he'd never make it through the next few minutes let alone the next few hours. What he needed to do was get out, leave now before it got worst.

Owen breathed through his mouth to calm down and not take in the reek of over heated scents and colognes and the perfumed bouquets centered on the tables. There was a sickening excess of everything: food, music and drink all back grounded by sharp sparkling glass, starched white table clothes and silverware polished to a frightening blindness.

The department has depleted the coffers for this one occasion he thought, disgust rolling through him at the wasted excess held aloft around him. For just this one night of the much vaulted Policeman's Ball we—the supposed rising stars in the department—pretend in our fractured-fairy-tale world we're surrounded everyday by light and beauty, that we deal with only those who love us, who welcome us with open arms and lay flowers at our feet upon our arrival so that when tomorrow comes and we wake with hangovers and gluttonous bloated bellies to face again the realities of human depravity and the soul-destroying darkness of the human condition we cull for a living, we can at least be thankful the night before we had a great time. Insanity.

Just keep walking he told himself or you're going to fall flat on your face. He felt sweat slide down his back as he tried to keep from bumping into anyone. He kept his arms by his sides and his fists clenched inside his pockets as he tried not to concentrate on his inner turmoil, the rage that moved through him like shifting, world-destroying tectonic plates.

A laughing woman stepped back into him her stiletto heel puncturing his toe. "Sorry," she looked at him, embarrassed. He didn't acknowledge her, kept going. She watched him move off, "Didn't we just see him arguing with that pretty wife of his?"

Her companion, Alan Becker of the Internal Affairs Bureau, watched him too a frown on his face, "Cold as ice that one."

Owen hurried past a decorated lieutenant with gray hair and worry lines on his face who was talking to a deputy inspector from the two-four on the Upper East Side. "I just feel it's time to move on. I've done everything I can over at the three-two and can do better somewhere else, get into private security, more autonomy and not to mention more money," he laughed. "I guess I am mentioning the money."

For a heart beat Owen let the lieutenant's words capture him. He'd heard such talk many times: getting out, going private ever since the World Trade Center was taken down and so many lost. He understood it could be the best way, the easy way, to stay alive.

Maybe it was what he should do; leave the force before he ended up taking one of the two options left to him: a barely-there-pension or a bullet to the brain. God, he massaged his temples, his head hurt, it was too full of the other terrible thing to pile on any more sad facts of his life.

5

He passed by the raised platform at the head of the room and glanced at the top brass sitting at the extravagantly laid out table: Commissioner Simon Chandler, First Deputy Commissioner Timothy Rider, Chief of Department Oscar Willimet and other notable commissioners, inspectors, high ranking officials and high profile guests from around the city and state.

The distinguished group smiled benignly down on the troops as they talked among themselves. Owen's gaze rested briefly on Chandler, the Commissioner was the exception of course he sat stony faced as usual giving nothing away.

Forced to stop at a bottleneck around one of the buffet tables on the verge of collapsing under the weight of a mind-numbing array of food, he waited impatiently for the crowd to loosen up so he could get a much needed drink to deaden his nerves and maybe offset the terrifying weariness that threatened to overwhelm him. He was bone tired; he had put in a long day chasing bad guys and was eager to go home. He and Lorna needed to talk anyway and the sooner they got out of there to do it the better.

At the bar he grabbed a glass of champagne and downed it. Hell, he decided maybe this year would be the last ball he and Lorna would attend. They had made every one since his arrival on the force and he had grown jaded with the experience long ago. Here and now he pronounced in his head, he—they— wouldn't attend next year's ball if invited; cross my heart and hope to die.

Yeah right, he slumped against the bar's frame and stared at the loaded glasses in front of him with their shimmering, beckoning liquid. Who's kidding who here Cinderella? Lorna would have your ass if you turned down that invite. When it had arrived gold embossed on hand-made paper she had been thrilled as always and had shown him the perfect dress she'd be wearing. She had of course been right.

When she'd entered the living room where he'd been sipping his second whiskey of the evening letting the liquor clear his head, hoping it would give him the courage to tell Lorna they should skip the ball and talk instead, he had almost dropped his glass at the sight of her. She had looked gorgeous, perfect. Her reddish-gold hair had luxuriously surrounded her beautiful face. Her jade green eyes had glowed with excitement and her skin with sweet, ripe health. The gold dress she wore had smoothed over a figure from a dream.

He had stared and managed, "You look good." He had reached for other words but couldn't get them out as she glided over to him and put her arms around his neck, her body, her scent, enclosing him.

"Let's make this a wonderful night," she'd said her voice as enthralling as she. "We can do it. Just take it out of time as if it was no one's fault and it never happened. Please Owen, can you?"

He had looked into the face he loved and nodded.

At the hotel he'd let her precede him and had grinned with stupid pride as every eye it seemed to him had turned toward her, their mouths agape at the stunning picture she presented. Then and there he'd decided they would work their problems out just like she'd said. It would be different between them, better, with less heartache, anger and regret and he'd work hard at making them work because he couldn't lose her. Remembering all this he sat the empty glass down with a decisive thump eager to get back to her.

He walked pass a group of detectives intent on ignoring them. But Al Gunderson, a heavy set man with dark eyes and thick features and who'd been his partner for less than a minute when he'd first arrived on the Manhattan force spoke up behind him, "Long Island pig in the city; a big fucking joke."

Owen stopped as he felt heat push through him as their laughter rolled over him. The people who stood around them stopped talking and stared, waiting to see where this would go, but he had heard similar comments before and had done something about it which usually resulted in a bruised part of his body and trouble for himself. Tonight he didn't need to get into it, cause a ruckus and ruin his dress uniform and anyway he had more important things on his mind than dealing with a jealous big mouth. He didn't turn around instead he eased his shoulders down, relaxed the muscles in his body and walked on.

"Asshole," Gunderson called; his buddies laughter following him.

Okay, Owen breathed it out. So he wasn't liked by some of his colleagues that was their problem and always had been. He'd come over from Long Island six years earlier and not from another planet like those jerks believed but a detective third-grade and had quickly done well for himself.

Some of the others at the 1-9 who were at the same grade as he was but didn't work twice as hard as he did, who hadn't gotten a couple of good collars under their belts, who hadn't answered when opportunity had come knocking hadn't made detective first grade as he had with only one year in and because of that he wasn't asked to hang-out after work and wasn't invited to barbecues at the homes of the other cops, he'd learned to live with it and sometimes like now not give a rat's ass.

Taking his seat at the table he looked at his partner Stephen "Cush" Cushman who asked, "What took you so long?" Cush was a big-boned man with rough dry features, a few years older than Owen with amused grey eyes and thick black hair untouched by grey he considered his best feature.

"Had to get some air."

"You know what your horoscope said today?"

"Don't care," Owen answered as Cush's wife Connie, a pretty brown eyed blond said at the same time, "Not now, honey."

"All right," Cush smoothed a hand through his lush head of hair, "don't say I didn't warn you. The signs never lie."

Owen let a smile slip onto his lips as he realized he'd just walked up in time to hear fellow detective Mackey Walsh finish one of his infamous stories. He looked at the empty chair next to him then leaned over to Connie, "Have you seen, Lorna?"

"She didn't say, but I think she went to the ladies room," Connie laughed. "Isn't Mackey hilarious?"

Walsh stood in front of his eager audience, a whiskey glass in his hand his voice loud over the band's version of 'Moon River',"…so the guy's down on his knees in front of me in the knave," he gestured behind him with a thumb, "right in St. Katherine's around the corner."

His grin broadened, "As sexy as that sounds it wasn't. On the floor beside him is the Virgin Mary he'd ripped down off the church's wall. She's maybe two hundred pounds, six feet tall and was too heavy for the jerk to get out the front door before we got there."

"He's crying, begging and pleading," Walsh finished his drink and sat down the glass before he smacked his hands together in prayer, " 'God I repent my sins and if you get me out of this one

I promise the next job I do will be for the Lord and the Holy Mother'. I look down at this prick and ask him, 'Who'd you think I am the goddamn Pope?' He looks up at me wide-eyed and says, 'I know the Pope, who's the Goddamn Pope?'"

Laughter erupted around the table and it took a few minutes for the commotion at the ballroom's entrance to catch everyone's attention. Mackey laughed, "What's up over there; a cop have too much to drink? Since when?"

Some laughed though their eyes didn't stray from the front of the room. Most of the guests now stared that way, even the band had stopped playing the musicians watching. Owen stood like the others drawn to the disturbance.

A man, his voice high as he babbled in hysterical Spanish shot past two sergeants who stood near the doorway and moved up to a table where two women sat. Alarmed, the women stumbled out of their chairs as one of the two sergeants a head taller and sixty pounds heavier than the man grabbed him by the shoulder and shoved him toward the door.

The smaller man knocked off balance collided with a table knocking it over and sending everything on it crashing to the floor, the sound loud, harsh bouncing off the walls as the people at the surrounding tables jumped up and ran toward the back, gasps and squawks of dismay moving through the room.

The man staggered to his feet, his voice high on a plaintive sob, his words gibberish as tears coursed down his face. He stared back at the silent fear-filled faces staring at him.

Commanding Officer's Ronald McGinty from the five-two in the Bronx and Captain Arthur Ramsey of the one-nine hurried over and joined the tableau. Ramsey, a large vigorous man in his early fifties with ruddy features and wide salt and pepper sideburns spoke to the man in rapid Spanish trying to break in on the his tear-filled words and his calls to God.

Enthralled by the developing situation in front of them most of the guests had drifted forward to close in around the players drawn by the horror and fear in the man's voice and the growing realization something terrible had happened.

"Goddammit, no," Ramsey shouted his outburst causing an abrupt silence to fall over the crowd. He let go of the man and bolted out of the room followed by the sergeants.

The man sagged to the floor at McGinty's feet as the captain pulled a cell phone from his pocket and spoke urgently into it.

"The party's over," Mackey said.

No one laughed this time they were too busy asking each other if any one knew what was going on. The questioning voices grew more urgent as sirens were heard coming toward the hotel. Some of the guests hurried to the huge floor to ceiling windows and threw back the curtains; others ran out of the room their faces tight in uncertain panic.

"It's a string of cruisers and ambulances," someone shouted.

Owen watched the panic seize the crowd as he felt a stab of undefined fear shoot threw him causing hot tingles to stab his fingers and toes and his heart to gallop. He looked at Connie, "Where did you say Lorna had gone?"

"I thought the ladies room; she—"

Owen didn't hear the rest he ran.

CHAPTER 3

In the hall Owen barreled into Ramsey who was the color of new snow as he grabbed the detective tight by his right arm. Behind him their faces stretched sick stood the sergeants.

Panic flared in Owen's eyes as he grabbed at Ramsey's hand and dug his fingers into the soft flesh on the side of his palm making the captain wince in pain, "What the hell are you doing? Let me go, Captain."

Ramsey held on, "Owen listen, don't—"

"Don't what goddammit?" Owen tore away from him on a run.

"For god sakes go after him," Ramsey shouted at the men who took off. He put the side of his hand into his mouth and sucked at the blood that oozed from the gouges and turned toward the people who stood at the ballroom doors staring back at him in dawning horror.

There was a crowd outside the kitchen entrance, "Excuse me, please move," Owen pushed threw then pushed against the door that would not move. He pushed harder.

"Hey," said a voice from the other side before the door was flung open and a young patrolman stood in his way. "You can't come in here," he said as Owen pushed past him. The cop shut the door on the curious faces and glared at Owen, "Get out of here. No one can come in."

Owen stopped in the center of the room and faced the back door. Ribbons of emergency lights sliced the darkness and bounced off the alley walls. He looked around the spotless kitchen at its unmarred whiteness, the clean brilliance of the stainless steel. He smelled the perfumed soaps and the clean water, breathed in deep the clean harmlessness of the room as his eyes strayed back to the alley his stomach tumbling with terror at the thought of going out there in that cold rank darkness though he couldn't hear or see any reason for this fear, he knew once he stepped through the door to the outside he'd be stepping into the end.

"I can't allow you out there," the cop moved in front of him. "I got orders to keep—"

"Step back," Owen stared at him, "Or I'll knock you on your ass."

Recognizing the barely-holding-on strain reflected in Owen's eyes, the cop stepped back. Owen went out the door as the sergeants bullied their way inside the room. They caught him as he rushed down the alley. One of them yanked at his shoulder and without looking his way, Owen elbowed him hard in the stomach and kept moving as the man doubled over.

"He's lost it," the other sergeant said going to his companion's aid.

Owen reached a group of men, detectives Mel Slater and Harry Scarborough from his precinct and two uniformed officers who stood encircling large doll-like objects lying haphazardly on the ground.

"It makes no damn sense," Scarborough muttered his voiced filled with gruesome amazement. "How the hell could this happen? Here? Tonight, goddammit."

An unlighted cigarette dangled from Scarborough's fingertips and this sight alone caused Owen's unnamed fear to rise into his throat and choke him; he'd never seen Harry without a fired up Pall Mall hanging from his lip. He broke through the group and stood frozen, his hands out as if warding off an attack and as the horrified group looked on he collapsed to the ground on his knees, threw his head back and howled, wailed to the sky in inconsolable pain and heartbreak.

"Oh, Jeezus" Scarborough moaned as a body pushed past him.

Ramsey clamped a hand on Owen's shoulder and shook him, "My God, Owen stop. Don't do this now."

Owen barely heard him as he stared at the impossible. He scrambled forward and took into his arms the lifeless body of his wife, Lorna. This can't be real, can't be happening his mind yelled at him in tormented disbelief as he began to rock her. He looked at her lovely face into her green eyes that stared blankly back at him as he smoothed a hand over soft hair that still glowed in the flash of emergency lights.

His eyes strayed over the rest of her but retreated at the sight of the hole in her stomach surrounded by black blood. If I don't focus on that open wound, he rocked her faster, if I don't focus on it or the blood it will be as if she has just fallen down and is unconscious or even asleep like Sleeping Beauty. His lips touched hers they were so cold and stiff it iced his heart.

His eyes swept over the two other people and took the man in first, what he saw stood up the hairs on his head. The man was in dressed blues; a cop. He lay on his side; a ragged black hole at his temple, the rest of his face was dotted with red flaps of torn flesh. Owen looked at the other victim recognizing her. She was face up, her expensive red dress darkened in front by a large black patch. Her eyes were open and staring.

Ramsey bent down into Owen's face; his own hard with sympathy and determination as he put steel into his voice, "There's nothing you can do for her; she's dead. This is a crime scene now." He pointed toward the mouth of the alley, "There are a hundred people ready to take care of her: forensics, crime scene, ballistics, you name it; all standing down there waiting to do their job. Let's go inside and leave them to it."

"It," Owen stared up at him his voice tight with grief, "is my wife; Lorna; my wife." He pulled her body deeper into his own, "I'm not leaving her."

Ramsey stood and looked down at him before he nodded at the two patrolmen. They advanced on Owen and jerked him to his feet. Their actions forced her body from his arms.

"Lorna," he lunged for her but she plopped to the ground like a bag of wet rags and at this a high keening sound of rage came out of Owen's throat and he went wild.

With the strength of the insane he bucked out of their grasp and rounded on the bigger officer slamming a fist into the side of the man's head. The officer's hat flew off as he screamed and clutched the side of his face, his legs pumping up and down in his pain as he left the remaining officer to Owen who took the man in a headlock.

Ramsey, watching the disaster along with the stunned detectives and sergeants looked at them in disgust, "Do I have to do everything myself?" He stepped forward, pulled Owen off the cop and punched him in the face. "Ah shit," he clutched his throbbing hand as Owen crashed backwards into the officers who roughly caught him. He then nodded at the open-mouthed patrolmen, "Now, you think you can handle him? Take him inside." Sorrow and pity touched his voice, "The poor bastard."

The officers, the bigger one's face swelling on one side carried Owen toward the hotel as all eyes turned back to the horrific scene at their feet. Ramsey abruptly waved a hand and an army of people moved forward to begin the gruesome, arduous task of dissecting a triple murder scene.

CHAPTER 4

Someone shook him and without opening his eyes Owen said, "Okay, I'm all right." He heightened his voice as he became aware of the sounds of anger and protest sailing around him. He opened his eyes and stared up at a worried Cush; Connie stood beside him her face wet with tears.

He touched his throbbing jaw and grimaced at the sting; his boss had a hell of a hook. He closed his eyes again and when he opened them they were filled with bone crushing sorrow, "Oh jezzus, Lorna. What about Pop? How am I going to tell him?"

"I'm so sorry, Owen" Connie touched his face as tears slid down her own. Her voice quivered, "Why would someone do this?"

Owen didn't answer, instead he wiped at the smears of blood on the front of his dress blues. It's her blood. He held out his smeared fingers, "She's dead, Cush." He thought if he said it out loud it would finally sink into his mind instead of recoil from it, "Lorna's been murdered. And there were others too."

"I know," Cush nodded, "We all want to know how three people are murdered practically in front of a room full of cops; it makes no damn sense. But we're on lockdown, Owen; they're keeping us prisoners in here." He thumbed over his shoulder, "Can you believe this shit?"

Across the room Adrian Reynolds and Ralph Kopalski, commanding officers of Midtown North South stood in front of the closed ballroom doors and in front of them stood a mob of angry shouting cops and their guests. Owen looked around and saw others commanders standing in front of the other exits letting no one in or out.

"Shut up," Reynolds, a solidly built man the color of a road tire raised an authoritative voice over the others, "There's nothing you can do; it's a crime scene."

"But a cops been shot," a female officer yelled, frustration stung along her words.

"True, but we've got people working it already and you won't help anything by messing around out there. We're trying to keep this thing under control so the media won't go crazy until absolutely necessary. So back off people; now. Don't make this harder than it already is."

The crowd grumbled and backed off a few steps from the doors though their agitation and outrage filled the room like the mad buzz of enraged wasps seeking victims.

Kopalsi, a short man with a bald head said, "Have another drink for chrissakes."

Owen looked at Cush with desperate eyes, "Lorna's out there and so is the person who killed her. I have to get out of here."

"They're not going to just open the door for you or anyone else."

"I have to get out of here now," Owen's gaze swept from the barred doors and halted on the commissioner who still sat on the dais surrounded now by twice as many of his minions all urgently talking at him, "One of the other victims was Chandler's wife. I'll talk to him and he'll get me out."

As Owen started away from the couple Cush stepped in front of him, "Wait, what are you gonna say? I mean why do it now?"

Owen grabbed Cush's shirt front as Connie burst into tears, "Because he's out there, this minute," rage rippled across his words, "walking around, getting away with killing her and he has to be stopped."

"I know but—" Cush broke off his attention caught by the new action taking place in the center of the room. He pushed Owen off him and took Connie into his arms, "What's this shit now?"

First Deputy Timothy Rider, Chandler's second in command stood in the center of the room waiting to be noticed. He was thin and gangly with a receding hairline over brown darkly ringed eyes that haunted a bony face that never seemed touched by the sun even in the height of summer.

The street cops called him The Undertaker, he reminded Owen of Dracula. He was Chandler's right hand man and guard dog rolled into one. It was rumored he'd been with the Commish a long time and would cut the throat of anyone in their way, literally and figuratively given the nod by his boss.

"Ladies and gentlemen may I have your attention please," his voice was patient and as he waited for quiet, his eyes swept back and forth around the room. "You know we've had a terrible tragedy here tonight and at the moment we have more questions than answers…"

Owen's gaze flickered off Rider as a man walked up to Cush and whispered in his ear. He recognized him as a lieutenant from the Homicide Bureau. The man's eyes ran over Owen's uniform coat, over the blood dried there like dark shellac. He whispered into Cush's ear before he hurried off.

"They're asking some of us to start interviewing the guests in case one of them saw something," Cush said.

"Of course somebody saw something," searing helplessness ran through Owen like a tidal wave at the immediate and devastating fact that at this moment no one was being hauled away for his wife's death and he was helpless to do anything about it. "Look, there must be two hundred people in this room and God knows how many out in the street tonight making it damn near impossible that someone didn't see the person who murdered three people."

"There're a hundred guys canvassing the area already; we—"

"Sh," Connie cut in, "Rider's saying something important."

"…Please do not try to leave the ballroom," Rider's voice rose over the angry insistent shouts of the crowd.

"You can't keep us here all night," someone yelled.

"We want out," a voice rang from the back of the room.

Glass broke; bodies were shoved around as a woman sobbed loudly among the frantic shouts escalating the tension that made the place, once serene and beautiful with happy people now a stifling airless gathering on the edge of total chaos.

Rider's lips closed in a colorless slash of annoyance as the crowd, belligerent, pushing for action, pushed around him. He raised his hands to keep them back, "Hold it. You all can leave soon I promise. Right now you need to talk to the detectives approaching you with their questions and as soon as they're done you can—" cries of protest rose in the air cutting him off. "Be quiet," the words were terse, icy. "All I'm saying is that as soon as you're interviewed you can go home; we'll even provide an escort for those of you concerned about your safety."

Owen couldn't listen anymore he paced trying to hold back from charging the commander's at the door. His impatient gaze was again drawn to Chandler who still sat surrounded by his people. The guy hadn't moved; Owen couldn't believe it.

Here he was barely able to breathe let alone stand because Lorna was out there alone lying on the cold ground with a bullet hole through her and Chandler's wife lay there too, yet the man hadn't gone to see after her, to confirm she was gone. Was he just too broken up? Too grief stricken to believe it or to look at what had been done to her? Or was he really made of stone as everyone believed?

He watched Eddie Blume, one of the detectives from Chandler's personal security team walk over and whisper to him seconds before Chandler grabbed him by the lapels and threw him backwards. Eddie hit a chair that skidded across the floor and tumbled off the dais. The people surrounding them stared as Chandler sat back down, his head dropping into his hands.

So the old Commish did have blood flowing through his veins, angry-as-hell-blood from the look of it Owen thought. What had Eddie whispered to him? Something about his wife of course. The incident replayed in Owen's mind even as his attention was forced back to the now exasperated Undertaker who was being bombarded with anger filled words from the belligerent crowd.

"No, no, you're not prisoners here," Rider shook his head. Oscar Willimet the Chief of Department, his face beaded with nervous sweat stood beside him.

"Hey," a big red-faced cop, his jacket off, his sleeves rolled up shouted at Rider. "I can protect my wife. What I want to know is, has the bastard been caught yet?"

"Yeah, has an arrest been made or what? We can't get any news while we're locked in here," said a lieutenant his fists clenched at his sides.

"Yeah," the red-faced cop added, "And if he's still out there why the hell are we still in here with our thumbs up our asses instead of out on the street doing something? Any damn thing. Let us out of here for chrissakes."

"They killed one of us," someone bellowed.

Furious yells of agreement went around the room as the crowd advanced on Rider to surge pass him and force their way out.

On the dais Chandler stood, pushed past his people and jumped to the floor. Everyone froze, went silent as he strolled to the middle of the room; the Undertaker sliding back as his boss took center stage.

"I don't think the killer's still in the vicinity," Chandler stated matter-of-fact; his voice composed and reasonable lessening some of the thick awful tension filling every corner."

"He'd be crazy to stick around don't you think? This place has been cordoned off for three miles in all directions; Park Avenue looks like a used car lot; no one's getting in or out without being searched and questioned. You know I mean what I say." He paused weighing his next words against the vigilante mood in the room, "Yes, it's true my wife has been murdered, is lying out there being stared at, photographed and handled," he said unflinching.

"And I can't make myself go out there and watch what's being done to her, to stare at her lifeless body knowing she's been taken from me so tragically and this fact infuriates me; so there's no one—I mean no one—in this room, in this world wants that bastard strapped down to the needle more than I do but it won't happen until he's caught and that can't be done without your cooperation so let the detectives do their job; we have a killer to catch."

He waited in the silence then nodded once to the crowd before walking back and joining his people.

Beside Owen Connie shook her head, "The poor man. He has no choice but to put on a brave face for us."

'Brave face', Owen thought, not buying it for a second; it felt wrong. He'd heard a trace of false grief in the Commissioner's voice though he couldn't imagine why; the man's wife had just been murdered. But he knew he hadn't heard what everyone else had and felt confused and agitated to the breaking point because of it.

19

What was really happening out there in the pursuit of the animal who had murdered Lorna? How could anyone know what was going on? No one could get out to investigate. Well, he was going to get some answers and from the man himself or he would break down the door and get out there to find out.

He started pass the couple and Cush again cut in front of him, Owen's face darkened, "I'm going to talk to him."

"Let me see what I can get; they want me over there anyway."

"I'm a big boy; I can do this on my own."

Cush gestured in Chandler's direction as Owen moved off, "Look how they gott'em roped off; you won't get within ten feet of the guy."

"Watch me."

Focusing only on his destination Owen didn't stop until he reached the steps leading up to the dais and Eddie Blume stepped in his way.

Eddie held up his hands, "Whoa hot shot, you can't see him he's busy."

"I understand but I need to talk to him."

"You're hearing must be off," Blume jabbed him hard in the chest with a thick forefinger, "I said he's busy."

He's getting back some of what the Commish dished out Owen suspected as his hand shot out before he could hold back and took hold of Blume's neck tie. The man had picked the wrong day to mess with him, he was struggling to keep a grip on his sanity as it was but this jerk had to come along to provide the spark that tipped him over the edge. Wrenching apart the two ends of Blume's tie, Owen sent the knot punching into the man's throat, Eddie gagged as his face gushed red then purple; his hands scrambled at Owen who swung him around and aside before releasing him to move up the stairs.

"Commissioner Chandler," Owen stopped a few feet away. "I'm Owen Story. My wife is out there with yours."

Chandler's people turned almost as one and looked at him before shuffling aside to present Chandler. The Commish looked to him like the actor Christopher Walken, thin, loose-limbed, his skin pale, his hair going not gray but a controlled silver. His most striking and frightening feature was his eyes which were a predatory ice blue and as humorless as those of a praying mantis. He looked tired, his skin's paleness more pronounced, his mouth flat with tension though his gaze was as vibrant and intrusive as ever as he gave Owen a cool going over.

"You're out of the one-nine right? Homicide for five—no—six years; over from Long Island." A tight, brief smile fainted across his lips then was gone as his unrevealing gaze bored into Owen's, "One of these guys knew your stats. I'm sorry for you detective; that shouldn't have happened to your lovely wife."

"We have to get the son-of-a-bitch," Owen's voice wavered with anguish he couldn't hold down. Chandler didn't reply. "What's happening with—?"

Rider stepped between them, a cell phone held out to his boss, "The DA's on his way. Mayor Jackson is on the line."

Chandler took the phone and spoke into it as Blume and another man, topped the stairs and moved toward Owen. Cush as if on cue bounded up the opposite set of stairs and was at his partner's side a couple of steps ahead of the men.

"Can't you see he's grief stricken? Out of his head?" Cush pulled Owen down to the main floor and into a shadowed alcove beside an emergency exit door manned by Kopalski who looked at them—at Owen—then away.

"Leave it alone," Cush's voice was urgent. "Please, Owen. There's something up, all these rumors are flying around, crazy stories I'm trying to get to the bottom of—"

"You think I don't know something's wrong? My wife's dead and they're acting like its noth—"

"You're going to have to leave it for now."

Owen shook his head, he wasn't hearing him, didn't want to, he wanted only to fight: against Cush, against the people who wouldn't let him out into the action and especially against this nightmare he was living. "I can't. You didn't see what that bullet did to her, Cush. She's gone, I don't know why and until I do I'll never let it go." He turned away leaving his partner to stare after him with a combination of fear and pity in his eyes.

Owen walked up to the commander, "I need to leave."

"No ones going anywhere yet," Kopalski said his features heavy with wariness.

"I need to relieve myself then."

"Your wife—"

"Can I go or not? Or is right here good?"

Kopalski's features tightened as he pointed down the wall, "Back through there next to the storage room."

Owen opened the door and the rank odor that wafted out told him he was in the right place. A toilet and sink were in the corner to his left to his right was a generous sized window someone had opened in an effort to try and clear the room with fresh air.

He shut the door and moved to the window that looked out onto a narrow dark walkway between the hotel and the building next door. Climbing up on the sill he perched a moment listening before he hopped to the ground.

CHAPTER 5

The walkway was no wider than the bathroom. He let his right hand trail the wall for reference as he walked toward the light up ahead. As the light got more distinct he heard what he at first thought was…a party? No, it couldn't be. He hurried forward, stepped out onto the street and stared; it was as if the entire frantic world had converged on this narrow section of Fifth Avenue.

Fire trucks, ambulances and countless police vehicles of the marked and unmarked variety were lined haphazard in front of the hotel and along the street for at least half a block. Beyond all those vehicles sat R.V. styled news vans their antennas spinning on their tops.

Spectators were everywhere, walking, standing, talking and laughing as they ignored the numerous yelling street cops who tried to keep order with the use of endless numbers of blue sawhorses and gray portable fences placed around the area to keep the gawkers at bay. The street looked as if was hosting a summer festival instead of the scene of a triple murder.

Owen walked through the throng sidestepping a group of bike messengers carrying on a raucous conversation about rock bands and slowed as his eyes caught on a small group of uniforms standing beneath a book store's lighted canopy a few feet down from the hotel's entrance. They huddled around one of their own as he sat on the curb with his face in his hands; Owen could see his body shake as he wept. One of the other patrolmen gripped his shoulder his own face filled with sorrow. My God he thought feeling his own pain add another layer in his chest, everyone's been touched by what's happened here tonight; by death; Lorna's death.

He turned away spotting three parked ambulances. He walked up beside the driver of the first. The man, bald and of medium height with strongly built arms and shoulders leaned against the driver's door as he yelled on his radio mike.

"There's no way I can get Uptown; the streets blocked off. What can I do huh? What?"

"You have the bodies?"

The driver glanced at him but didn't answer; kept on yelling, "Get Harriet or Walosky, I don—" Owen snatched the mike out of his hand. "What—?" the man squawked as Owen tossed it inside the cab.

"Have they been taken away yet?" Owen asked, his voice level, his eyes on the driver.

The man opened his mouth to curse Owen and his parentage but snapped it closed as he took a good look at him, at the dark dried blood smeared down his chest and at the fierce look of rage and scorching anguish in his reddened eyes. The man took an involuntary step backwards. He'd seen that look usually before the guy was heavily sedated and put into a straight jacket; yet he'd never seen it so intense, so ready to escape and pulverize who ever was in the way; and to make matters worse this man was a cop; he killed people.

"I got nobody," the driver stammered and lurched back to open the rear doors. Owen peered in at its emptiness, "Somebody else gott'em."

"You're right," Owen agreed and moved off as the man breathed again with relief.

Owen stopped at the next ambulance and found it unattended and empty inside. If anybody else dies in this city tonight, he thought with black humor they'd have a long wait for that one-way ride to the freezer.

He moved to the last ambulance and opened one of the rear doors, inside atop two stretchers lay dark green body bags, filled. He looked at them for a long time before he stepped up into the ambulance. He slid down the zipper of the bag to his right, pulled back the tough folds and stared into the handsome face of the young cop marred by the patches of ripped skin and the deep black bullet hole on the side of his head.

He zipped closed the bag before he moved to the other where he pulled down the zipper, folded back the plastic and felt his mind loosen from its anchors. He reached out a hand and ran his fingers over Lorna's closed eyes and pale cheeks.

"Wait honey," he pulled the rear doors closed and locked them before returning to her side. From inside the bag he gently pulled out her left hand and let his thumb rest on her diamond wedding band. He put her cold fingers to his lips and closed his eyes.

"I'm sorry, Lorna; so sorry," he whispered and began to cry as if he'd never stop because he knew as a wave of despair rolled through him, his life had changed forever and from this moment forward his heart would be untangled and adrift.

CHAPTER 6

The guy behind the counter of the Dunkin Donuts on 42nd watched the man who stood across the street hunched against the pelting icy rain as he waited for a break in traffic so he could cross. The man stepped back where pots of fragrant coffee brewed and prepared a cup. He was topping it off when the buzzer sounded.

Owen moved up to the counter as the cup was pushed forward. He glanced out the window at the pounding rain seeming unmindful of the cold and his wet clothes, "It's not forgiving out there is it?" He looked at the counter man, "In here either it's barely warm."

"The heat isn't working right; the repairman's coming to fix it tomorrow. The coffee's fresh and hot."

Owen picked up the cup and sipped gratefully. He knew he looked in need of a gallon of the stuff. He was exhausted, couldn't sleep, no big surprise there; he was burying his wife tomorrow afternoon. Instead of lying in bed praying for the oblivion of sleep he knew wouldn't come, he'd gotten into his car and driven around, down familiar and unfamiliar streets, steering the car by rote until he'd ended up here to wait.

"How're you tonight, Joe?" he placed a dollar and change near the register.

Joseph Dunbar, round all over, his skin the color of melted caramel, his eyes hazel and steady, pushed the money back as he took in Owen's blood shot eyes and wasted pallor knowing it was the result of bitter grief and fatigue, he'd seen that look often enough in his own life.

"I'm doing better than you," he watched as Owen tried a smile that came off badly.

"Have they been in yet?"

"It's too early for'em."

Owen shivered. From underneath the counter Joseph pulled out a bottle of Jim Beam and generously aided the coffee. Owen started to shake his head then picked up the cup and downed half the cooling liquid; fire blossomed in his belly and put color in his face.

"You needed something from Kentucky not Columbia."

A companionable silence fell between them as he stared out the window at a homeless man who stared back, his face pressed tight against the glass, his eyes huge and frightened as if he'd seen the devil. The rain poured heavy and impenetrable, people barreled by tight into them selves defending their bodies from the deluge. He emptied the rest of the liquid into his mouth, his eyes closed as the welcome numbness spread through his limbs.

He looked at Joseph, "How's your mother?"

"Good, still visiting Gerald once a month."

Owen nodded. He knew not only Joseph's mother, Anna, but his older sisters Kim and Venessa as well. He'd gotten to know Joseph's older brother too, though at the end of his life; Gerald, whose grave Rose visited once a month out at Woodlawn.

Gerald had been the victim of a forty-five round to his head as he sat in his brand new BMW M3 waiting for the light to change; his brains had literally been blown out through the back of his skull. His two passengers had also been shot though survived the ordeal. From the few witnesses who would talk the perpetrator, a young black man who looked a junior high schooler, after unloading his rounds had nonchalantly crossed the street to the bus stop, had waited for the next bus and boarded it going on his merry way; that had been three years ago and the boy had never been caught.

The crime had occurred near the George Washington Bridge bus station between 178th and 179th in the area served by the 3-4. At the time, like the rest of New York, the crime rate had fallen significantly in Manhattan so much so that New York City was voted one of the safest in the nation and the powers on top had wanted to keep it that way; so Gerald's murder and the shooting of his passengers had become the department's top priority.

He had been assigned to help work out the case in conjunction with the two primary investigators and he had done so diligently, obsessively especially after the primaries let the case sour after they discovered Gerald had been dealing drugs for a couple of months along side his best friend, one of the neighborhood's convicted dealers.

The primaries had immediately dismissed any other facts regarding Gerald's life as the truth became known, facts they assumed hadn't been important to a dead kid gone bad; that Gerald had been a high school football star or that he'd had a smile that instantly made you a friend or the fact he'd been a member of his church youth choir and a mentor at the Boys Club; he'd let those facts matter to him; taken them to heart.

He'd sat with the family during the investigation and after, explaining—through their tears, curses and recriminations—why the case had been regulated to the cold case file and Gerald's memory battered to hell and back. He had tasted their pain, felt it settle in his belly and couldn't do much about it except watch over them, especially Joseph, a quiet young man he knew had an uneasy manhood to survive and whose choices were few and could mean life or death.

He had talked quietly but insistently and tried to explain to Joseph best he could that the streets—a world he saw for himself go mad from day-to-day—was not just careless and unforgiving but would leave his family forever broken and bleeding while it ate him alive as it his brother.

He'd figured his clumsy useless attempts to keep Joseph safe hadn't worked until Joseph had called on him. Joseph had told him he was looking for a job and needed a reference; he had gladly given it. Joseph had started at the doughnut shop with the owner, Mr. Tuttlemen during the day; that was two years ago. Joseph now ran the shop from midnight until eight, five days a week and was looking forward to opening his own in six months.

Owen tapped his empty cup against the counter, edgy, time was not passing fast enough, "I want to thank you and your family for the flowers and the card."

"I felt bad I never got to meet your girl."

Owen looked around at the empty coffee cups and donut wrappings tossed on the floor Joseph hadn't yet swept up, at the scarred orange wooden booths and at the ragged homeless man whose face was still pressed up against the glass his lips moving as he talked either to himself or the doughnut display. He smiled wanly, "She wasn't much of a coffee drinker."

His hazel eyes bright with concerned interest Joseph asked, "What was she like? I mean she was fine I saw that for myself from the newspaper picture but that don't mean nothing in the end. You don't have to tell me the too private just what about her kept the sparks flying."

Owen stared into his cup. He knew what Joseph was asking and now just realized how many "sparks" had made Lorna like no one he had ever known, "Maybe she was like other wives I don't know; but she wasn't like any one else." He looked at Joseph but his thoughts were far away, "There were times when she looked at me that certain way she had and everything I felt, I believed, clicked right into place and I knew I was exactly where I needed to be in the world. In the beginning, we were on the same wavelength with everything you know? If I had a half-formed question playing in my mind she already had the answer; sometimes it was strange but always special," his voice played with amazement, "and to have such a connection to another person was worth getting up for."

"And she liked to walk," Owen grinned, "man, could she move; these long eat-up-the-world strides you had to run to keep up with her. She hated being alone said it was because she was an only child not many friends growing up; my life mirrored hers in that way too, in many ways so that when we came together it was magic; at least to me anyway." His head dropped, his eyes hidden. Moving away Joseph reappeared with another cup of coffee he added more Jim Beam to.

"You believe in God?"

Owen looked at him, cautious, "Yeah, sure."

"Then find comfort in this fact," Joseph tapped his large right bicep, "He forgives us sinners; our pasts so that whatever we've done it's as if it never happened and all is clean and new. Think about it."

Owen looked at Joseph's arm where tooled in exquisite vibrant detail a tattoo of Jesus Christ, his head crowned with green thorns; his eyes wide and vivid with raw beatific agony as startling red blood coursed down his hands and feet which were nailed onto the cross on Joseph's solid upraised skin.

29

"I'll think about it," Owen took up his coffee. "Thanks for the refill. They should be here soon." He moved to one of the tables by the window and stared out onto the street. It was maybe that easy for Jeezus to forgive past transgressions because of his divineness, but mortal that he was he couldn't forgive anything or anyone especially not himself for what had happened to her.

As he sipped his laced coffee what he felt warring inside was a jumble of terrifying emotions that pushed him to the edge of a breakdown. His first tormentor, guilt, had a stranglehold on him so tight it was a fiery pain pulsing through his body that made his hands shake as he sat down the cup. He should've been there to protect her. He should've insisted they not go to the ball especially after the terrible thing that had played out between them that morning. He should have immediately gone to look for her when he found her gone. So many should haves, could haves; the wanting to change a past he damn well couldn't was a living hell inside him.

And to make sure there would be no let up soon—if ever— from his growing list of torturers, hot on the tail of shark-toothed-guilt was aching loneliness. He was haunted not only by the persistence of being physically alone but the crushing weight of being emotionally alone; the one true connection he'd made to another had been cut so abruptly, brutally he felt himself cut and bleeding and was positive he'd never get over it. The fact he'd spent so little time with her in the past year yet missed her so much now was the bitterest of cosmic jokes.

Guilt and loneliness, those two bastard tormentors were bad enough, worse was the stabbing, hounding need for revenge. Here he sat staring out; people occasionally glanced at him as they walked by. They saw a guy maybe just off work enjoying a cup of coffee but like most everyone else, he was presenting his normal-I-wouldn't-hurt-you-mask to the outside world.

The real scary action was going on inside him; the king, revenge was a huge and nasty beast that ran through him like a madman overseeing an insane asylum. He would thoroughly enjoy killing the man who had murdered Lorna; dreamed of it. His minds eye conjured up a drooling, wild-eyed lunatic he would rip apart and slay in defense of her; he'd vowed over her bloody body to do nothing less. The buzzer on the door sounded and his head snapped around toward the door.

The two men he'd been waiting for had finally shown. He knew they had deals going on in every borough and spent their nights traveling, seeing to their various customers.

They were emissaries for a highly evolved company called TruSuitors that sold illegally confiscated guns and military weaponry up and down the East Coast to the highest bidder. The police and the Feds were well aware of their activities but hadn't been able to catch them at it, hadn't tried hard enough in his opinion.

These two had long records mostly for petty crimes, misdemeanors, no major infractions; they were low-level operators in a multi-layered and complicated scheme of money-for-guns so their status was overlooked and tolerated in the hope of some day grabbing the bigger fish.

Owen no longer assumed it would happen; they were criminals he would love to get something on to send them to prison because the way he was feeling now they were a link on the short chain that led from them to the gun and the man who'd used that gun to kill his wife. Whether it was true or not he didn't give a shit; he had no reason to feel generous lately.

"Hi ya, Officer," Antonio Esposito said as he slid into the seat across from him. He was over six feet tall and slim with large black eyes set off by a halo of blue-black hair. He wore his usual white T-shirt, jeans and leather, he looked like a character out of Brando's the "Wild Ones"; the only difference was that Antonio wore bright red lipstick on his generous lips and dangly chandelier earrings.

His companion Dougie Reese was a different story. He was short and stout, a toad in a black Nike jogging suit. He had a suntanned face and the heavy lidded eyes of a sun lizard lying on a rock, all combined to give him an appearance of permanent shadiness. Dougie glanced at Owen from underneath his eyelids before he turned his head and blew his nose onto the floor.

"Hey, man," Joseph shouted.

"Clean it up for me, Ant," Dougie grinned with small discolored teeth. Owen stared at him in disgust as Antonio grabbed up a hand full of napkins and cleaned up the mess. Dougie sat down across from Owen and stared out the window.

Antonio slid in beside Dougie and sipped at his drink his lipstick staining the straw, "I just love icy drinks all year round;

that rush of cold through my blood," he quivered, "makes me shiver all the way to my toes." He looked at Owen, his gaze liquid and serious, "We heard about your missus. Sor-ry," he sing-sang.

"Anybody on the streets saw what happened? Who did it?"

"A lot of people are saying they saw the three get chopped, but it's cool to say that right now," Antonio glanced at Dougie who continued to stare out the window ignoring them. "But there was this one dude said he was there and he didn't change his story either and was he scared out of his bikini briefs. He's gone now. Disappeared. Bye-d-bye."

"You know him?"

Antonio shook his head causing his earrings to swing like pendulums, "A new face. Probably just out of Rikers or from Upstate."

"The words out a cop did it," Dougie grated with such menace it made them jump. He stared at Owen his eyes wide and Owen saw for the first time they were green and as cloudy as swamp bile, "The crime; but won't do the time. The way I figure it—you," he stabbed a clawed finger at Owen, "should take a look in the mirror."

It took a few seconds for the words to make any sense and when they did Owen launched himself across the table toward Dougie grabbing him by the front of his shirt and dragging him forward sending their benches bouncing backwards and their cups flying. Antonio screamed, his hands flying to his mouth like a scream actress in a B horror flick.

Dougie clutched at Owen's arms but Owen held him tight, face-in-face, the man's body lying across the rickety Formica table like a jogging-suited-sacrifice, "You don't know what you're talking about you piece of shit," his voice shook with rage. He shoved Dougie back into his seat before bending over him, "You'd better watch your mouth before you find yourself without it." He left them staring after him Antonio with his arms around Dougie as he soothed him in that sing-song voice as if he were the words biggest upset baby.

He stopped at the counter, "I'm sorry Joseph" he cocked his head back the way he'd come. "I didn't mean to leave a mess."

He left the shop moving quickly through the rain. Half a block away he stopped unmindful of the hard drops pelting him and replayed Dougie's words in his head. How dare the little ass wipe accuse me of anything. And why do I care what some human waste product said in the first place? How could anybody think I was involved in any way in my wife's death? It's nuts That prick doesn't know a damn thing.

A gust of icy rain blew into his face and penetrated his clothes to his skin. He stepped into a tiny sheltered recess between two buildings, shivering, his teeth chattering. And if it starts to snow right now proving God doesn't like me then they can just call me George Bailey and follow me over to the Brooklyn Bridge and watch me jump. Jump? Not pushed or thrown off but voluntarily toss myself into the deep dark water. Suicide. Am I really thinking suicide? He tightened himself against the cold and let it play out.

Was he actively contemplating killing himself because someone killed her? It reached up out of his mind and caught him not unaware, it had been down there. Stop it; it's stupid to even wander down that road. But Lorna was gone and what did he have left to live for? Not much. He let the thought simmer. But for now he had the twin causes that took precedence over everything else: finding out whom killed Lorna and killing the bastard; anything else had to wait, to simmer. Realizing he'd stopped shivering he left the protection of the building.

The man following Owen skidded back into a darkened doorway and plastered himself against the wall as his subject went on the move again. His stomach roiled in anger at almost being caught due to his lapse in surveillance. He balled up his right fist and punched himself in the midsection; a rush of air whistled through his teeth at the exploding pain. How could he be so stupid he berated himself as he huddled in the shadows his stomach throbbing as he watched the detective hurry on.

He'd stood underneath a cinema marquee surrounded by a sea of moviegoers watching the cop through the donut shop's window and half listening to the movie patron's grumblings about the rain as their black umbrellas knocked together like funeral clouds. They had swarmed around him as they talked, bumped him with harsh words and elbows without apology and he'd asked for none knowing to them he wasn't important, was virtually invisible; he'd gotten used to it and learned over time to use it.

When the cop had exited the shop he'd crossed the street behind him and had somehow lost sight of the man as he'd rounded a corner. His heart had raced in panic and he had quickened his pace only to find the detective had vanished.

How was he going to do this if he couldn't keep track of the guy? His heart had frozen as he realized the cop might have known he was being followed and had doubled back to trap him. He wouldn't put it past him; he'd heard the detective was determined and relentless meaning he wouldn't of course leave his wife's death to others to solve but would do everything he could to find out what happened to her and when he did, he'd come after him. The detective terrified him, threatened his very existence so if the time came—no if, when—he would have to act first for once and get the detective before he got him.

For now though he would wait an easy thing to do; he was the Invisible Man right? And if the detective got close too fast he would be ready. Death wasn't something new to him anymore; and his being the cause of another one? He was surprised how the possibility didn't bother him at all anymore, so surprised he chuckled before clamping his hand over his mouth his teeth biting into his tongue to stop the sound. Blood squirted; he tasted it and swallowed his eyes closing on an ecstatic whimper before they flew open and he looked fearfully around. He was still alone on the street not another lost to be seen.

CHAPTER 7

Commissioner Chandler stood in the room at One Police Plaza he'd co-opted to run his mayoral campaign from and perused the three poster boards that featured his image. His assistant, a young woman with Ivy League blond good looks stood off to the side.

On the walls were hung numerous charts, graphs and banners that didn't list crime statistics or precinct rating sheets instead depicted the progress of the mayoral race including a percentage of guesstimated votes he and his opponent would win along with charts featuring all kinds of demographic information from the racial makeup of each borough to which of the city's newspapers were read by what cross-section of New Yorker at what income level. Chandler used a tech from the Command Center to gather this information and chart it out on a weekly basis.

He knew polls and trends, blogs, videos and web hits were becoming the most important indicators in any political race these days—other than the scorecard cash—that defined the candidate's success and he meant to keep up with them all. He figured not paying attention to even the smallest most insignificant blip in public perception or opinion could mean losing and he wasn't going to lose; though in truth it had never once crossed his mind he wouldn't be the next mayor of New York City; his hubris was untouchable.

On the floor and a top a table sat boxes of campaign buttons, bumper stickers and flyers with its familiar black background featuring his name in stark white letters and his slogan: "The Truth. In Black and White." He of course thought it perfect though he was apt—for his own good reasons—to "shift" that rickety plank of truth depending on what he needed accomplished.

He didn't believe in "shades of gray" it was either his way or no way though he did have to compromise once and a while, after all he was a seasoned politician; he just hated to do it and avoided it by hook-or-by crook whenever he got the chance. But he'd do whatever he had to, use whatever means at his disposal to become the next mayor of New York, he loved this city and in his vaulted opinion of himself, it deserved him.

Dressed in pressed dark blue slacks, a crisp white shirt and a blue and green striped tie he felt signaled to the world he was ready for anything; he'd woken feeling great with the kind of energy he hadn't felt in years and had arrived at his office two hours before his staff. Once there he'd planned his day, made phone calls waking his advisers, completed a stack of reports he was a week late submitting to the present mayor and had even outlined a new angle for his campaign before his administrative assistant, Teresa Bowles had arrived and presented him with his first cup of coffee.

"None of them are any good," he frowned over at his new campaign manager Randall Sidowski—the old manager he'd fired a week earlier—who stared from his boss to the screen of the laptop computer on the table in front of him. "I wanted to look friendly, trustworthy, like J.F. K, instead that photographer you got made me look like John Wayne Gacey; he wouldn't know how to take a picture at a kiddy party. Get me somebody else."

There was a rap on the door before it was opened and Teresa Bowles entered. She was a brown-haired, middle-aged woman with sharp blue eyes, an MBA from Northwestern University and a whip in the guise of Blackberry scheduler she used to oversee Chandler's office with ruthless efficiency.

"Your ten o'clock's here and it has to be kept at forty-five minutes," she said in a no-nonsense voice as she studied the small screen. "You have Comp Stat at ten forty-five which must end at eleven-thirty if you want to make it to lunch at the City Club." She looked up at him, "Anything else?"

"Call Eddie and tell him to bring over my gray suit and burgundy polo tie, I want to look fresh. The people who lunch at the City Club are some of the liberal elites we need to woo—at least their wallets—over to our side. "Okay Teresa let'em in."

She opened the door and stood back as Chandler's top chiefs and deputy commissioners entered to take took their seats around the conference table. Most of them had been summoned only an hour earlier and they'd arrived with the exact same feeling the president's cabinet must get when summoned to discuss war.

Chandler signaled to the young woman who quickly picked up the poster boards and left the room. "Everybody's here," Chandler nodded. "Good. It tells me you all view this matter as urgently as I do." He rolled up his sleeves and took his seat in the Captain's Chair at the head of the table. He settled back as his eyes swept over his top staff, "Have you found the person who killed my wife?"

Their gazes bounced off one another as tension slid around the room. Jason Zivich, the Chief of Detectives, leaned forward his well-known easy smile absent, "You know—"

"I know," Chandler cut in, "you haven't found her killer. So what're you all doing about it?"

Eliza Truegood, the Chief of Department cleared his throat, "This is of course a delicate operation sir…sensitive. And my division is trying hard to make sure it proceeds without any mistakes or misinterpretation of procedures. We don't want the public or the media hammering us over any little thing they believe smells like harassment or strong-arm tactics so it's taking longer than we anticipated."

"No suspects?"

"We've hauled in around two hundred suspects; just not the person or persons we believe did it."

"This is ridiculous," Chandler's gaze stormed around the table, everyone stiffened in anticipation of the blow up. "You get me something; yesterday. Those were major crimes for chrissakes not some drugstore holdup. Our citizens want this monster caught and jailed for the rest of his life; if not worse. And they want it done now."

"How many times have we've been touted nation wide for how we've significantly lowered this city's homicide rate so that tourists feel safe, we feel safe and now how do you think we look? Like assholes who have a goddamn triple murderer on the loose."

"And if that's not good enough for you," he leaned toward them with checked menace, "I'm running a mayoral campaign here which is a delicate business. Right now I have public sympathy on my side but it's not going to last long if you keep bullshitting and that son-of-a-bitch stays on the streets."

"Our action sheets do back the Commissioner's point," said Ellen Watson Doherty, the Deputy Commissioner of Public Information, the only woman in the room. "Approximately sixty-eight percent of the hundred calls we've received seem to be in support of you, sir. The rest want the killer caught before he murders again and I quote many of the callers: 'If the police aren't safe. Who is?' "

There was silence until Chandler asked his voice cool, "So boys what are we going to do?"

No one answered until Rider sat forward so that his bony head and shoulders hung over the table, "What's the story on Detective Owen Story? No pun intended," he added with no trace of humor on his sallow face.

"What're you talking about?" asked Michael Floriano the Chief of Detectives his face flushing an angry red. He was a tall acerbic man who knew every policy, rule and regulation that floated the bureau yet was known to gladly break a few of those edicts when it came to protecting his men. He glared down the table at Rider, "Story's not involved in this. If anything he's another victim. His wife was murdered too if you've forgotten."

"What's your take on this, Dave?" Chandler questioned an intense looking man who opened a file on the table in front of him.

"He's connected to all three victims," said David Hague the Deputy Commissioner of Intelligence; a lawyer by trade, twice divorced who spent most of his time at the Plaza. "Witnesses saw him arguing with his wife and apparently it got somewhat physical. They also saw officer Tynon try and go to her assistance but Detective Story wouldn't allow it. Later, he was seen—excuse me Commissioner—having a quick but intimate conversation with Mrs. Chandler."

"He disappeared for approximately ten minutes during the time the crimes were committed," Rider tossed in. "And there's not one witness to corroborate his alibi."

"Sounds cut and dried to me," Chandler said.

"So what he had a spat with his wife in public," Floriano said. "Who hasn't? And of lot of people came and went that night some doing God knows what and they aren't suspected of anything." He stared down the table at Truegood for support and received a cold stare in return.

"True, but his wife—you just pointed it out your self Mike— was one of those murdered." David gestured at the folder, "And he'd been having problems with her; unfortunately I don't have it here exactly what those problems were but from what I could gather they were substantial."

"A lot of people have problems with their wives," Floriano insisted.

Truegood piped up, "And they solve them by killing said wife."

Chandler laughed, "Said wife."

"It sounds all well and good his being seen with all three victims—and not favorably—yet from a legal standpoint it's still a weak premise to have to defend in court," Hague said.

"Then we have to get solid evidence he was involved," Rider looked around the table. "Let me say it if no one else will: there's no doubt in my mind Story's our prime suspect. All the bodies point to him don't they? And there's no one else is there? All we need to do is get our proof, present a case to the grand jury, go to trial, celebrate the inevitable outcome then wrap up this nasty business as quickly as we can and get it off the public's mind."

"Sounds like a plan and I have no doubt we can get it done," Chandler nodded confident. "What about his record? Any complaints of police brutality, domestic violence?"

"No," Hague shook his head.

"Oh well," Chandler said disappointed. "We tried. But I still like what's been put on the table."

Truegood cleared his throat again, "We have to be careful," he threw a nervous glance toward Chandler. "We may see negative repercussions from the rank and file if it looks like we're trying to railroad one of our own."

"Whoa," Chandler held up a hand, "You all aren't going scared over what needs to be done are you?" He waited for a moment in the ensuing silence for someone to answer him. "We're talking about a cop true, but a cop who has murdered his brother-in-blue. And this time instead of the department covering up this terrible act like the public believes we'd do, we're going to surprise them this time—without hesitating or wimping out—and have that cop arrested and prosecuted like we'd do any other stone-cold killer."

"You realize how good this would look for the department? Hell, let me be even more frank; how good it'll look for me? And since this is a high priority the FBI should be involved; it'll only emphasize how seriously committed the department is in rooting out evil in our own backyard."

Except for Floriano there were nods of agreement around the table as Chandler settled back down, "And to add even more to Story's criminal resume, he may be connected to organized crime right Dave? The Giordano family.

"This is crazy," Floriano shot to his feet unable to go along with the insane case they were manufacturing. "You're blowing this way out of proportion. Story's a good cop. I can't believe you want the FBI of all people to go after one-of-us when nothing's been proven yet. Too many entities are getting involved here. This should be an IAB matter first—"

"Mike," Chandler's arctic blue gaze struck him like a razor, "I admire your loyalty, I even understand it; he's one of us at least for now but as this investigation speeds ahead I want to know right here in front of everyone and no bullshit Mike; if you're with us or you're out." His words were coated with ice, "What will it be?"

Floriano opened his mouth but nothing escaped. He shut it to an angry bloodless line and dropped back into his chair.

"Good choice," Chandler gazed around at the rest of them. "The ball's in the air folks and I don't want any fuck-ups. I want every step followed legally straight by the book and whomever you assign to this make sure they understand that. I don't want Detective Story walking away on any technicality because he didn't get his rights read to him loudly enough or because the warrants were signed in blue ink instead of black or because he got a rash from the toilet seat in his jail cell; not one goddamn fuck-up."

"All right then we're all on the same page. And as the rule goes: what was said in this room stays or you'll be hearing from me." There were quick nods as notebooks were closed and pens capped. He stood and the others followed suit. "I'll see most of you Comp Stat," he glanced at his watch, "in ten minutes." He smiled, "Teresa is going to be tickled I stayed on schedule."

As his staff left the room, Floriano bolting first, Chandler said, "Timothy, a minute." Rider, who'd been almost out into the hall did an about face and slid back into the room.

"This could—" Chandler broke off and swiveled his head around toward the side table. Randall who'd sat silently through the meeting, almost becoming part of the furniture stiffened at Chandler's gaze. "Go get yourself a glass of milk."

They watched as he got to his feet gripping his laptop computer to his chest and looking at Chandler with part awe and the rest undiluted fear as he quickly exited the room.

"He okay?" Rider asked.

"He understands what side his bread is buttered on."

"You know this could be dangerous," Rider got straight to it.

A crazy glint flashed in Chandler's eyes as he laughed, Rider ignored it; he'd seen it before too many times.

"It's funny how you didn't say anything about it not being right; dangerous I can handle. You just make sure this thing is airtight and all the arrows point the right way. I can't afford any loose ends." He took in Rider's usual closed and watchful expression, "This is good for us," he said with enthusiasm before stamping his words with a ring of entreaty. "You know what they were doing to me—to us," he gripped the man's arm for emphasize ignoring Rider's stiffening at the contact.

"You know what she was like. Trust me on this like you've done on everything else. We have to get this thing going and done as quickly as possible so there are no obstacles in our way. I'm going to even help it along, get that ball in the air by calling Riviera personally."

Chandler picked up the phone. Dialing, he winked at Rider, "This is going to be fun."

CHAPTER 8

Dennis Riviera, Agent-In-Charge of the New York City office of the Federal Bureau of Investigation hung up the receiver and felt the engine inside him that ran at one-hundred rpm's, rev up high in anticipation of a new chase. Opening the door to the outer office where his agents and staff sat working he said, "Williams, Berniak and Carter in my office."

He glanced at his assistant, a young male agent, "I'll need this written up and copies distributed to ensure all the proper procedures are followed."

Back inside his office he stared out the window. A crooked cop. A murderous cop was loose in the city and the police needed the investigative skills of the Feebs as they called them to help capture him. He smiled at the thought, reveled in it. The local boys couldn't handle one of their own and needed their assistance. Priceless.

There was no love lost between him and the commissioner, he thought the man arrogant and too sly for his own good yet he would overlook his many failings because this was business, the law had been broken and that was his only concern. He stretched a body taunt and muscular from daily swims at the local YMCA before dropping his children off at school. He was full of high energy; it sparkled in almond colored eyes in a handsome face due to a pure mixture of Mexican and American-Indian blood. The look in those eyes was turned inward as he clicked over how he wanted this investigation to run.

He insisted his technically savvy, analytically thoughtful agents run smooth operations where their prey was thoroughly researched and any problems effortlessly solved garnering the only acceptable outcome: capture and conviction. This was the way he ran his piece of the bureau and though the bureau heads might not be keeping score, he was and would tolerate no losses.

He had arrived at FBI Headquarters in Washington two directors after Hoover was put under and a few years out of Yale Law School on a full scholarship. He was a minority in a highly patriarchal-white-male-dominant-system abhorrent to change and had to fight his way through, not only to become a law enforcement standout in its hallowed halls but to eventually win the position of AIG of the Manhattan bureau, one of the most coveted positions in the bureau, in the most popular and prized cities in the world.

He still fought battles and not only to maintain his present status or because he was the kind of man who didn't like open cases on his watch but because he believed in the fundamental doctrine of good versus evil. His foundation rested on the conviction that when you committed a crime, you deserved to be punished for it and to make sure you paid were people like him.

After the country's greatest terrorist attack was perpetrated on this city, his convictions, his ferocity that had advanced him through life to where he now stood had morphed into an obsessive zealousness centered on his need to make sure such an attack never happened again.

His feverish vigilance saturated every case that fell into the Manhattan bureau's hands: a synagogue blown to bits killing all inside, a family of innocents murdered over baby toys full of heroin, a ships cargo hold filled with suffocated illegal immigrants, a life ripped apart by computer hackers stealing personal information and now to catch a murdering cop, these were cases he would lose sleep over and oversee their every detail because in his 9-1-1-minted-voluntarily-narrowed mind solving all the bureau's cases upped the score on his side of liberty and freedom and directed a blow to the cowardly monsters who would try again and again to make the United States a vast wasteland.

The agents entered and sat in chairs encircling his desk. His assistant, last in took an unassuming seat by the window a laptop computer in front of him.

Rivera got right to the point, "The police commissioner just called about those three murders; no ones talking about anything else and I believe it's one of the factors that prompted the call.

Plus the tragic fact one of the victims was his own wife. He wants our help in finding the killer; the trick here is he believes they know who it is or at least the most likely suspect, a Detective Owen Story, one of their own."

"You're kidding?" said Daniel Williams a career agent in his mid-forties whose growing baldness and baggy features advanced his age ten years.

Riviera nodded, "Did he kill the other two to get to her? He's the only one can answer that but if he did he's a dangerous man. The Commissioner's taking no chances so neither am I. Story's free though a wide net has begun to grow around him; but if he somehow figures it out he might run making him a fugitive which could get him on the most wanted."

"We're going to put him under surveillance while we check out every crack and crevice of his life. There's another side to this," he added his face forming into a mask of distaste. In many ways he considered himself the modern day version of Thomas Dewey believing anyone touched, tainted by the putrid rancid odor of organized crime he swore was the root of much of the evil in the city, deserved to be brought down and brought down hard. "This Story may be connected to Richard Giordano."

"Jeez," said Lee James Carter William's partner, a thin man with tiny gray eyes and a Georgia accent. "That's enough right there to arrest him."

"Giordano has never been convicted of anything," Riviera said more than familiar with the Giordano family. "He's never even spent a night in jail. If we can somehow connect them to something we'll get two for the price of one."

Riviera glanced at the youngest man in the room who sat laconically back in the chair drinking coffee from a mug with the words: EAT ME, splashed around it in red letters. The agent's tie was askew and his shirt wrinkled as he stared out the window. He liked his agents clean, neat, professional and this one was none of the above.

"Berniak, I want you to do your tricks and track Story. Know where he is at all times and I want meticulous records kept."

"Yeah," the agent replied then, "Right," as Riviera threw him a dark frown.

Insolence was the prime characteristic of these new recruits Riviera had decided long ago. Though most were one hundred percent computer literate, gadget savvy and language diverse they were zero competent on just about every other essential aspect of bureau life. He knew you had to usually give up something to get something else but what the bureau had given up to get these new agents was not worth the price.

"Williams, you and Carter will be the primaries and can assist the police if necessary," Riviera said then quietly, "Remember, three people have been murdered in cold blood. One suspect. A cop with dirty connections who believes he's gotten away with it. It's abhorrent to me to know he's walking around this town, eating, sleeping, thinking he's free, beyond the law; we can't let it continue."

"Our duty to the bureau, to New York is to do whatever it takes to make sure this cop's days are numbered. No one will be safe until he's put down. Get to it."

As everyone filed out Riviera turned to look at his extraordinarily clean and innocent view of the city, the world below, a view only those at the top get to see. He felt confident Owen Story's world would soon come crashing in on him; it was his duty to make sure it happened even if it took all of his personal resources, the bureau's and then some.

CHAPTER 9

"She was a lovely girl," Lorna's Aunt Ruth said as they gazed at the flower laden casket. After giving Owen's shoulder a solemn squeeze she moved off.

Other mourners, some of them cops stopped beside him and gave him their platitudes he accepted without taking his eyes of the casket.

"I'm sorry…" someone said the voice so low it barely penetrated the bleak thrashing rolling sea that was Owen's mind. A hand gripped his right one the palm soft and warm, the contact like a splash of cold water in his face waking him from a dream. Someone stepped in front of him cutting off his view so that he stared instead into the sallow face of a young man in an officer's uniform with tears running unashamedly out of his reddened brown eyes.

"…Sorry about your wife," said Officer David Murphy, Owen read off his police issue nameplate. He looked to be in his twenties with an unassuming face crumpled with sadness.

"Thank you," Owen said uneasy with the young man's visible grief. He didn't know the man and wondered how he knew Lorna.

"Bobby Tynon was my partner."

Owen nodded feeling instant sympathy for him. "I'm sorry for your loss. Are you going to be all right?" He reached inside his coat pocket and handed Murphy a wad of dry tissue.

Murphy wiped his face, "It's hard too—"

"Owen," a sergeant from the 1-9 named Van Atkins moved up between them and gripped Owen's left shoulder. "I know you'll miss her but we'll get the bastard who did this to her; we'll get 'em"

"Yes, I will," Owen said and realized he'd spoken out loud the thought that had been playing over and over on the screen of his mind since he held Lorna in his arms for the last time.

"She was special," added another cop standing beside Atkins.

Pushed to the side Murphy lingered a moment like an uninvited guest before he walked away as those remaining mourners crowded around Owen to wish him well before moving off to their cars. Owen's father-in-law, Abraham Kaplan, eyes red-rimmed, his face years older glanced once at Owen as he placed a hand on the lid of the casket before he moved off with Ruth at his side.

Starring at the casket a little longer Owen made himself turn and walk away. Cush, who had been standing off to the side joined him knowing that any thing he could say would be useless to his partner in the world of grief he was now living.

"It was a beautiful day for it," Owen said though he barely felt the warm rays of the sun and the gently blowing autumn breeze. It was almost laughingly ironic that everyday since Lorna's death the late October weather had been perfect.

"Connie's sorry she couldn't be here but funerals scare her while I'm comforted by the fact my soul will depart to my ancestors."

Owen didn't answer instead he watched his feet move one beside the other. He felt numb inside, frozen. He knew he had to get it together—prayed he could—because there were things he needed to do and he couldn't do them walking around like his head, instead of his heart, had been crushed. "That's a good looking jacket," he glanced at Cush and smiled a little.

He had managed to do one conscience thing through out this horrible day and that was notice his partner's lime green suit jacket. It made no sense of all the things going on around and inside him he'd managed that feat, it more than anything else pointed out the one thing he couldn't ignore, he was still alive and Lorna wasn't. Though he didn't think he or anyone else could have by passed Cush's awful wardrobe choice even if they had tried.

The jacket fit his partner like it was made for a man two sizes smaller making Cush look like the Jolly Green giant and it was an awful neon green, a color he hadn't seen on anyone since the eighties.

He knew Cush could care less how he looked to any one else; it was all about how Cush felt, how as he put it his "inner life force" was reacting on the particular day and for him it was usually beaming. Cush liked himself and it was one of his partner's many attributes Owen had admired from the first moment they had gotten together.

Cush had a steady and secure sense of his place in the world. 'The worlds a living, breathing entity' he always said. So he considered its feelings, its emotions, its vibes as well as the unsaid of the people around him and he factored this into all the cases they worked. He'd never brought one hundred percent into what he referred to as Cush's "medium capacity" though he never discounted it.

When they had first partnered up, the other detectives had likened them to Steinbeck's Lenny and George. They of course believed he was the archetypical George, the smarter one in their partnership, the ringleader who did their talking and thinking while Cush as Lenny did the brawn work. They were wrong.

He had come to rely on Cush's strength of mind not body, his honesty, his instincts, most of all his ability to dismiss all the cowering bullshit when all seemed lost. They were a team of equals, good together, and he was grateful for that and not just for the days on the street, but for everyday of his life.

"Yeah," Cush admired his jacket, "got it just for this. I consider this as a home going ceremony, a celebration of the spirit returning to where it's life began so I dressed up for the occasion." He tapped Owen gently on the shoulder, "You seem to be holding up okay?"

Owen nodded, "Holding up."

They neared the road that led out of the cemetery and looked up at the sound of laboring engines coming their way. They watched two news vans, one emblazoned with Channel Three on its side, the other Channel Five speed toward them.

Owen's face twisted in irritation, "The same assholes from the funeral home."

The vans threw up pebbles and almost side swiped each other as they screeched to a halt in front of the locked gates. A distinguished looking blond-haired man Owen recognized from the evening news stepped out of van Channel Three and was

48

followed immediately by a small blonde pixie of a woman from the Channel Five van.

Both wore Burberry overcoats and the exact same expressions of terrifying eagerness. Behind them followed equipment-laden cameramen who looked perpetually harassed.

Owen and Cush turned their backs on the gamboling news people and walked away over the well tended and still green lawn overlooking the sea of gravestones.

"You shoulda known they'd hound you after you refused to give them anything at the funeral home," Cush said.

"Dammit, I don't know anything."

"Then they're gonna follow you like maggots follow a corpse if just to catch your tears or you cursing God and the department for their evening idiot hour. You think this is bad?" Cush rolled his eyes, "Wait until Jocelyn Chandler's send off."

"All this is so nuts," Owen took a couple of agitated steps away from Cush before stopping to stare off toward the elevated highway a few miles away, his words rimmed with shocked disbelief, "It's as if I've been hit by a tornado. One second I'm in my house and the next it's a pile of bricks and I'm just standing there, screaming."

"But alive."

Owen's eyes were bleak, "Not by much."

Cush hoped the look wouldn't last long. He had known Lorna of course and wasn't sure she warranted such devotion; yet he hadn't been in love with her.

"This is insane. A couple of days ago I was hoping she'd take some time off and we'd take a second honeymoon, get to know each other again, instead I'm burying her."

Cush stepped close to Owen forcing him to take a step farther away from the reporters shouting his name, "You've got to get your shit together." Owen opened his mouth to agree, but his partner didn't give him the chance. "Wait a minute, hear me out. This is worse than you think. This is big, huge and you're right in the center ring."

"Tell me something I don't know. My wife and two others are murdered practically in front of a room full of cops—cops everywhere—and if it wasn't so damn crazy do you think those vultures," he jerked a thumb back at the reporters, "would be here?"

"Right. And what happened is not only being carried by those asses, it's everywhere you turn; national papers, radio and Web coverage even the international press has gotten hold of it. MSN has been reporting on it every time Jackson holds a press conference and he's been holding them almost every hour since it happened trying to keep the citizens from panicking; or at the very least, pointing a finger at him for not reigning in crime a-la-Giulliani. This thing is so damn explosive, shit sensational, it's hard to tell which way it's gonna go and because of that, I think it's going bad for you. So you gotta be careful."

"Why? What's changed in the last few days?"

"Plenty from what I hear. Listen, I don't have any details. People are whispering your name, allegiances are being broken and power is being shifted; things are happening and not in a good way."

Owen stared at him used to Cush's psychic sounding pronouncements but what he was saying now rang with the sound of truth and it scared the shit out of him.

"Maybe I'm being promoted," he tried for a touch of humor he didn't feel in an effort to break-up the dread building in his stomach.

"No one has come out and said anything—you know how the department is—but that tornado you're riding? It's gonna feel like a summer shower compared to the bloodbath that's coming."

"For chrissakes how?"

"Hell, if I know. I've got my ear pressed to the ground so when I know something you'll know. In the mean time just watch your ass and watch it good."

Owen believed him, there was no doubt in his mind his partner was right; Cush was well liked and respected by their fellow officers meaning he had connections in the department, was privy to top notch information quietly passed from one privileged cop to another, unconnected cops like him only received the information second hand after somebody's ass was in a sling. Cush was right, something was coming, he could feel it blowing against him like the wind that swept across his skin. He had no idea what it would be other than it wouldn't be any fun. He couldn't worry about it now—wouldn't—he had other concerns.

They turned and walked toward the waiting family car sitting in front of the gates, Owen its only passenger. As they closed in the driver turned from watching the yelling, gesticulating news people as if he was watching reporters-gone-wild and opened the passenger door for Owen before he went around and took his place at the wheel.

The reporters screamed louder as soon as they saw them, thrusting their mikes through the bars like crazed monkeys grabbing for bananas at the zoo.

The female reporter whom Owen had seen on the news once or twice shoved her mike forward while she pushed hard at the larger male bodies surrounding her. "You know who killed your wife?" she shouted over the others.

Surprised by the question Owen straightened from bending into the car, "No and neither does anyone else."

The Channel Five reporter not to be out done by a woman from the rival station raised his voice, "That's not what we've been told. Did you know there was a witness?"

"What?" Owen stared at him.

Cush put a hand on Owen's back and urged him into the car. "Forget about them; people are waiting at the house." He nodded at the groundskeeper who unlocked the gates and pulled them open. With one last look at the reporters Owen got into the car. Cush watched it out through the gates before he looked at the news people who hurried after the departing vehicle.

"Hey you," he called. They turned and looked at him expectantly. He didn't say a word instead he pointed two fingers of his right hand, one covered by a ring with a deep gray stone, toward the sky before he swayed those fingers back and forth across his chest while he mumbled something they couldn't hear as they stared at him.

"What are you doing?" asked the pixie reporter, her made up face smile free.

Cush shook the fingers three times toward the ground before he answered, "It's an old Aztec curse called the Co'pil; the guy it was named after had his heart cut out by his own uncle."

"What's supposed to happen to us?" asked the reporter from Channel Three his face fumbled a frightened confused smile.

"I don't know," Cush grinned. "Because you people have no hearts. Bye and have a nice day," he waved at them with the two fingers the stone winking.

"What the hell was that?" asked the female reporter's cameramen.

"I'd say it was the best 'fuck off' we've gotten all week," she smiled then with admiration. "Let's go; we can't let Story get too far ahead."

CHAPTER 10

O wen sat in the bedroom that had belonged to Lorna which Pop had turned into a catchall room filled with boxes of old magazines, receipts, paid bills, whatever he didn't want to trash; putting five years worth of tax filings and old magazines in date order. Busy work to keep his mind off the people downstairs who were eating, drinking and whispering about the dead. Once he caught a glimpse of his face in the mirror above the dresser and noticed it was wet meaning he was trying not to think about Lorna and it wasn't working.

The door opened and Abraham Kaplan whom most called Pop, stepped inside. They looked at each other their faces remote, "How long are you going to be here?" the old man asked.

"In this room? Or in your house?"

"Both."

These were the first words the old man had said to him since he'd told him Lorna was dead. He'd asked no questions, made no comment had just turned and walked away. Owen had known he'd grieve long and hard over his only child, wallow in bitterness and anger yet he hadn't figured he'd turn it on him.

The first time he had met Pop (Lorna's mother Patricia having died years earlier) the meeting had been tense and unforgettable. The old man had looked through him with eyes the color of faded green leaves and ignored his gestures of friendship. Two days later he'd come out of the station house and seen him across the street wearing an orange Hawaiian shirt that had made him stand out like a traffic cone in the snow.

Believing he'd come to make amends, he'd crossed to him and in place of a normal greeting the old man had asked, "You two gett'in married?" When he'd nodded, Lorna's father had laughed then walked away shaking his head, "You marrying her."

He'd gone to Lorna angry over what he'd called "his confrontation" with her father upset the old man didn't like him and had what he believed were issues letting go of his daughter. She'd commiserated of course, her hands soothing him as she'd told him Pop had drifted into long silences after her mother's death until she'd grown up in a house where she'd become invisible, where they rarely spoke, laughed or even shouted so that it built up something huge inside her screaming to be seen and heard.

"So this is how it's going to end?" Owen put down the old paper and dusted off his hands.

"It? If you mean your being part of my family that ended the moment you told me Lorna was dead."

The word's hit Owen in face but he didn't flinch, "I tried to get along with you for her sake—"

"You wasted your time."

"What's your problem?"

"You were my daughter's choice, not mine."

Pain twanged through Owen; he'd known of course how Pop felt about him but to hear it out loud spiked him nevertheless, "No matter what you think of me I can't just abandon you." He wanted to mean those words though he wasn't sure if he could carry it out in the face of the old man's hatred of him.

Pop reddened, "I don't need your pity or you I'm not some old piss bag dying at some backwater nursing home praying for a visit from somebody, anybody; even you. I can take care of myself. You did everything to appease her, to look good in her eyes and not because you meant any of it."

"I'm not just anybody," Owen didn't want to attack but couldn't help himself; he had a few bugs up his ass too. "And what about you? How'd you show her you cared about her? Loved her? I visited you more than she did; she could barely stand being in the room with you because you treated her like a stranger. It was a miracle she didn't hate you for it. You're mean as hell and deserve to sit right here in Kew Gardens silently rotting to death."

Owen pushed pass ignoring the stunned look on Pop's face and the bony hand that reached out to touch the air. He was at the door when a heavy thud, a body hitting wood made his heart jump. He turned and saw Pop faced down in a box of dust covered linen.

"Oh God," he ran to him and on his knees rolled him over. Pop's face was as gray as the old linen he lay on. He felt for a pulse, life, with a cold finger and got a thin reedy rhythm that could have been his imagination.

He snatched the phone off the side table and punched in 9-1-1, "I need an ambulance at 2962 Kew Gardens. Pop—the victim—has had a heart attack or stroke."

He dropped the phone and pulled the blanket off the bed his hands shaking with reaction as he covered him. He checked Pop's pulse again praying it hadn't been his imagination.

CHAPTER 11

He sat beside the hospital bed listening to Pop breath. Guilt weaved through him as he bit at this thumbnail. He'd caused the old man to have a heart attack or stroke he didn't know which, the one thing he did know for sure he'd almost killed him by being an asshole with a big mouth. God, he dropped his head to Pop's side, the thin coverlet cool on his sweaty face. Please don't let him die, please God.

Cush stepped inside and handed him a cup of coffee, "Thank you," he said then asked, "You got anything stronger?"

"You don't need anything stronger and anyway I think the doctor is coming down the hall. At least a guy in a white coat who looked impressed with himself is coming this way."

Owen looked at his father-in-law who was the color of the white pillowcase. His stomach roiled with nerves. He hated to hear what the doctor would say but needed to be pinned with the crime he'd perpetrated against his own relative; needed to be beaten with it so he could accept it and crawl away.

The door opened and as Cush had said a man who looked impressed with himself entered with a manila folder under his right arm. He was slim with brown eyes in an evenly structured face that held a flat mole near his bottom lip.

"I'm doctor Everett Powell Mr. Kaplan's oncologist." He moved to Pop's side and studied him a moment gently touching the side of his face and fore head as if he were a mother checking a child for a fever the old-fashioned way. It was an oddly endearing gesture that made Owen feel worse.

"I'll wait outside," Cush exited the room.

"How long have you been his doctor?" Owen asked.

56

"More than a year." He straightened from Pop and looked at Owen, "You're Mr. Kaplan's closest relative?"

"His son-in-law. He doesn't have any blood relatives, at least not in state; one sister lives on the other side of the country." Owen gripped his knees, "What happened to him? Was it a heart attack or stroke?"

Powell didn't answer, he took out an opthamoloscope and opened one of Pop's eyes then the other looking into them no more than a few seconds. "I can't let him go home alone, not until someone can be with him to make sure he's careful, doesn't fall or hurt himself when he has the next reoccurrence of the lost of consciousness."

"He didn't have a heart attack? A stroke? He only fainted is that it?" Owen felt such a wave of relief pass through him he thought he was going to faint.

"Yes, he's in a coma though slowly coming out of it."

"How could passing out put him into a coma?" shock made Owen look form the doctor to Pop.

"Losing consciousness didn't put him into a coma," Powell frowned at him. "Mr. Kaplan has cancer, a brain tumor." The words hit Owen like a two-by-four in the face; his mouth fell open with an audible pop "A malignant astrocytoma growing on his temporal lobe Mr. Story. It's inoperable. And 'passing out' as you call it is a symptom of his condition."

Owen laughed deepening Powell's frown until the mole near his mouth seemed to pull all the way to his chin. Owen laughed until he grabbed the plastic covered wastebasket at the side of Pop's bed and threw-up the coffee and sour stomach juice that was all he had inside. After he was done he took the basket into the bathroom and flushed the contents.

"Excuse me doctor," he reentered wiping his mouth with a Kleenex. "I just can't believe this fucking day."

"He didn't tell you about his condition?"

Owen forced the heels of his hands into his eyes as if he were going to put his eyeballs through the back of his skull making Powell wince. When he dropped his hands from his face lines of strain ringed eyes that were as crimson as if he'd shedded red tears, "He's spoken twenty words to me in seven years; most of them today and all of them bad."

Owen's mind whirled. Had this man who seemed to him like some actor playing a doctor said "brain tumor"? It hadn't sounded real; couldn't be real goddamit. Pop had brain cancer. They'd just buried Lorna and now to learn her father may not have long to live; this day had gone from awful to suicidal. "How long has he had it?"

"A year."

"A year," Owen laughed again the sound as unfunny as a tsunami. "And not once did he say a word as if it wasn't important. Or maybe he thought if he didn't say anything acted as if it weren't happening it would go away." He looked at Powell hope darkening his eyes, "Will it go away?"

"It's in an area of the brain that controls his—our—motor functions. His kind of tumor expands out like creeping spider legs putting pressure on his brain until it may eventually cause him to go blind or become paralyzed."

"Oh, jeezus. You sure there's no chance?"

"No," Powell gave the word a stab as if to wake Owen out of a useless day dream, "it won't, though miracles do happen but in this case, no. It's as I've told you, inoperable. As soon as Mr. Kaplan awakens he'll want to go home but I won't allow it."

"He won't let you stop him. He'll walk away whether you like it or not."

Powell's face hardened, "Then it'll be against my professional advice based on the knowledge that if he's home alone he could suddenly lose his sight while walking down the stairs and fall and break his neck. Or become paralyzed while in the bathtub and drown. Or lose the ability to walk while holding a boiling pan over the kitchen stove. And there would be no one there to save him."

The pictures Powell's words sketched heightened Owen's helplessness and horror, "What about full-time care?" The words were quiet and vulnerable those of the lowly confused patient conceding to the mighty expertise of the God-like professional in the white coat, "How much do you think it would cost?"

"Expensive. Especially if you don't have long-term care insurance which Mr. Kaplan doesn't. Since going into a nursing facility is not an option the only alternative is for him to go home or to the home of a relative who would care for him, make his remaining days productive; make them count with assistance from a visiting nurse once or twice a day of course to check his care." Powell looked over at Pop, "It's a shame he lost his daughter I'm sure she would've done all she could to care for him."

What would have happened to Pop if Lorna hadn't been killed? The question stomped through Owen's mind. Would we have moved in with Pop or him with us and she care for him? The answer kicked both questions in the teeth with no. She hadn't done well with illness or specifically caring for others if they were sick; it made her clumsy, uneasy and afraid, she hadn't had a Florence Nightingale bone in her lovely body. She would've insisted he go into a nursing home, a good one. The problem, it wouldn't be where he wanted to be, the home he owned outright where he'd lived with the wife and daughter he loved.

Can I do it? I can't do it I'm the reason he's in the hospital now; no, the tumor's the reason but I haven't brought any sunshine to his life either have I? He looked at the old man who lay smaller, shrunken as if he were already giving up the ghost unaware his life was going to be different when he woke whether he liked it or not.

"When he wakes up I'll be here. I'll take him home and see after him."

Powell's face warred with skepticism and relief, "Will Mr. Kaplan be okay with it? With you? Will he want it?"

"Doctor," Owen stared at him, "How often do we get what we want?"

CHAPTER 12

Three days later Owen stood in Pop's living room reading out loud the obituary section, "Pillson Iola aged seventy-six, passed away October twenty-first. Beloved husband of Ida Iola. Beloved father of Judy Iola of Seattle, Washington. Funeral Services will be held at Thursday, October twenty-third at Lymon and Sons Funeral Home—," he stopped and looked at Pop who lay on the couch with his eyes closed.

"What's the point in your hearing this? It freaks me out reading this stuff out loud."

"It's not about you but me. It makes me feel good to know those folks are gone and I'm still breathing."

"That's morbid."

Pop didn't say any thing for a long time, "You don't have to stay with me; I can take care of my self."

Owen looked at the dust that coated the floor of the fireplace and the grey stone of the mantelpiece; both hadn't been dusted since Ruth had left. The past two weeks worth of newspapers were sliding off the stack by Pop's chair onto the floor. Dirty cups lay on the coffee table and television stand where Pop had left them. A plate smeared with dried ketchup sat in the middle of the floor as if it were a piece of art work. He tossed the paper aside and picked up the plate.

"And maybe I don't want to be at my place with Lorna still in every room, so I'm here—with you. Get used to it old man," he turned toward the kitchen, "I'm going to get a drink."

In the kitchen, instead of the drink he took a stack of Tupperware tubs out of the fridge and stared in at what seemed like forty or more sitting on the shelves. Condolence food; tons of it. He sat the ones in his hand on the counter and read the name stenciled on the lid: the Ramsey's. Lasagna, he smiled briefly; it was well known his boss made the best pasta in the department.

It seemed years since he'd last seen him though Ramsey must've been at the funeral then at the house, he'd just been too out of it to notice. It had been more than a week since he'd been to the office though he'd thought about it in a round-a-bout way, at least the part of it that mattered to him, the mechanics at play surrounding Lorna's murder investigation

Questions rotated in his head: Was the investigation being worked around the clock? Were Harry and Mel getting anything useful? Were they pulling every angle? Who was this so-called witness? He kept calling the detectives but had yet to receive a call back so he'd moved on to visiting his snitches and Cush's and asking a thousand questions about that night and getting no answers that satisfied. He'd even called an acquaintance at the Daily News but the guy had been more interested in getting information out of him than giving any up.

He took out enough of the pasta to satisfy Pop, his own stomach was tied up in too many knots to even wish for an appetite. He was going crazy in this helpless wait for answers; this sitting around doing nothing while he was being eaten alive by hot grief and loneliness and the one soul destroying monster question that jumped him in the blackest part of the night keeping him from sleep.

Why had Lorna been in the alley in the first place? It haunted him. He'd assumed she'd been in the wrong place at the wrong time yet this explanation wasn't good enough; wasn't right and none of the slipshod answers he came up with managed to satisfy his marauding brain but led to even nastier questions.

Why had she gone to the alley and not the lounge or the lobby? Why hadn't she mentioned she was going outside in the first place? Why had she gone alone?

"Stop it," he muttered as the front doorbell ring. He hoped it wasn't someone with more food they couldn't eat all they had as it was. He called, "Get the door would you Pop?" He shoved the food into the oven before he opened another tub hoping it was a salad to go with the rest of the meal, the old man needed his vegetables to keep up his strength.

Pop moved across the hall, at the door he pushed aside the thin gauzy curtain that covered the unadorned panel of glass and frowned at the three men on his porch. Two of them were looking up and down the street while the third who looked like he'd just come from the beauty shop, studied the fingernails on his left hand.

All of them wore dark suits and ties; con artists he figured. Owen had warned him time and time again about rip off artist who preyed on the elderly and these three looked like nothing but swindlers.

He left the chain on and opened the door a few inches. The one studying his nails grinned at him with large teeth, "Hello," his voice politician jovial. "My name's Fontaine. Your son-in-law home?"

Pop looked him up and down, "Who'd you say you were?"

"Fon-," Pop slammed the door in his face and Fontaine's smile slipped away.

Owen opened the door a moment later managing to keep to the surprise off his face, "What have I done to deserve such an honor?"

"Just lucky I guess," his grin revived Fontaine said, "Can we talk? Inside."

Owen hesitated. What was Internal Affairs Bureau doing on his doorstep? They went after bad cops not grieving widowers. He'd never had anything but superficial contact with the IAB crew who had a reputation—warranted or not—as underhanded and as slick as Fontaine's hair for getting cops corn holed; but the only way he was going to find out why they were here was to ignore the alarm bells shrieking in his head and let them in.

"It's all right Pop; they're cops."

He pushed the door open and led them through into the dining room, "Have a seat," he told them, "I'll be back in a minute." He walked Pop into the living room and settled him in his easy chair before handing him the remote which the old man ignored. "Don't start worrying," he gently admonished.

Mystified at the men's—cops—presence in his house and right after his daughter's funeral, "Why are they here?" Pop asked, not liking this at all. "What the hell cops want with you?"

"Good question so when I know you'll know."

"Couldn't they have left you alone for a few more days? For chrissakes you just buried your wife."

Owen put a hand on his shoulder, "It's all right," he took the remote and clicked on the television. "These guys should be out of here before the news is halfway over. Your dinner is warming but we can go out if you're tired of condolence food."

"Not hungry," the old man grumbled.

"A beer then," Owen glanced at the men at the table, "We'll both probably need one after this."

Owen took the seat across from Fontaine who said, "You know Becker and Jeter."

He nodded; he'd met them before and hadn't been impressed by either one. Alan Becker looked tough with a marine-to-the-scalp haircut blocky shoulders and a hard ass direct stare. He would bet the farm Becker had walked off some military base and right into the department.

Jeter was younger than the others looked a day off a college campus where Owen decided he'd been the head of the campus Republican Party. He had the air of someone who constantly sniffed around not in the pursuit of justice but for the smell of opportunity he'd kick down doors and arrest cops to grab.

"What can I do for you?" he asked Fontaine.

"First we'd like to extend our condolences for your loss. This may not be the best time for this but some in the department felt this should be done before you got wind of circumstances that could be unfavorable."

"What circumstances?"

"The controversy surrounding the death of Jocelyn Chandler, Officer Bobby Tynon and of course your wife."

Guilt flooded over him, "Jeezus, I still haven't gone around to his precinct house. Is he the reason why you're here? I have to tell you I don't know anything about Tynon."

"You didn't attend his funeral," Becker's voice was gruff as he sat with arms folded across his chest his gaze focused on Owen. "Though his partner was at your wife's paying his respects."

Owen decided not to take offense and laid it out simple, "I didn't feel up to it."

"Tynon was all of twenty-four years old, popular at the one-seven; well-liked. He'll be missed by everyone who knew him,"

Fontaine said. "And what happened to him and the others has of course affected every precinct in this city and the boroughs like nothing since the Trade Center."

"Detective, we want to help you," earnestness tapped Jeter's face; "because this situation is nuclear I hope you understand that. Everybody is demanding answers—yesterday—and since we don't have many we can't leave any stones unturned."

In the other room Pop ignored the television. He sat on the edge of his chair and strained to hear the conversation going on in the other room. It sounded as if those con men—he couldn't think of them as cops—were trying to involve Owen in something that stank to high heaven. He pressed the volume button down until no sound emitted from the set.

Owen felt the muscles in his chest tighten, he didn't like the direction they were headed, "What stone am I?"

"How much did you have to drink that night?" Becker asked. "You were seen fighting with your wife; physically attacking her."

Anger shot through Owen, "That's a lie."

"You have anything to do with your wife's death?" Jeter asked point blank.

Owen got to his feet sending the chair skidding back. He wanted to jump across the table and strangle them all. Where did these jokers get off accusing him of anything?

"I'm not going to answer a question like that from you or anybody else. And what the hell makes you think I'd unburden myself to you departmental snitches?"

"Because it'll be the right thing to do," Fontaine answered.

"Bullshit," Owen tossed back.

"You—" Fontaine broke off and glanced at Pop who'd moved to Owen's side. "Can have a lawyer present," hardness wrapped his words, "though I'm advising you to be up front with us because we're the only ones on your side."

"I don't know who killed my wife and that's the truth."

"What about Jocelyn Chandler?" Becker asked.

"I don't know who killed her either and I didn't' know her personally."

"Really?" Becker's brows rose into a bushy line. "I could swear I saw her talking to you at the ball; after I saw you fighting with you wife out in the corridor."

"I don't know what you thought you saw," shock surrounded Owen's words at Becker's admission. He wondered if for some bizarre reason the guy had been spying on him; he'd been so involved with Lorna at the time he hadn't noticed anyone else. "There was no fight and like I said I didn't know Jocelyn Chandler. She spoke a few words to me in passing and that's it."

"Tell us everything," Fontaine leaned toward him eager. "What did she say to you?"

"No more questions. This little condolence visit is over."

Fontaine stood," Owen you—"

"No," Owen slashed the air with his hand, "You should be out finding the bastard who killed Lorna and not trying to hamstring me." He turned and walked away.

"And get out of my house," Pop added. The men hesitated then stood and trooped out with him on their heels, "My son-in-law didn't do anything."

"It's okay Pop," Owen stood with the front door open and watched the men move past him out onto the porch.

"There's no need for this hostility," Jeter's face was pink with anger. "We were sent here to control a badly spiraling situation that is if you'd cooperated."

"Right, get off the porch," Owen said, Jeter's words sounding hollow as he began closing the door.

Fontaine threw up a hand and kept it from shutting in their faces, his manufactured grin long gone, "Being a pain-in-the-ass won't win you any allies. Remember, we approached you first."

With a shove that sent the man back Owen snapped the door home in its frame and stood in the hall with his head down unsettled by the encounter.

Was this what Cush had warned him about? Why hadn't someone let him know IAB was coming and not to his home but his father-in-law's in Queens for godssakes. They'd tracked him down and questioned him like some street thug without telling him the truth and then they'd topped the damn thing off by threatening him.

He tossed the threat around in his head until the answer dropped his heart to the souls of his feet. Of course idiot, you looked at the husband first; looked him up down and sideways because he's always the first suspected in a spouse's murder, it was procedure, they were just following procedure meaning he was in deep trouble.

He glanced in the other room making sure Pop was gone before he walked over to the hall table pulled open the top drawer and removed his Glock weighing its hefty warmth. It had been four days since he'd carried it and as he held it he realized he'd missed the sense of security it gave him, of control, both he needed now.

Owen found the old man at the kitchen table. The warmed over lasagna sat on the stove looking like a large and glistening bloody eye ball. The Times and the Post sat unread on the table and even from where he stood he could read a headline: Few Clues in Police Ball Triple Murder.

He glanced away and looked at Pop who was flipping through a discount supermarket circular, "How're you feeling? Do you need to lie down? I'll—"

"If I wanted to rest like some cripple I'd let you know," the old man continued flipping pages now and then licking a thumb before putting it to paper.

"You mind if we put off dinner for a while? Though there's plenty of other stuff I can heat up if you want. I need to go down to the station."

Pop looked at him then, "I thought you had a few more days off."

"I do but I forgot to go over some things with Cush and I don't want to do it over the phone."

Pop stood and moved to the refrigerator, "Since we aren't having dinner I might as well have those beers you promised."

"Beer," Owen said on his way out, "I said a beer."

CHAPTER 13

Owen parked in the precinct's lot and as he got out of the car he gripped the folds of his jacket closed with one hand against a cold wind that sliced him to the bone. After days of perfect warm weather Indian summer had fled leaving behind a bitter withered fall of gray skies, fearless cold and brittle darkness. The weather goes perfect with how I'm feeling he thought as he entered the building.

He gave a brief wave to the sergeant at the front desk who was trying to coral a bunch of upset tourist whose tour bus had been stolen, "Calm down folks we're going to get you some transportation as soon as we can. Yelling is not helping and it's giving me a headache."

Owen maneuvered around the crowd, started up the stairs to the detective unit and was forced to stop behind two clerks who had halted in intense conversation. As he moved around them a middle-aged man with red hair and brows, his eyes on the business section of the Times started down toward him.

"Mel," Owen said. Detective Slater looked up wariness sliding across his face just as fire alarm bells peeled through the building.

"Crap," Mel said folding his paper up underneath his arm as he moved down toward Owen. Others holding coats, bags and packs of cigarettes came out offices and down the stairs pass them.

"Why haven't you called me back?" Owen asked having caught the look that slid off the detective's face ensuring him something was wrong. He hurried down the stairs beside Mel.

The sergeant stood on the first floor hustling people outside as sirens were heard coming up the street, "Come on people out, out. Everybody has to go."

"What set off the alarm?" Mel asked.

The sergeant jerked a thumb toward the group of tourist, "A couple of them got nervous, started smoking in the bathroom and lit the trash can on fire. Idiots."

In front of the building where the employees and visitors gathered watching the fire trucks assemble Owen asked, "You got anything new?"

"Over there." Mel led him down the sidewalk out of earshot of anyone and away from the light of a streetlamp and even then he spoke low, "We're not on the case anymore."

"Why not?" Owen was stunned; it was worse than he thought. "What happened? You and Harry—"

"Had the case taken away from us."

"Why?"

"Sh," Mel looked around, "This isn't public knowledge. They didn't tell us why just dismantled the task force and left us out in the cold. But from what I've heard they found something they could use and were running with it."

Owen tried dissecting Mel's words but none of it made sense, "Zivich and Truegood wouldn't dismantle an ongoing murder investigation would they unless they had a viable suspect ?" Mel shrugged. "You sure you're out?"

Mel slashed a finger across his throat, "Out. Let's go before someone notices us."

Confused, Owen walked back down the street as Mel disappeared into the crowd watching the fireman run back and forth into the stationhouse. Someone gripped his shoulder Owen turned and looked at his boss.

"I was just about to call you when the bells went off," Ramsey said releasing him. "I needed you to come down so I could do this in person," He looked around his face rigid with preoccupation, "Let's talk over there." Ramsey led him around the side of one of the fire trucks.

Owen spoke first, "Mel and Harry have been taken off my wife's investigation. Why?"

Ramsey sat his bulk down on the lip of the truck, "They haven't been taken off it's just become a bigger team effort and they've be assigned to a different task." Sounding irritated, "Listen I didn't bring you over here to talk about them." He let out a loud puff of air as if readying to take a leap.

"Say it. I promise not to go crazy."

"You promise ha?" A wry smile slashed across Ramsey's face "I'm going to do this in my own good time thank you, because I hate this shit." He rubbed his hands up and down his fuzzy sideburns, "Happy Halloween it's so cold. I heard Fontaine and his bunch came to see you."

"It wasn't a visit I'll remember with any fondness. Did you know they were going to call on me?" At Ramsey's nod, "You could've let me in on it."

"I had my own problems to deal with like suspending you until further notice."

Owen thought he hadn't heard right. He couldn't be receiving another body blow in the same afternoon could he? "Excuse me? I thought you said—"

"Until further notice."

Owen threw up his hands against the truck as if he was being frisked, "You have to be kidding me? Just because IAB paid me a visit? They're jerks who don't know their own assholes from a hole in the ground."

"It's a big deal or you wouldn't be here. You've been running a side investigation—no surprise to me—you're one of my best interrogators so people are going to talk to you, pass along information the task force should be handling that's the way it is, I understand it but there are people who don't and they let me know about it."

"I didn't get much."

"You shouldn't have been trying to get anything at all; that's the problem. Then you went and talked to Peterson."

Owen didn't say anything because his boss was right. He'd spoken to James Peterson the chief medical examiner just forty-eight hours earlier. He'd come out of the morning fog and Peterson had jumped dropping the cup of take-out coffee he'd been clutching. He'd stared at the man who seemed to have materialized out of the fog shrouded air who stood between him and the morgue's entrance.

"Detective Story nice to see you," Peterson said recognizing Owen. They'd had close dealings with each other on a number of unfortunate occasions.

"I didn't mean to startle you and make you drop your coffee."

"There's more inside."

Peterson was a big man, raw boned with thinning wheat blond hair and weathered gray eyes surrounded by hundreds of tiny sunburst lines. He reminded Owen of an Iowa farmer with his large blunt fingers that looked ready to sift bags of wheat and barley instead of the human entrails and body parts he plied through for a living.

"What were the results of your autopsy on my wife?"

Peterson's eyes shaded over, "You're here then in your official capacity detective? We usually go over such information in my office."

"It's not official and I think you know it; you've already met the primaries on the case."

"Since I have I can't tell you the results can I?"

"You were called in that very night to perform the autopsies on all three weren't you?"

"All right," Peterson shrugged, "I guess it won't hurt to admit it. They were given top priority so I worked them one after the other."

"With the same results?"

"Same manner of death. Same cause. Bullet wounds to the vital organs."

"Same gun then."

"I don't do ballistics but in my experience, yes. One shot each. It looked—" he said softly, "I'm sorry, detective—as if your wife was shot first then Jocelyn Chandler; similar entrance wounds and last the young officer who was shot in the head."

"The head?" Owen was surprised until he remembered the ugly hole in the side of the cop's face. Why had he been killed differently? What had happened in those brief moments after Lorna and Jocelyn's deaths?

"A surprise to me too. The killer got up tight and close."

"One more thing and I'll let you go," Owen stepped closer his dark gaze steady. "Was there a reason you weren't supposed to talk to me? Were you ordered not to? And by whom?"

A humorless smile crossed Peterson's lips, "That's more than one question detective."

Owen flashed back a humorless smile, "Come on," his voice had a we're-all-buddies-here edge to it, "You can tell me."

"No one can order me to do anything I'm the chief remember? But let me put it this way, I was informed these were special—very special—cases and keeping information under a strict need-to-know basis was imperative."

"I need to know."

"What are you after, detective?" The chief's eyes narrowed as if he were staring at a blazing Midwestern sun, "Closure? The killer? Or worse, vengeance."

Owen turned away, "Thanks, I won't forget this."

"I wish you would," Peterson called relieved he'd gotten off so lightly as he watched the fog roll into the space the detective had stood.

"You scared him half to death," the edge on Ramsey's words captured Owen's attention. "You can be downright scary when you want to be. He didn't want to snitch but he didn't want to jeopardize an on going investigation either. You're interfering Owen and the people in charge don't like it."

"All right," Owen said straight faced. "I'll stop."

"Don't fuck with me Owen. And that's not even half of it; they got you on assault of a fellow officer."

"That sergeant? Or the skinny uniform in the alley?"

"Listen to you, a list; there's enough right there. But it's neither of them; it's Blume."

Owen rolled his eyes, "I just cleaned his clock a little, school boy stuff I'm sorry about now so why hold it against me?"

"Of course he's not going to file charges against another cop, he'll never live it down but he could have and it's enough it's out there. Listen Owen I don't blame you for any of this, it was your wife but this is beyond you and me. There are explosive questions stomping around without answers and without serious suspects and its got people edgy, so until they've got something my hands are tied here." Ramsey sat back against the truck his face drooping with fatigue and sympathy, "So you're out."

"This can't be happening," Owen threw up his hands in angry exasperation, "I'm really out?" At Ramsey's nod, "Who ordered it? Was it Truegood? Or did it come from the Undertaker? Or better still, Chandler himself?"

"What're you going to do? Beat'em up? Just let it go and look at it as an extended time off due to bereavement and if anything changes I'll call you."

71

"This is shitty."

"Yeah and it's a done deal," Ramsey waved a weary hand at him. "Please, just walk away and go home."

"I don't have to go along with this," Owen said unwilling to accept what his boss said.

Ramsey shrugged as shattered glass hit the sidewalk a few feet from them. They jumped back as a large floor heater crashed to the ground splintering steel.

"Hey," they shouted looking up.

Two firemen looked down at them from a hole where a window used to be, "Sorry," one said as they both laughed.

"Firemen, I swear they're born with a trash-something gene; and goddammit I think that was my office heater. Go home Owen," Ramsey repeated and hurried away.

Owen watched him go. Does he think I'm going to sit on my ass and not investigate Lorma's murder? Impossible; they'll have to kill me first.

"You almost got brained there, partner. Your days are numbered," Cush appeared beside him.

"Where did you come from?"

"I was waiting for the boss to take a hike. We gotta go."

Cush hustled Owen through the cold and complaining crowd still waiting to go back inside and around the western corner of the station house just as the man he wanted to avoid saw them and tried to push his way through to them.

"Come on," Cush glanced back as he urged them through a break in the wall used as a shortcut into the sheltered end of the parking lot. "Hurry it up," Cush nodded at a few of the early arrivals for the shift change as he stopped at his car and opened the passenger door for Owen. "We gotta leave before Gunderson shows up."

Owen stood at the open door his puzzlement at his partner's behavior instantly replaced by suspicious anger. This time he wouldn't put this down to Cush-just-being-Cush, something else was going on and he wasn't taking another step until he got at least an answer to one of his questions.

"Why should I give a rat's ass Gunderson knows I'm here?"

It was true he wasn't buddy-buddy or even fairly chummy with a lot of the people he worked with—Cush being the one exception—and had long ago given up trying to win them over.

YOU DON'T KNOW ME

Instead he got along best he could with the other cops, except for one Alfred Al Gunderson.

Al hadn't wanted to get along, as a matter of fact he'd disliked Owen the moment he'd set eyes on him and the feeling had been mutual which had been too bad because they had found themselves partnered up and unable to make it together for more than six months. They had clashed from sun up to sun down, one not giving an inch to the other and not giving a shit if the other didn't like it.

And when he'd begun—despite Gunderson's efforts to sabotage and backstab him—to make his mark causing the people at the Plaza to take notice, it had gotten really ugly then. Gunderson had begun to do some actual work though mainly trying to knock his rising star out of the sky.

"What's this crap about Gunderson?"

"Get in," Cush got in the car and started it up. "And I'll explain everything." Having no choice and wanting to talk about what Ramsey had said and IAB's visit Owen got in.

As Cush pulled out into the street and down the block, Owen looked at him, "So what's—", he didn't get the rest out because a man popped up from the back seat and scared him into screaming, "Holy shit."

CHAPTER 14

He grabbed for his gun as one of the man's hands flew over the seat and clamped over his.

"Oh hell," Cush, his eyes still on the road, reached out a hand the size of a bear's paw and clamped it over theirs, "It's Harwood; with the night shift."

Owen smacked down hard on his partner's hand Cush let go and Owen threw off Harwood's hand, "Stop the car," he said and gripped the door handle as if readying to fling the door open and jump out.

"Owen—."

"Stop the goddamn car, Cush."

Cursing again Cush ignored the horns barking on their tail and shoved the car to the side of the road.

Owen threw open the door and had his right foot on the sidewalk when Hardwood spoke his voice as cold as the look in his dark stern eyes, "If you want to keep living you'll get your ass back in this car and shut up."

"What did you say," Owen felt his mouth go spit less as he stared back at the man and the dead serious look in his eyes. 'If you want to keep living?' What in God's name was he supposed to do in face of that disturbing pronouncement? Get back in the car you jerk and find out how it'll effect if you live tomorrow. Or not. Damn.

"You need to hear him out Owen," Cush said. "Now," he got them going again. "Your horoscope said today your life would be rife with dark mystery or was it mayhem? Like one's fucking better than the other."

That was the last thing said for some time as they rolled along in a tense silence from avenue to avenue, street to street until they became the streets of Harlem then one West 116th, "Is this the place?" Cush slowed.

Owen glanced once in the mirror and found Hardwood's gaze on him the look as closed and as darkly remote as an ice flow.

"The building on the corner," Harwood answered.

Cush wheeled the car around back of a three story newly renovated office plaza and parked in one of four reserved spaces. "Be patient for once in your life," he said to Owen and got out of the car.

"You weren't scared into a goddamn heart attack," Owen muttered as he reluctantly followed them into the building.

After he disengaged the alarm Harwood led them up a short flight of carpeted stairs and down a hall. He stopped in front of a door with: Norman Mitchell DDS and Associates printed on it. Inside he led them through a decorated reception room, down a short hall and into the last room in the back, an examination room. He turned on the lights and closed the door. Cush positioned himself back against it as Harwood pulled out a stool, sat and pointed to the patient's examination chair.

"Have a seat Story."

Owen glanced from the impassive face the color of teak to the chair. He'd always hated visiting the dentist, they seemed to give him nothing but bad news and he guessed this visit would be no different. He stiffly straddled the chair planting both feet on each side for balance.

"Why here?" he tried a brief smile that felt stiff as cardboard. "What are you going to do? Pull out all my teeth or x-ray me to death?"

"Just talk," Harwood hitched his chin toward the room. "My brother-in-law's new office; three times the size of his old place."

"Good for him."

"It's the only place I could think where we would be completely safe."

"Safe? From whom? Or what? Tell me what the hell's going on? I don't need this yanking me around—"

"I'm going to arrest you for triple murder," Harwood calmly broke in.

"No, "Owen shot out the chair as if catapulted almost falling over in his haste. "You're out of your goddamn mind, pal," he looked around at Cush, "You knew about this?" he slapped his forehead, "Of course you knew. This is a sick joke right?"

Cush shook his head, "There's nothing funny about what's coming. Believe me. I told you something was up, something wicked."

Harwood kicked the stool aside. "You're done," he cut the air with his hand. "Finished. You're headed for the needle—pal. And not only for the murder or your wife, for Jocelyn Chandler and Bobby Tynon too."

Owen's mind went dark as his insides turned to hot volcanic rock and dropped to his knees, "How the fuck are they going to pin their murders on me?"

"How?" Harwood's eyes narrowed until only pinpoints of harsh light shown, "You're talking about the cops here," he stabbed a thumb at his chest, "Us. We can do whatever we want and turning out a lightweight like you is done over lunch. The DA's foaming at the mouth for your ass right now; the grand jury is sitting down as we speak and a warrant is being prepared for your arrest; even the FBI's in on the game looking to hang you up. And when you're arrested—not if—when, you're going to get the royal treatment from body cavity searches on down. Need more?"

"Son-of-a-bitch," Owen's hand went to the top of his head as if to keep it from blowing off, "I don't believe it. Son-of-a-bitch."

He was positive now, absolutely one hundred percent sure he was walking a nightmare. His wife had been murdered and the police department—his supposed brothers-in-blue—thought, no, believed he'd done it. He turned on Harwood desperate, "There was somebody who saw something or someone. Who can prove it was not me. I can find him—"

"We already have," Harwood snapped. "A junkie thief who barely knew his name. He didn't see anything and half of what he told us he made up. He was cut loose within hours, as useless as a pile of dog shit. Bottom line Story you were the one seen with all three victims. The fight with your wife—"

"It wasn't a fight," Owen evened out the panic in his voice as he fought for control, "it wasn't a fight. People were going in and out all evening so why look at me?"

"None of those people ended up with a dead wife."

Wrong; the word exploded through Owen's mind. He hadn't been the only one with a dead wife. Chandler is standing right there beside me but it's obvious he isn't suspected, I'm the only one in front of the bull's-eye.

"I didn't kill anyone."

"I didn't kill anyone," Hardwood mimicked hot skepticism flowing over his words, "What else are you supposed to fucking say?"

Owen paced the tiny space in front of them as Cush fingered the gleaming instruments of dental torture on the sideboard next to him, "I can't believe this is happening to me though the signs were there; right there, shouting at me like world's largest neon sign. I suspected something like this when IAB showed up that goddamn Fontaine and his 'remember-we-approached-you-first' ass; they just wanted to be the first on my ass."

He glanced hastily at Cush, "You even tried to warn me but I let it go, didn't think it through." He stopped pacing and glared at Harwood his anger barely leashed, "Again, why me? Of all those people in that ballroom why me?"

Harwood's face twisted, "Are you blind as well as stupid? All signs point to you Story. You were the only one in the room who had contact with each victim no matter how brief you say it was; and why not you? What makes you so goddamn special?" He spat the words at Owen who reared back.

In that instant Owen realized Harwood wasn't just furious at him he hated him either for what he thought he'd done or the nasty situation he found himself in; which ever one it was Owen knew if the man had his way he'd grab one of his brother-in-law's sharp dental tools and eviscerate him, leaving his guts swimming in the spit bowl.

"You're a nobody from Long Island who walked right in with your daily planner and progress charts and pushed your way around and up."

"There's nothing wrong with going after cases instead of sitting around twiddling my thumbs doing paperwork until retirement or a bullet up my ass," Owen shot back figuring his anger outweighed Harwood's by ten tons.

Harwood's face hardened even more until it looked carved of burnished wood, "You act as if you don't halfway give a shit yet you're moving up the departmental ladder."

Owen stared at him in disbelief before glancing at Cush, "What is this personal crap?" To Harwood, "It sounds personal to me. I'm about to get fried and you're talking this."

"You got promoted before me and three other guys who'd been around longer than you."

Owen made a face as he waved a dismissive hand at him, "Take it to the grievance board."

Harwood stabbed a finger at him, "That's it right there—"

"Get over it—"

"Shit like that rubs people the wrong way."

"That's not my fucking problem."

Cush looked up from examining a range of wicked looking scalers, long needles with thick handles, " He can't help it he's a good interrogator and most of the time without having to say more than ten words. They just open up to him," he grinned, "It's like magic."

"Yeah, I heard how you can make shit holes tell you where they buried the first kitten they strangled," derision flowed over Harwood's words. "Something to truly be proud of."

"It works. And for those who don't like it too bad."

"Your attitude makes you enemies in the department like Gunderson who was number one boy before you showed up. He thinks you'll make captain before he does and he's running on a very dangerous combination of paranoia and ambition."

"He's a fat son-of-a-bitch who can't run anywhere."

Harwood straightened, "He's my partner."

"Oh, I get it now, "a humorless smile passed across Owen's lips. "At this moment I feel sorrier for you than I do for myself. Luckily I bailed after six months with him and for good reasons or I was going to kill him—"

"A ha you see," Harwood crowed. "Shitty attitude."

"Or he was going to kill me. We got along as well as Cain and Abel."

"You're both ambitious—"

"But I work for what I want while he sucks up to get it or gets somebody else to do the work while he takes the credit."

Harwood shrugged, "Not the worst cop in the world though a possible first runner up. Nevertheless, he's still my partner and I stand-by him."

"You should call Manny," Cush said.

"I'm going to need a truckload of lawyers."

"A truckload won't help you either," Harwood leaned down into Owen's face, his words freezing his blood, "Don't you get it? There's nothing you can do; nothing. A sacrificial lamb was needed to throw to the tax-paying-scared-spit-less-voting-public because if the Commish's wife can get axed in a public place surrounded by cops then they're hamburger." He taped his cheek thoughtfully, "So what to do? What to do? What can we give them to make them sleep nights again? A crack-head out of his mind? A serial killer? No, how about something much better; let's give them a bad cop, a very bad cop they'll eat that one up because it'll prove their suspicion most cops are monsters anyway."

"And you Story, you made it so easy: your troubling contact with each victim, no corroborating witnesses, a flimsy alibi and best of all nobody gives a shit about you except maybe Cush here. So you're fucked," he laughed. "Fucked."

Owen stared at him with a mouth dry as dust as his heart beat like it would implode from sheer terror so struck by the ferocity and the supreme surety in Harwood's voice. He was wrong, he had to be. Owen swallowed forcing out a pained click, "I don't have a motive."

"That little show you put on with your wife. Then the opportunity to get rid of her presented itself and even though the others were in the way you didn't let it stop you for a minute," Harwood whispered. "You did it anyway."

"That's lunatic; you can't—" Owen broke off as sweat coated him like a wet sweater. He couldn't go on and they knew it. He'd put together the same scenario countless times, fitted what he thought happened together like a puzzle, linked it step-by-step, one-two-three and somebody is going to prison; as easy as that just like Harwood said. It was just this time he was the some body.

A heavy corrupt silence filled the room until Harwood added, "There's one more thing."

Owen groaned and sagged, "There couldn't be." Helpless exhaustion hit him until he was ready to curl up into a tight ball on the floor.

"Richard Giordano."

"What does he have to do with any of this?"

Contempt flared in Hardwood's eyes as he looked him up and down, "Most cops aren't friends with mobsters; both on your way up in your

present positions—or at least you were."

"I can't believe it," Owen shook his head in total bewilderment, "All this because I went to take a piss."

"Alone right?"

"I should've had an entourage?" Owen countered fury and shock running through him. This must be what a caged animal feels with no way out. "This is so....so nuts. I've been loyal to the department, done everything—everything—I thought right. And dammit," His voice was harsh with raw grief, "I loved my wife."

"You wouldn't be the first man to lov'em and kill'em."

That was it Owen boiled over, "Fuck you."

"No, fuck you," Harwood tossed right back and Owen rushed him.

Cush just managed to step between them a fleshy wall in the small space as the tray of dentist torture tools toppled over as Owen tried to go around Cush to get at Harwood, surprising the man who was at least thirty pounds heavier and a couple of inches taller.

"The hell with this," Owen raised his hands to shoulder height giving it up, "Okay, I'm done." He straightened his jacket, "I'm walking out of here but not before you answer me this." He stared at Harwood. "If you hate my ass why do this? Why let me know what's coming?"

Harwood's brown face filled with a storm of resentment as if Owen had asked the worst question in the world, "Because you're a cop; one of us. Why else would I do it?"

"Thanks for the warning," Owen opened the door then looked at him, "For the rest, kiss my ass," he slammed it on his way out.

CHAPTER 15

Night slid over the city with a slyness only coming winter brings. After misjudging stops it took Owen two trains and a bus to get back to the 1-9 and retrieve his car.

After calling Pop to check on him he headed to his own apartment not ready to go to the old man's yet wanting to be alone to think. He reached home still furious and calmed only after he'd walked through the hollow empty rooms turning on all the lights while he worked out a plan.

A couple of hours later he was leaning against his car's roof gazing through binoculars at one of the most beautiful and holy places in the city, Trinity Church. He was parked at the open end of an alley between an empty store with a for sale sign in the window and a closed pizza joint.

He watched the crowd that milling around the church's entrance and the mourners who'd arrived to attend the funeral of Jocelyn Chandler. Now and then his gaze would move toward "Ground Zero" not far from where he stood. Even after all this time he still felt terrible sadness at who was lost and what was forever changed.

He put down the binoculars and picked up one of the four remaining beers from the six pack sitting on the car's roof. After he took a healthy swig he checked his watch, he'd been studying the church and its guests for more than an hour though his thoughts were centered on Harwood's words.

Could he believe them? It was crazy, nuts. Yet did he believe the entire department considered him a murderer? Pictures flashed in his head: arrested, put in lock-up and secluded because he was a cop and his life was worth one cent definitely not two. A speedy trial, the courtroom full of people eager to see him given

81

death not life; the unsteady walk to the death house, laid out on the gurney, strapped down and the needle full of lethal poison poised on his throbbing purple vein before it sinks in, his last breath in then out and he's gone. He gulped the rest of the beer in one swallow.

Lights flashed at the church and he took a look. Oh great, the media, acting as if they were at a movie premiere instead of a funeral. "Ah," he said aloud, "here comes the mayor and good old Commissioner Chandler."

He sharpened the glasses focus and watched Cardinal Richard Donohue take one of Chandler's hands in both of his as they stood beside Mayor Ezra Jackson, a bald stout man with a bristly black mustache who was looking respectfully somber. Owen focused on Chandler until he could count his teeth.

"The luck of the devil," he muttered. He scanned the faces streaming out of the sanctuary then those of the heavy contingent of uniformed officers and gawkers watching the famous.

Could the killer be down there? Right there. He focused again on Chandler who was laughing as he talked to a wealthy looking couple the woman in a huge black fur coat and matching hat. Yes, the killer was there all right and if no one believed it then too bad, he knew it was true, felt it, and he'd make Chandler pay.

A hand reached around his shoulder and plucked one of the two remaining bottles out of its holder. He turned and collided with Cush who tossed the bottle into the air.

"What are you doing Owen?" his voice was casual. "Sight seeing? I knew you wouldn't be able to stay away from Jocelyn Chandler's send off. What if you get caught spying on the funeral? Somebody could see you and call—" Cush broke off and closed his eyes shaking his head, "Am I psychic or what."

A patrol car pulled across the alley. The cops in their early thirties with sharp marine haircuts looked at them, then at each other and spoke in low tones as their car radio squawked a series of calls.

"Barry, how you do'in? I thought that was you," Cush said.

The driver stared at him then smiled, "Hey Cush, it's been a while since I've seen you down here." The smile dimmed, "You okay over there?"

"Fine, you ever meet my partner Owen Story?"

Barry looked at Owen, his partner tipped his head forward and stared at him too. No one said a word. Barry looked away and put the patrol car in gear, "We'll see you around Cush. Be careful, there's a lot going on down here tonight."

Cush put a hand to his forehead as if he had a headache, "Owen you gotta be more circumspect."

"Why? I didn't do anything?" Owen felt anger swell in his belly. "Chandler's the one," he gestured down the street. "He's the one who had something to do with Lorna's death."

"You've had too much of this shit," Cush grabbed the bottle out of Owen's hand and tossed it along with the one he still held into the nearest trash can.

"I'd bet my left kidney Cush, he's involved up to his scalp and I'm going to prove it."

Cush's saturnine features were pinched with aggravation, "Do you hear yourself? You're accusing the police commissioner of New York City of triple homicide. Don't you at the very least—," he held his thumb and forefinger up close together, "—think it's just a tiny bit farfetched?"

"Hell no; he's dirty and I'm going to prove it." Owen turned away and stared back toward the church, "And anyway you know you suspect the husband first like they're suspecting me; I'm going to give Chandler the same treatment."

All of a sudden the fierceness that had fired his words drained out of him and he picked up the last unopened bottle and almost dropped it as he stumbled back against the car. His coordination was off he realized. He was tipsy off four beers, couldn't hold his liquor anymore. What a sorry ass he was turning out to be.

"Look," Cush gently took the bottle. "Let me drive you home."

"No, I'm not finished yet. I'm going to follow Chandler; see what he's up to."

"Don't do it Owen."

"He can't get away with what he's done."

"Look," his partner glanced around, "We need to get out of here before somebody else calls the cops. I'll drive you home so you can start over tomorrow. I'll call somebody for my car."

"Tomorrow," Owen laughed weakly, "Life has been such a treat, such great fun lately I'm so looking forward to tomorrow."

Cush led his now subdued partner around to the passenger side of the car retrieving the keys from his pocket before installing him inside.

Owen put his foot on the door holding it open, "And another thing: I didn't like the way Harwood talked to me like I was New York's Jack-the-Ripper."

"He's trying to save your life."

"I don't need his help."

"Oh man, Owen you're some piece of work." Cush closed the door, got in the driver's side and turned to him. "Lorna is dead. Dead. You hear me?" he stared into his partner's stunned eyes. "And there's nothing you can do to bring her back."

"Right now you have to take care of your own ass or you'll be seeing her sooner than you think. Is that what you want? Is it?" When Owen didn't answer Cush jerked the car to life and with a roar of gas shot them out the alley.

Cush opened the front door to Owen's apartment turning on the lights before he led him through to the darkened bedroom. He pushed him down onto the bed removing his shoes and coat before he let him fall back into the mattress. "You gonna be all right?" his look of concern was illuminated by the light coming from the lamppost outside.

"No but I'll deal with it; tomorrow."

"I'll lock up and slip the key under the door," Cush tossed the car keys on the dresser. Owen didn't respond.

His partner turned to leave and stopped when Owen said out of the semi-darkness, "Thanks Cush; for all of it. I'll see you tomorrow." Cush nodded and left him alone.

When the clock struck three Owen's phone rang and rang on the twelfth ring he came out of his pickled-sleep-state into a kind of awakened-dream-state and even then it rung four more times before he realized what the sound was and reached for the receiver.

"Yeah?" his voice was thick with sleep and dissipating alcohol. There was no answer from the other end only heavy almost rushed breathing that caused Owen's eyes to open, "Hello?"

"I know you were watching," he recognized the voice and sat up in bed pressing the phone to his ear.

"I'm not calling during business hours because this has nothing to do with daily business," Commissioner Chandler said as if he called everyday. "And don't you worry about this call I'm on a secure line so no one knows we're talking."

On Riverside Drive in an exclusive neighborhood he stood in front of the patio doors in his library the phone at his ear, a highball glass of whiskey in his right hand as he looked out onto his security lit backyard. He had removed his suit jacket and dislodged his tie right after the funeral.

On the other end of the line a rush of stark disbelief rolled over Owen, "What do you want?" How had Chandler known he'd been watching him? Because you're being watched that's how. Was Chandler coming for him now? Owen got off the bed moved to the side of the window to stare out; nothing moved in the street.

"Don't you think I know what you're up to?" Chandler spun away from the view and stalked across the dimly lit room to his desk where he dropped his glass, it thudded against the marble like a hammer against the skull. "You're a goddamn amateur so I'll make this short and sweet: stop screwing around in the investigation or I'll fuck you up."

The fuzz in Owen's brain was blown away at Chandler's words, "What's wrong with you? I'm——"

"Jeopardizing," Chandler rode over his words, "the investigation and I won't have it. The team working these cases is doing a fine job and don't need your interference. I thought I took care of you but it looks like I haven't done enough. If I hear you're sticking your nose where it doesn't belong again, I'm going to cut it off and I can do it too because I'm the goddamn police commissioner." He pressed hard the "end" button then tossed the phone onto the desk.

He picked up his drink and twirled the dark liquid staring into its depths, "I want this Story thing wrapped up as soon as possible; sooner."

Rider who'd been sitting in a deep stuffed chair his face shadowed and angular said, "I'll push it hard." He held aloft his glass, "Congratulations Police Commissioner Chandler for bravely getting through such a no doubt trying day without a tear or an unseemly bit of emotion."

Chandler giggled, "Didn't I play it beautifully? So stalwart and strong."

"I won't be long before you can replace Commissioner with Your Honorable Mayor."

"Don't you just love the sound of that?" Chandler grinned as he downed the rest of his whiskey.

Owen listened to dead air for a long time before he let the receiver slip from his grasp. Chandler, top cop and raving maniac had just threatened him by way of a late night call. No one would believe it. Yet why was he acting surprised? He believed the man was a party to murdering three people so his insane threats were for him all in a days work.

Owen lay stiffly back in the bed as his mine played over the menacing call; the truth was, Lunatic Chandler had the power to make his threats come true. Owen listened to his breathing as he tried not to listen to the soft sneaky sounds of the presence of his dead wife gliding through the darkness, the disquieting thought making him listen harder.

Stop it you fool. It isn't Lorna's gliding ghostly form creeping you out but Chandler, the man scared the daylights out of you. Owen got off the bed and searched for his shoes. He couldn't sleep there tonight, possibly never again; the surety of this stayed with him as he grabbed his keys and was out the apartment seconds later.

CHAPTER 16

After a circuitous route to Kew Gardens feeling the hairs on his neck rise every time he thought he caught someone tailing him, Owen stood trying to find the key hole in Pop's back door in the dark; it took several tries before he home, unlocked the door. He was definitely going to get Pop a security light because trying to find a tiny key hole in pitch dark was like trying to drive blind.

Inside the kitchen he locked the door behind him before moving to the fridge and taking out a couple of beers. Without turning on any lights he walked into the front hall and took off his coat before placing his gun in the top drawer of the hall table. As he quietly made his way up to the second floor he hoped his father-in-law was asleep because he didn't feel like explaining anything but as he stepped onto the landing Pop stood framed in his bedroom doorway.

The old man took in his son-in-law's face and the beers, "You gonna make it?"

"I think so. You eat okay? Take the pills? The doctor said you have to take them at least a half-hour after you eat. I'm sorry I should've been here to make sure." Pop didn't say anything just looked at him with a complicated watchfulness, "Don't worry," Owen said quietly. "We'll be okay."

At this Pop rolled his eyes and retreated back into his room. Owen heard the springs of his bed creak as he lay down.

I don't think I'm doing too badly Owen congratulated himself as he dropped onto the bed in the other room. Lorna would be proud of him; he'd made it this far without shooting himself or anyone else. Propping himself up on the pillows he

87

drank the beers one after the other carefully sitting the empties on the nightstand.

Settling back against the pillows he hoped it would take only seconds before the combination of fatigue, fright, an empty stomach and a pretty hefty amount of alcohol dropped him into the hole of sleep without his having to think about anything or anyone, especially not his dead wife.

It seemed he'd hit black oblivion for a few precious seconds before he was shaken awake. He rolled off his face and stared bleary eyed up into the face of a gargoyle. It took a moment before he recognized Pop who looked simultaneously amazed and furious.

"Someone's in the house," he whispered.

Instantly alert and sobered as if he'd been dunked in an Alaskan stream Owen swung his legs off the bed. He put a finger to his lips as he urged Pop into the bathroom before handing him the phone off the nightstand and mouthing the numbers: 9-1-1.

He quietly closed the bathroom door before he moved out of the room on to the landing to listen. No sound came from downstairs though it didn't make him doubt Pop; the old man knew his house; an intruder was inside. The question rolled through his mind: what was he going to do about it? Was this a burglary? Or worse? Come on who gives a shit, he ran an agitated hand threw his hair if it's a burglary or a surprise house warming party there isn't a damn thing you can do because your gun is down there in the hall drawer.

He backed into the room and picked up the table lamp, a heavy thing with a steel neck and base wrapping the cord around its bottom before moving out to the head of the stairs where he peered down into the front hall whose gloom was broken only by the ambient light coming from the streetlamp. Nothing moved. No sound.

He slipped down the first two stairs and froze as he heard a familiar sound, one he'd heard a thousand times; the grating shift of glass-on-glass. The intruder had replaced the top of the candy dish filled with fruit Life Savers sitting on the mantle piece; an intruder with a sweet-tooth?

He went down two more stairs his back against the wall. If I can just get over to the table and grab my gun before the asshole appears—sirens pierced the air shattering his thoughts as a masked man ran out of the living room. He glanced at the front door then directly up at Owen pinning him like a butterfly held by a butcher knife. Owen threw the lamp at him before vaulting over the banister. The intruder knocked it aside as if it was a feather and hurled himself at Owen just as Owen's fingers pulled the drawer out slamming him into the wall underneath the stairs; Owen felt his back scream as they crashed to the floor.

The masked man pulled on top of him, his gloved fingers spidering around his throat to clamp like steel bands, his hot breath panting into Owen's face smelling of cherry Life Savers and panic. Owen scrabbled at the fingers cutting off his air barely hearing the heavy blow to the front door that shattered the inset glass.

The intruder let go and scrambled off him as Owen coughing and gagging grabbed for a hold on the man's anything, caught his right pants leg and dug his fingers through the fabric into the man's flesh as if he were digging through hamburger. The intruder fell forward with a grunt rolling on his back and quick as a cat kicked back with his free leg; his boot connecting with Owen's left cheekbone; Owen went down writhing in solid pain.

Desperate, crawling now the masked man shot to his feet and ran for the kitchen just as the front door blew open hammering against the wall. Two uniformed officers ran in their flashlight beams spearing Owen as he clutched the side of his face with one hand and pointed toward the kitchen with the other. They pushed around him, stumbled over him; one of them stepping on Owen's right hand in their haste, he howled as they took off for the kitchen.

Owen collapsed onto his back his eyes scrunched closed at the white-hot agony that raced between his hand and cheek. He heard footsteps coming down the stairs but didn't open his eyes until light hit his eyelids. He looked at Pop hanging over him his face white with concern.

"God almighty you all right?"

"Never better," Owen touched his cheek, it was raw, bleeding and twice its normal size though he didn't think the bone was broken. He glanced at his hand, the skin on his knuckles was gone leaving an open bloody sore.

Pop helped him stand and they moved to sit on the stairs to wait for the cops. Twenty minutes passed and still the officers hadn't returned.

"Wait here," Owen got carefully to his feet and moved into the darkened kitchen over to the wall beside the window that looked out onto the back yard. He peered at the cops who stood near the hedge separating the yards whispering to each other, their flashlights aimed at the ground. What were they doing? Had they been standing there all this time instead of going after the guy? One of them moved through the hedge and was back a moment later. They then headed for the house.

Owen quickly stepped away from the window, out of the kitchen and back to sit beside Pop just as they appeared, their shoulder radios squawking. He didn't know them. They were around his age, height and weight one black the other white.

The black officer, Maxwell Dumas Owen read off his nameplate spoke first, "We went through your backyard and the next out into the street and nothing. If there—"

"No if," Owen cut in, "Someone broke in and when I caught him he tried to kill me."

"Broke in?" Dumas frowned. "The lock's still in place; doesn't look tampered with it. Was the door locked?"

Owen thought about it. He was positive he'd locked it after he'd come inside; he hadn't been too plastered he'd forgotten to take that precaution, "Yes, he must've picked it."

"A he? You sure?" the other officer asked wiping sweat off a face that needed a shave. His name was Russell Thome off hand Owen wondered if he was related to the former Cleveland hitter.

"No, I'm not positive; whoever it was wore a mask," Owen loaded irritation on top of the words, "but fairly certain because if he was a woman she'd be the poster child for steroid abuse."

"You didn't get a look at him," Dumas concluded.

"He wore a mask," Owen's irritation slid into anger.

"He must've kept it on as he took off," skepticism edged Dumas's words as he glanced from his partner to Owen. "We searched around and didn't find anything. I've called for patrols in the area to be on the look out. Anything missing?"

"I don't know. Pop?" Owen turned to him. "Could you look around in case he took something so it can be reported?" Pop nodded and disappeared into the living room.

"You're kidding," Thome's face soured. "If you make out a report we'll have to do one too and it'll take half the night."

"I'm going to make a report and put in whatever I think necessary. Anything else you have to say about it?"

"Nothing missing in there," Pop called and headed into the kitchen.

"How far are you going to take this?" Thome asked his anger out in the open. "I suppose you're going to have to talk to a detective too and make more work for us."

"I don't need a detective," Owen tried not to sound condescending but they were making it too easy, "On my own I was able to figure out someone was trying to kill me. So if you—" he broke off feeling as if he'd just been clocked in the forehead with a ball peen hammer. They didn't believe him. It was why they had stood in the backyard instead of looking for the intruder. They thought he was a liar who'd made the guy up. Or was it because it had already gotten around he was person non-grata? And if they'd caught the guy taking his head off they might've clapped.

"Okay," he said resigned there would be no help here. "Tell you what: leave. Go. Write it up, don't write it up; do whatever you want I don't care. I'll put in my paperwork later."

He turned toward the demolished front door and pushed aside the broken glass with his foot fingering the broken locks. He would have to secure the door but first thing tomorrow he would get Pop an alarm system with flood lights if he had to no matter how badly the old man kicked up about it. He pushed open what remained of the door and watched the cops pass by him out onto the porch.

Dumas looked at him, "So it's all right we—"

"It's not all right but there's nothing I can do about it."

Thome shook his head and stomped down the stairs to the patrol car. Dumas stayed back, "Okay someone broke into your house; we're not idiots you know. The guy was fast or knew how to get around us because there was no sign of him either way. There is nothing we can do here."

"Even if you'd wanted too right?" Owen watched Dumas down the stairs. "You guys have a problem with me."

Dumas didn't stop walking as he shot back over his shoulder "We're not the one with the problem."

Back inside the house Owen filtered the cop's words. He was positive now he was a topic of conversation at every roll call, over police radios, at every shift change meaning he was now on his own and in dangerous trouble.

He turned to go get wood for the door and almost collided with Pop who stood behind him a look of alarm in his eyes that threw Owen's already careening heart into over drive.

"From the rack," Pop said, "the butcher's knife's gone."

CHAPTER 17

He let himself into the detective's house and ran to the bathroom. Flinging open the medicine cabinet door he knocked cold medicine and toothbrushes into the sink until he found a roll of bandages and a bottle of rubbing alcohol.

"He had the fucking nerve to hurt me; the fucking nerve," he gritted through his teeth to his mirror image.

Sitting on the lip of the tub he rolled up his right pant leg and examined the wounds. Ripping off a clod of toilet paper he doused it with alcohol. He put his foot up on the washbasin and starring at himself in the mirror, he put the dripping wad to the deep gouges and pressed it hard into his flesh. He didn't scream as his wounds shrieked on fire instead he pressed harder and watched as the raw harsh pain made him drool, the spittle dripping from the corners of his mouth down his chin.

After more agonizing seconds he pulled the wad away and stuffed the blood soaked mess into his pocket before he studied his wounds again and decided he was lucky to have gotten away because if the detective had held on he would be in jail right now or worst.

The cop was a tough son-of-a-bitch. He hadn't wanted to let go until he'd gotten that kick in the face; he smiled at the memory as he wrapped his leg in a bandage and contemplated what he should do next. From his pocket he took out rubber gloves and pulled them on. He would have to clean before he left, start at the front door and erase all traces of his presence leaving not even a ghostly disturbance of the air in his wake.

First though he'd take something from the detective in retaliation for the pain he'd caused him. Walking into the bedroom he stopped and giggled; hadn't he already taken something from the man? He smacked his hand over his mouth to stop the sound from growing. Well in a way, so what was that compared to taking a few trinkets.

He opened the drawers in Lorna's French armoire and waded through her silk underwear admiring a few pieces before his fingers unearthed a round plastic manila colored packet. Flipping open the lid he counted what was left of Lorna's birth control pills. She'd been on schedule up until the day she had died; she'd been determined not to give life and ended up losing her own. He pocketed the case; it would make a nice keepsake.

From off the top of Owen's dresser he picked up a jeweler's blue velvet ring box. Inside were two sets of gold collar pins fashioned into the numbers one and nine. Cops wore them only on special occasions he knew so the detective would probably not miss a set. Yet his fingers hesitated over the pins, he could hear his own breathing loud in the room and froze glancing around. Had he been there too long? Should he leave? But he hadn't decided if he'd take these souvenirs or leave them behind because the detective was a smart ass and might miss them and wonder if someone took them and who that someone might be. He stroked the pins unable to keep his hands off; but by then it'll be too late for the cop.

"I'm going to have to kill you Detective Story," he said out loud with no regrets at all. "I just know it."

CHAPTER 18

Owen woke an hour after falling asleep without realizing it and three hours after a aggravatingly useless trip to the local station house where he'd made out a report and was told with bored unconcern by the desk sergeant, break-ins had recently occurred in the neighborhood and Pop's place had just been next on the target list.

He sat up on the couch with his head hunched forward in his hands as he listened to the answers his body gave as he questioned it. Am I all right? Do I need to see a doctor? Does every thing still function as it should or should I lie back down and just let the day drain away?

His insides were right side up. His brain was on track and his head didn't hurt much was just a little wonky. He touched his cheek it ached along with his hand but he could live with both. Pop had mixed up a salve smelling of lemons and rubbed it on the wounds. Standing he squared his shoulders as he worked through a few conclusions he'd used self-pity, liquor and exhaustion to avoid.

After a long shower he dressed in jeans and a Tribeca Film Festival sweatshirt before checking on Pop. He knocked on his bedroom door and when he got no answer walked in. The old man lay on his back still dressed and snoring. Pop had stayed up with him most of the night until he'd pleaded with him go to bed afraid the nights antics would effect his health in some terrible way. He pulled the blankets over him before leaving the room.

Downstairs he made a few phone calls, one to Doctor Powell who reassured him Pop didn't need to come in and the rest buying a replacement door and an alarm system. He then wrote a note to the old man telling him someone would be installing a front door and a motion-detecting lighting system leaving it on the hall table before retrieving his gun from the drawer and grabbing his coat. He was out the back door when he hurried back and added a postscript to the note: Have the oatmeal, no fried eggs. I'll see you later.

At half-past nine he stood staring out at a small barge making its way down a narrow isolated stretch of the East River. He sipped from a large of coffee as he braced himself against the pushy blasts of fierce wind not in the least blocked off by a row of blackened and crumbling buildings looking as if they'd grown out of the ground and were sinking back into it.

He heard the crunch of tires and turned as Cush pulled up. His partner wore a long brown leather coat with a thick white fur collar that ran down the lapels to the waist and cocked on his head a brown fedora with a long thin white feather that waved frantic in the wind.

Owen grinned at him, "You look like a pimp."

"At least I'm a warm pimp. What the hell happened to you?" Cush stared at Owen who's face looked like a kicked around Halloween mask. "Who beat you up?"

Owen shrugged, "Some asshole who broke into Pop's house and tried to knock out the few brains I do have."

"Why didn't you call me? I woulda—"

"I know I know. The precinct rollers showed up and went after the guy who of course was long gone. That wasn't the scary part. Earlier I had a call from Chandler."

"You shitten me? What did he say?"

"He threatened me. He's the one behind the break-in."

"What does he have against you that he's sending out a hit man?"

"He's setting me up because he's involved in their murders and I know it so he wants me on death row or just dead." He threw down the coffee, "Listen to this; I'm suspended and windup the only suspect in a triple homicide, I'm told any minute I'm going to be arrested by my fellow detectives who hate my guts and if that isn't enough, someone breaks into Pop's house and tries to rip my head off and the way the only way someone could've known I was there was because I was followed. I'm not dreaming this up Cush; it's happening to me—to me—right now."

"Okay okay, Owen" Cush soothed concerned at seeing his partner so distressed. "Calm down and let me think. All right what's the first lesson you learn on the job?"

"What's this? Detective school one-o-one—"

"Come on."

"Start where it begins: with the victim. Find out as much as you can about him and work from there." Cush nodded as Owen stared at him not saying anything for a long time then shaking his head, "I can't—"

"Then ask Connie about Lorna."

"Why would I ask your wife about mine?" hurt rolled across Owen's face, "I knew Lorna better than anyone else in the world."

"Then what's this 'I can't shit'? What are you afraid of?"

"Nothing," Owen's face paled. "She wouldn't like it if I pried."

"Prying is too mild a word for what you need to do Owen and hell if you don't know it. You have no choice here."

Instead of looking at Cush, at the truth, Owen stared after the barge that had almost disappeared around a bend in the river. The wind picked up strength in its icy fingers and catching him off balance, urging him forward as if God was pushing him to go forth and uncover his wife's mysteries.

CHAPTER 19

In the gloom of the wintry afternoon the temperature having dropped enough to frost window glass, Owen walked from one beautifully decorated room to another feeling Lorna's presence in every crevice and corner of the place his fellow detectives would be convinced he'd held up mob bagmen and drug couriers to outfit. There had been days when he'd wished he'd pulled off a couple of dubious jobs for the cash to pay for the extravagances Lorna had filled their home with; instead of working those long endless hours of overtime to buy all these things he couldn't care less about but Lorna couldn't seem to live without.

Sweeping past a Caruso floor lamp he sent the shade bouncing to halt off kilter. She had never let him forget she'd worked just as hard as he at making their home "presentable" as she had put it. He righted the shade that was coated with a layer of dust; Lorna would've been upset his home making skills had lagged since she'd been gone.

She'd been a real estate agent, her territory Chelsea, Tribecca, Clinton and Midtown. She had sold small condominiums and mid-ranged apartments hating every minute of it despite the fact she'd sold more than anyone else in her office.

She had been determined to get from a mid-range seller to the big league selling super luxury properties of twelve rooms plus in exclusive buildings on the Upper East and West Sides for a cool five million or more depending on the market and the size of the client's wallet.

He'd felt uneasy with her ambition at least with what the thought of her elevated success and its trappings and obligations would do to them. He had tempered his feelings by conveying to

98

her, sometimes with more annoyance than he could hide how he didn't care if their place looked like a replica of a Pier One storeroom as long as they were happy.

She had literally become nauseated at the very idea then angry at what she considered was his lack of sophisticated taste and ambition. She had then gone about obsessively making their home a show place, putting in wallpaper by Chris Paschke and furniture from the Isamu Noguchi collection. He had asked her once if the people whose collection she'd taken the things from would want them back. She hadn't thought the question or him funny.

Threading his way from the bedroom to the living room through the study, he stopped in the kitchen that resembled a set-up out of a New England Country Kitchens magazine and stared out at the thin naked tree branches scratching against the window pane.

He'd known almost from the beginning he needed to start with her, she was the beginning; she was all he truly had. It was ironic that before her death he hadn't tried to hard to find out who she really was, the person behind the mask he loved so well and now it was like Cush said he had no choice. He couldn't run anymore from the questions plaguing him surrounding her death and if he couldn't stomach the answers as a husband then he would try with all he had to look at them from his professional, his detective's supposedly objective point of view. The victim after all got it rolling and the investigator carried it through by finding out as much as possible about her and her life which in most cases led to those two vital answers: who did it and why.

He smacked the counter with his fist. Yeah, fucking right; my problem is the victim is not a stranger but the woman I love. And no matter how hard he tried this fact stayed his hand, kept him from doing what he had been trained to do. But that wasn't the entire truth; he was afraid, yet maybe he didn't have to be. Could he be thinking this all wrong? He ticked it over in his mind coming to a conclusion that momentarily lifted the weight of his pain. Maybe there was nothing to be found out, no nasty surprises to be discovered about his wife. All he needed to do was get through this quickly and finally put all the questions to rest so he could get on with finding her killer.

Walking back into the bedroom he glanced around at the Ralph Lauren collection of drapes, bedding and rugs before moving over to her armoire and opening the doors. He ran his hands through the party dresses before pulling out the top drawer and was immediately assaulted by the scent of Tea Rose, the perfume she had used to scent her lingerie something her mother had done; it was one of the few pieces of information she had ever volunteered about her mother Patricia.

Pop had told him Patricia had been a shy woman with a quiet smile that lit her face to beautiful. He'd never gotten over her death and now he's lost a daughter leaving him to a son-in-law who was rifling through her silky and expensive underwear the same way he would though a murdered prostitute's last possessions. He went through the remaining drawers didn't find anything to trip his heart and was closing the last one when something or better yet the lack of something caught his attention.

He searched all the drawers again puzzlement drawing his features tight. It was not there, Lorna's packet of birth control pills was gone. For as long as he could remember she had kept them on the right hand side of the third drawer never forgetting to take one each morning with her orange juice. Had she run out? Not possible he decided. She had been killed October fifteenth so sixteen pills remained meaning the packet should be here. Maybe for some unfathomable reason she had decided to change where she kept them and he just hadn't come across them yet. But after all these years?

Maybe the question wasn't why her pills were missing but why he was wasting time worrying about them; he would come across the pills at some point. He dry washed his face with his hands; the way his mind worked sometimes made him sick.

Sitting on the bed he opened the drawers on the antique table Lorna had used as a nightstand and picked through fashion, home design and real estate magazines then clipped together newspaper stories and pictures from the city's society pages showing people, most of whom he'd never heard of, dressed in expensive clothes as they stepped out of limousines at charity functions or lavish parties. Had she known these people he wondered. Were they people she hoped would someday become her clients? Or had she just wanted to be like them? The fact he couldn't answer the questions made him toss the clippings into the trash can beside the bed.

Picking up her laptop computer he turned it on and typed in: mangoes, her favorite fruit and password watching as her personal settings loaded up. Her files appeared twenty in all and he opened them one by one. In the first two she'd recorded their joint banking and bill paying records everything in order by submission and return dates. Opening the eighteen remaining files he found they were all work related. She had tracked Manhattan's real estate market over a five-year period with her goal market carefully researched and the findings recorded; she had been meticulous about everything in her life making him in no way doubt that if she'd lived, within a couple of years she would've been selling five million dollar homes and making a fortune. He checked her e-mail messages and found only those from other agents or business associates, nothing suspicious or out of order. Nothing. The tension that had tightened his belly relaxed.

Pushing aside the louvered doors of her closet he started in the middle of her wardrobe and worked his way through her things the job made easier because Lorna had everything organized by type of clothing and color. He checked shirt and pants pockets, dropped to his knees and slipped a hand into each shoe, boot and matching handbag even the umbrellas she collected were shaken out; not a thing.

In the lavishly decorated bathroom with its jet stream air bathtub, crystal glass wash basin and heated towel racks, he walked over to the first of two floor-to-ceiling cupboards where she'd kept towels, soap, toilet paper and other bathroom paraphernalia and checked through the contents finding only what should have been there.

He opened the door to the second set of cupboards situated between the bathtub and the wall and contemplated its contents. Truth be told he'd never paid any attention to what she'd kept there, the seasonal clothes and other odds and ends a woman like her accumulated but didn't necessarily need or want to toss out.

Off the top shelf he removed a plastic bag of thick woolen sweaters and shook them out one by one only to stop in mid shake; this was ridiculous. He hadn't found anything so far to implicate Lorna in anything wrong no matter what Cush implied, so why didn't he stat it here, leaving well enough alone he thought as he reached for the items on the next shelf removing a smaller bag filled with winter hats and gloves he riffled through, sadness and guilt pushing at him as he did so. Someday he would have to either give these—her things—away or get rid of them. Pushing the bag back in place he encountered resistance. Pulling it out again he dropped it to the floor before reaching into the shelf up to his shoulder his fingers making contact with a flat smooth object he pulled into the light.

It was a small black valise its paint peeling off in places to reveal thin white cardboard. It looked to be twenty years old its handle worn though the gold latch looked new. Sitting it on the floor he dropped to his knees staring at it. Fear washed over him like warm water. Why couldn't he have stopped three minutes earlier like his brain had told him.

He didn't touch the valise. He'd never seen it before and Lorna had never mentioned it. What was inside she'd felt needed to be hidden from him? This was nuts; all he had to do was open it. What did he expect to find dead babies? With his heart beating so loud he couldn't hear his own breathing, he unsnapped the latch and threw up the lid.

Not dead babies but close; dolls. Not fancy collectable porcelain figurines with perfect made up faces in elaborate costumes but discount store plastic baby dolls, three of them. All had big green eyes and dark reddish hair. They wore plain dresses of light blue, yellow and mint green with white collars and matching bows. On their feet were white bobby socks and plain black Mary Jane's. Their clothing was worn and thin but preserved as were the dolls though he could tell by the style of dress and the look of them they were years old. An ivory handled comb and brush set lay with them filled with the dolls reddish hair or was it Lorna's hair?

Were these remnants of a childhood she didn't talk about? What reasons did she have for keeping them secret? He shook his head at the dolls and the new set of questions they presented. He laid them on the bathroom rug before looking through the rest of the valise's contents.

The dolls had lain on a piece of white cloth printed with black Japanese characters; Lorna had loved all things Japanese; he pulled out the cloth and found underneath an ordinary brown grocery store bag. He unfurled its top feeling like a man faced with a basket that may or may not contain snakes and put his hand inside pulling out a red leather notebook and a handful of what he at first thought were movie tickets but realized were pawnshop stubs from a place called Better Times in Times Square. He looked from the tickets to the dolls, thinking: is there even a question where I'll be in the next forty minutes?

CHAPTER 20

After changing into his work clothes: jacket, shirt and tie, Owen walked into the pawnshop the motion detector sounding a ping at his arrival. An emaciated fiftyish man in a Harley-Davidson sleeveless t-shirt with an unshaven face, thinning hair and wearing large red framed glasses stood behind a wall of cage which swept from one side of the room to the other.

"This can't be a bust," his voice was back woods twangy. "You guys show up in twos and threes like a bad comedy team."

"You sound more like the comedienne. I have a few questions."

"That's what they always say. Okay if it ain't gonna cost me noth'in."

Owen took out a photograph and pressed it up against the wire mesh. The man squinted, his eyes almost closing shut. He stared for a long time then grinned showing perfect teeth. "Oh yeah," his voice twanged dreamy as he watched Owen pocket the picture. "Really good look'in that one; knocked your socks off the minute she stepped in the place."

"When was the last time you saw her?"

"A month ago maybe? Yeah," he chuckled causing his glasses to bob on his nose. "She wore this green dress belted at the waist, you know cinched tight, tight so it rounded out everything. And black do-me-good-heels. Man," he shook his head, his grin widening, "her in that outfit got me through some pretty lonely nights."

He laughed out right this time, the sound bulleting across Owen's skull, "Keep your dirty little fantasies to your self and tell me about these."

He shoved the tickets through the small cleared space carved out of the cage. Instead of touching them the man bent his head down until his nose was inches away from the tickets. He then reached a bony hand down the counter and pulled over a thin black ledger flipping it open to the middle.

Sliding the first ticket down the center of the page he stopped halfway, "Uh huh, this one was a Piaget watch, a beauty too; large diamonds around the face." He peered at Owen over the top of his glasses, "I gave her seventy-five for it. I didn't cheat her. She get busted?"

Owen didn't answer as his stomach lurched. Lorna had been pawning jewelry. Where had she gotten it from because he'd never seen it in his life. "What about this one?" he slid him another ticket. The man went through the procedure again on a page near the back.

"A diamond pendant that coulda come from Tiffany's it was that good, worth about three grand and we settled on half."

"You ripped her off."

The bony shoulders went up reminding Owen of a bat settling in a cave, "If she'd wanted a fair price she shoulda taken the stuff to one of those joints or Fifth or Madison instead or—"

"How much she pawn off on you? How many times was she here?"

"I don't remem—"

Owen shook the cage with both hands, the steel protesting with loud alarmed thuds. The man's eyes widened as Owen leaned forward his mouth inches from the metal, "Think about it."

The man backed from the angry face pressed toward him, "I wouldn't say she was a regular customer though she came in often enough for about a year with some good merchandise."

"How much in total?"

"Around five or six could've even been seven. Like I said she was a real good customer."

Owen turned away, "Thanks for the information."

"Ain't I suppose to cooperate with the law?" the man called his humor returning now the scary cop was leaving. "Help you fellas out whenever I can like a good citizen should. Hey, if you see her tell'er it was a real pleasure. I could tell she was something special."

Outside Owen felt a film of sick sweat coat his face as his thoughts pushed enough fear through his veins he could feel it tipping his heart into further darkness. Where had she gotten jewelry worth a small fortune? Had she used the money to set up their home? If not, where was the money?

Hell, for all he cared she could've used every cent to pay for a trip to the moon; what he needed to know was where she'd gotten the jewelry in the first place. He could think of only two ways: she'd stolen it or stolen the money to buy it. Her clients had given her thousands of dollars in exchange for property. Had she skimmed off those payments? He shook the thought from his mind, no, no way. And how would you know you ass? The same way you knew about the valise, the dolls, the pawn tickets and don't forget the little red book.

He needed answers, confirmation of something—anything— that would prove what he was feeling and thinking about his dead wife wasn't true. Okay, she had made a good living by anyone's standards so maybe she'd splurged here and there, Lorna did what she wanted. Then why pawn it later? Because the jewelry hadn't belonged to her that's why. He had to calm down and think this out. He'd found the valise at home; what about her office? What had she hidden there?

"Dammit, I blame Cush for this," he said and sprinted for his car.

CHAPTER 21

Parking on Vestry Street in Tribeca famous for its Italian actors, pricey restaurants and expensive warehouse space he opened the door on the small red brick building sandwiched between a Gelato shop and a store that sold brass beds. Zoss First Realty ran in formal nuptial script across the top of the building.

The bell over the door tinkled his arrival into the front office that was set up to look like someone's living room with nubby rug on the floor, two sofas with a coffee table between them and a quilt covered armchair rounding out the cozy picture. On the table next to a large red poinsettia plant were thick photo albums filled not with pictures of family vacations or newborns but with properties for sale or rent.

The room was bisected in the back by a long counter and behind it sat a wall with a door cut in its center. It opened and an attractive woman in her late twenties of medium height walked through. She wore a plum colored suit tight on a frame carrying thirty excess but attractive pounds, the color complimenting a head of black curls, light brown eyes, generous lips and nose emphasized by lipstick and eye shadow the exact color of the suit. She frowned at him.

"Hi Brigette," Owen tried a smile that immediately fell apart.

Her frown deepened aided by a spark of anger, "I didn't know you were coming today, Owen. You should've called—"

"I was in the neighborhood and figured I'd come and pick up some of Lorna's things.

"But if you'd called first we would've gotten them ready for you."

"What would you have needed to get ready Brigette?" their gazes locked. "Anything you didn't want me to see you would've taken care already. I'm just picking up her personals nothing more."

"I'm not accusing you of anything?" her voice rose. "I'm just telling you it would've saved us both trouble if you've called first. The way you're coming on its like police harass—", she caught herself; Owen watched her face darken until it was the color of her suit. She was embarrassed he realized at how she must sound not to a cop but to a man whose wife had been murdered.

Her hand went to her mouth, "I'm so sorry Owen I must sound like some insensitive ass." She came around the counter and embraced him her body lightly touching his then away. "This is awkward. Lorna and I—"

"I know," he cut into her words. "You've stored her things away?"

"No, we kept her office the way she left it... until something happened," she said. Leading him around the counter she pulled the door open.

They entered a large room with three closed office doors a long one wall. Two women in power suits and two men in jackets and ties stood behind desks in the center of the room talking furiously on their phones as they eyed them.

Lorna had been a part of this he remembered, one of these tense tight individuals who acted if their lives as well as their jobs depended on that big sale; he remembered she had thrived in this atmosphere.

"We keep it locked," Brigette said as they moved in front of the second closed door, her voice low as if this was a state secret, "The police have been here several times."

"Could you open it? I didn't think to bring her keys. I guess," he shrugged self-consciously, "because they were her keys."

"Oh no," she put a hand on his arm. "I understand. I have one that opens all the doors in this building anyway." She glanced back at the others then looked at him, "I guess its okay to tell you with your being a cop and all."

He wondered about the "and all" as he watched her produce a rubber band with a brass key looped through it. She unlocked the door, Owen stepped inside and flicked on the lights.

Brigette remained on the threshold looking as if she was going to run away, "I'll leave you alone then. Just close the door when you're done it locks automatically." She backed into the hall, didn't say anything for a while then, "I'm sorry she's dead Owen I really am. We didn't get along though I tried—hard—to like her but for some reason I was the one who didn't suit her." She twisted the rubber band in her hand, "I guess it doesn't matter with her gone does it?"

He looked at the guilt swimming in her eyes and felt it too even as he lied, "You're right, it doesn't matter. Everything's fine Brigette." She nodded her face still solemn as she left him.

He closed the door before turning into the room. This was the first time he'd been there in what, six months? Or was it a year? The last time had been on one of his rare couple of hours free during a workday and he'd driven down to take her to lunch but she'd been out.

The place looked the same what he'd half jokingly called the War Room. Bookshelves crammed full took up part of a wall; comfortable but basic black office furniture filled out the rest. Maps of the city were pinned on the walls and along side those were snapshots and information sheets on properties for sell and properties sold their dollar amounts meticulously written on swaths of colored paper tacked beneath them. Between the maps and informationals were her real estate license, a few awards and the degree in political science she'd earned from S.U.N.Y of Albany.

Along side the snapshots were framed photographs of Lorna: smiling and shaking hands with the former mayor; dancing with a state senator at a lavish dinner; laughing as she sat at a conference table with the attorney general. For some reason she had loved being surrounded by these moments, with these people of power and influence. He looked around having now only noticed there were no photographs of them together; as a matter of fact there were no pictures of him anywhere and was suddenly stung by his absence though he kept one of her prominently displayed on top of his desk.

Walking over to her work table he studied her beloved and prominently displayed Japanese woodblocks, scripted scrolls and prints. He picked up favorite, the beautiful Uikyore prints, pictures of the "the floating world" named for the licensed pleasure districts in the Japanese cities of Edo, Kyoto and Osaka. She'd once told him the striking beauty of that world made her feel clean.

He studied her rows of books which ran along two themes: politics and self-help for getting-what-you-want-when-you-want-it. Fiction, she had informed him didn't suit her sensibilities; yet squeezed between these tombs were thin volumes of Haiku she had enthusiastically read and too his surprise occasionally written. She'd once told him how she felt connected to Haiku's definition, its ideals, its seemingly clean and precise transparency which in truth she had said, was a façade hiding deep and complex meanings a contradiction she'd admired.

He recalled looking up the meaning of the word and being alarmed at its meaning: an independent poem complete in itself rather than part of a whole. The word seemed to define their relationship; they were independent of each other not interdependent as a stable happy couple should be and at the moment of the reading he'd decided to change things but by then it had been too late.

Pulling the books out one-by-one he searched through the pages and as he reached for the next his hand halted in midair, a monstrous thought presenting itself. Their home, the jewelry, the money and even the photographs taken with the influential and powerful pointed toward a life far different from the one they'd made together, from what a salaried cop could give her. Had he held Lorna back from a more fulfilled life? Had she resented him? Had she hated him for keeping her down? As quickly as the thought solidified it collapsed under its own weight of absurdity because if he didn't know anything else about Lorna he knew she hadn't been the kind of person who let anything or anyone get in the way of what she wanted; not even herself.

She had considered going into politics after college and had worked for the senatorial campaign of Robert Elliot Deacon, believing in him and what he believed in, his politics, his promises and when he'd won and left for Washington taking his family along and leaving her behind, she'd never spoken of him again and whenever she'd caught him on television she would turn him off, her face hard.

She had ended up working instead for Benet, Benett and Lawton the most prestigious law firm on Long Island; it was there he'd first laid eyes on her. He'd chased an assailant into the firm, one of their clients the man having failed to halt at a red light at a four way intersection before speeding through a school zone ignoring the order to stop. He'd had to take the distraught man down by force, slamming the guy to the ground when he charged him, pinning him on the floor with a hard knee and cuffing him tight with Lorna avidly looking on.

She had been the most spectacular woman he'd ever seen, had looked the most unattainable, so startling beautiful he'd had trouble keeping his eyes off her. She'd been wearing a summer dress printed with small red roses that fit her perfectly and was caressed by her long reddish gold hair. The look in her green eyes had felled him and ruined him for all time for anyone else. He'd gotten his man that day and to his surprise and amazement he had gotten Lorna too.

At her desk he picked up the empty trashcan figuring he would use it to deposit her things and began sorting through the drawers. A part of his mind registered the items he tossed into the can: two bottles of body lotion, the reading glasses she hated wearing, the Harry Konick Junior CDs; with the rest of his brain—the part always on the job—he was fearfully anticipating coming across a fateful clue to her life, her death that would cut him to pieces.

A knock on the door jerked his head up, "Come in."

Brigette entered holding out an empty computer paper box, "I wasn't sure if you'd find anything in here to carry her things out."

He sat down the trashcan and took the box, "Thanks for getting this for me."

She smiled something brittle with anxiety, "You find anything important?"

"No," he said then, "Thanks again, Brigette." She nodded the brittle smile then turned and left closing the door behind her.

He stared with at it, at the black shoe holder with twelve sleeves for six pairs of shoes. He dropped the box and walked over. From the first two pouches he pulled out a pair of black sling backs she would've worn to business lunches; he returned them then checked the next set pulling out a pair of Manolo Blahnik sandals. He continued pulling out shoes until he got to the third row and the last pouch where he removed along with a black Marc Jacobs pump an untitled dvd in a cheap clear plastic case.

Turning on the computer he slid the disc in the player and waited the longest few seconds of his life for the bits to add and images to appear on the screen and when it finally did he blinked at the sight of a man he'd never seen masturbating on top of a bare mattress. He watched the man's mouth working and didn't want to hear what was coming out of it but clicked on the volume any way. The man was moaning, the sound mixing with voices, women's voices coming from somewhere off camera; he heard them clearly and was shocked to hear they were talking about shoes.

He raised the volume, the man moaned louder then grunted as he spurted. The man glanced toward the camera as the women laughed the screen going black. Owen stared at the nothing. He had heard the laughter of one of the women before; it was Lorna's he was sure but that was impossible.

What he'd seen had been pornographic and his wife would never be involved in anything so dirty, so nasty and corrupt. But he didn't know his wife did he? No matter how hard he tried to convince Cush of the opposite. He didn't know what she had really been capable of. He wasn't sure of anything regarding her life—their lives; he'd never asked too many questions about what she did and who she did it with; hadn't wanted to sound like some psychotic possessive loser of a husband who didn't trust his wife to even go to the grocery store. His head dropped to the desk, his eyes closing as a tidal wave of memory filled his head. The one time, the one chance to delve deeper and he'd let fear paralyze him and done nothing, nothing....

Unlocking the front door he looked up and was pole-axed by the sight of his wife walking toward him looking so radiant and beautiful he could almost dismiss the fact it was 4:30 in the morning. She wore her long and expensive faux fur coat that glistened as black as night, her hair lying against it like wild fire. On her feet were those shoes, the black ones with the four-inch heels with only a front and back strap holding them on; he couldn't take his eyes off those shoes.

She stopped in front of him a smirk on her lips, "Aren't you going to ask me where I've been?"

He looked up at her then back to those shoes staring for a long time before he'd answered, "I'm too tired for it. I've been trying to find the person who murdered Isadora Sanchez. She left behind three—"

"My God stop it Owen," the smirk whipped away as anger suffused her face. "The dead aren't the only ones who need you."

"When this case is over—"

"There'll be another, then another, save your promises, those aren't what I need from you. And anyway if I told you where I've been you wouldn't believe it."

They stared at each other until she said with a sigh, "Oh, hell." Pushing in front of him she opened the door, on her beautiful face was an expressive mix of exasperation and frustrated love he recognized but was helpless to do anything about. "Come on in." She gently pulled him inside, "You're about to pass out on the doorstep. Go get some sleep and I'll wake you in a few hours so Isadora can have you back..."

Owen pulled out the disc and held it with two fingers wishing he'd brought in his rubber gloves. Twenty-minutes later he left for the last time clutching her things as his head whirred with dark and compelling images of her. He glanced at the dark blue Ford Explorer parked a few doors down and forgot about it an instant later as he drove off.

Inside the SUV agent Oscar Berniak reclined, his feet up on the dashboard as he watched the detective drive off. He looked at screen on his laptop computer allowing his eyes to follow a tiny white dot traveling across the screen.

"There he goes," he said out loud still irritated at the fact he'd been given this assignment in the first place. Babysitting a cop. Big deal. He knew he'd been given this detail because he was the new kid on the block though Riviera had repeatedly pointed out what he was doing was important; he just wasn't buying it. In his opinion Riviera was the kind of guy who thought being assigned coffee and doughnut duty was a high priority; his boss took everything that damn seriously.

Yet here he was wasting his morning tracking a crooked cop. He wiggled in his seat in aggravation. He should be working the important headline inducing assignments like chasing laundered money through the city's hallowed financial institutions or tracking drug and illegal immigrant smuggling routes worth billions through New York's ports, harbors and trucking lines instead of trailing a loser city detective. Junior league bullshit.

His fingers smacked the computer keys producing an illuminated street map of the five boroughs. As he watched the dot move toward Staten Island he reached for his third white chocolate mocha coffee of the morning. The dot steadied; stuck in traffic he decided and sipped. The tracking device he'd planted on the undercarriage of the cop's car was working like a dream, he could follow the cop anywhere without having to put the SUV in drive.

"Ah, he's on the Goiamus Freeway, headed for...?" Berniak tapped the keys and a street name appeared: Pelican Road. Residential he thought. Finishing his coffee he settled back into his seat for a nap. By the time he woke up the cop should be on the move again and where he was sure to roam he would be easily followed.

CHAPTER 22

Owen stood outside of Cush's front door unsure how he'd gotten there. He rang the bell and a moment later it was opened by a dark-haired version of Connie, her eyes huge and blue as she smiled so sweetly Owen couldn't help but smile back.

"Uncle Owen," Sophia Rose launched herself at him. "I hoped it was you," she planted a loud kiss on his cheek.

He held her in his arms and gave her a gentle squeeze, "Hi, Funny Face. Long time no see."

"I missed you." She took his face in her small hands, put her forehead to his and looked into his eyes, "You've been gone a long time and that wasn't nice."

"I'll never let it happen again," he carried her into the house closing the door. In the comfortably furnished living room he put her down then kneeled on one knee, "Listen Funny Face could you do me a big favor? Next time try and wait until Mommy or Daddy is with you before you open the door okay?'

"Why?" a puzzled expression settled onto the child's face, "If I wait I won't be the first person to see who's there."

"True, but there are some people Mommy and Daddy need to speak to before you say hello that's all." He grinned, "But lucky me I got to see you first and got a great big kiss too." He tickled her belly and she giggled.

Connie walked into the room a load of laundry under her arm she tossed on a nearby chair before approaching him, "You all right? Where'd you get that ugly bruise under your eye?"

"It's nothing. I know Cush is at the station—"

"Don't worry about him," Connie waved his words aside. "I'm glad to see you." She hugged him and so did Sophia Rose her arms wrapped around their legs. "That's sweet honey. Why

115

don't you go have your chocolate milk and orange? I sliced it in triangles the way you like it."

"Okay, Mommy," Sophia Rose looked up at Owen her face bright and happy, "See ya Uncle Owen."

"See ya, Funny Face." As she skipped out the room he called, "Remember what I said about opening the door." She nodded and then was out of sight.

"Thank god Stephen wasn't here," Connie sat on the sofa, "If she'd done that with him around he would've had a fit. Stephen thinks there're maniacs on every street corner. Sit, Owen."

He took the chair facing her, "I don't disagree with him, Connie. Listen I came to ask you about..." he stalled a wobbly grin of embarrassment passing across his face. "God, I feel stupid because I don't know how to start this." He rubbed his hands together, his face all pale lines and hard bones.

"I mean I just never expected to have to ask anyone about my own wife. Sure we had our problems like any other couple; some hard ones that forced us to grow apart for a while and with my job and hers," he shrugged, "it was difficult sometimes. Regardless of any of that I thought I knew everything to know about her, at least the important things."

"It's impossible to know everything even about the person you love more than anyone else."

"Maybe," Owen said impatient, "but she was my wife for seven years and I suspected nothing." The words were spoken on the tight edge of distress. "Connie, she might've had a life other than ours, the kind I can't get my mind around and I don't think I've even scratched the surface of her world yet. You were her friend; tell me how I could miss so much?"

"We weren't close, Owen. I don't think Lorna wanted to be close to anyone other than you. I believe one of the reasons for her," her mouth tightened as she tried to find the right word, "distance, was because she was so pretty and knew how to use it. People—women mostly—took offense at that. Another reason she didn't like anyone to get close, the most important one I think was because if you couldn't do anything for her she couldn't waste her time on you. She was an ambitious woman, too ambitious if you ask me." Connie said relieved to be able to identify what she had considered a reckless flaw in Lorna. "I'm not saying anything was wrong with it but she could be obsessive. The funny thing is that it didn't all revolve around her but you."

"Me?" Owen was taken aback. "Why me?"

Connie rolled her eyes, "Men can be so stupid. She wanted you to go as far as possible in the department. Didn't you realize it? All the way to commissioner and possibly further into mayoral territory."

"You're kidding?" Owen's face whitened in disbelief. "Lorna nev—"

"And I think she did things to ensure it could happen."

"No," Owen shook his head, "it's not possible. I never said anything to her about being anything other than a good cop. She knew it was all I've ever wanted; other than wanting her."

"You weren't hearing her then because that wasn't all she wanted for you; it wasn't even close. You were wrapped up in being that good cop and on the one hand that served her purpose because it was the groundwork for her ambition for you." Connie leaned toward him making sure he finally grasped what he had yet to understand. "Lorna didn't want to lead an ordinary life, to be ordinary; she hated the idea. And she didn't care much for people she suspected was ordinary like Stephen and me. Most of this is women's intuition I admit but twisted with it are a few of the confidences she'd occasionally give up to another cop's wife though rare and only when she was upset with you."

Owen's face went from bone white to silk scarlet, "I can't believe she'd treat you so awful, my friends—."

"Your friends not hers. She never said anything outright, she was too polite; too self-aware but there were definite boundaries. I think she felt badly about being the way she was but she just couldn't help herself."

"Do you think this…this obsession of hers to be—I don't know—more? Could lead her into something dangerous? Involve her with someone dangerous?"

"I don't think so. Of course it wasn't as if we were best friends but I believe if she'd been in trouble she would've told you."

He looked away from her, "But would she have told me the truth?" He stood needing to leave. He couldn't listen to anymore right now, take another bitter surprise.

"I'd better go, I have some things to do before checking on Pop," he moved toward the door Connie following.

"I wasn't any help to you Owen. I've just made things worse."

"No," he said opening the door and stepping out onto the stoop, "I still have more questions about her than answers though I can't figure how it's possible."

The devastated look in his eyes caught her. Connie took hold his arm staying him because she was certain, as certain as she was she loved her husband and daughter his search for answers in the closed darkness of Lorna's heart would lead to no less than his total ruin, "Why don't you give this up right now leaving well enough alone. Please, Owen."

"I can't, I wish I could but I can't," she hugged him tight as he gently patted her back comforting her this time.

She pulled back and looked into his eyes, hers dark with fear for him, "Aren't you afraid of what else you might find?"

"Terrified," he said giving her a brief awful smile as he left.

A few blocks away from Cush's house, Owen stopped at a small park across the street from a line of neat well-kept cookie cutter houses. Settling onto a bench he gazed at the serviced lawns and expensive porch furniture wondering which one kept a husband who beat his wife when she served chicken instead of fish; or which of the beautifully decorated dwellings lived parents who abused and tortured their child while on an alcoholic binge; or which of the cleanly painted abodes kept the mentally ill who worshipped razor blades and box cutters across their skin during the lonely hours of the night.

He clutched his head in his hands. My God, look how my mind works always on the dark and shitty side of the street. You have some fucking nerve when you have for so long been afraid to examine your own miserable dwelling. Had they really grown that far apart they'd become total strangers? Hadn't today proven it?

He took out the notebook and flipped through it. Down the right side of the first ten pages were letters and what seemed to be random numbering from one through ten. What did it mean? The only thing he understood—yet didn't understand—was the name, Lily which was written at the top of each page. He wondered if it was an associate of Lorna's, a client or something else.

He drove away from Staten Island under the heart breaking realization his marriage had been an illusion. He'd been living in a dream world of his own making, so wrapped up in himself he'd let their lives together ebb and recede believing it would take care of itself; ignoring it and now that life couldn't be improved, fixed, given another chance, it was completely no more and this fact haunted him all the way back to Queens.

CHAPTER 23

"It looks good—," Owen began as Pop opened the new front door but the expression on the old man's face dried up the rest and made him ask, "What's wrong?"

"We got company again; this place is turning into a bus station. And another jerk too." A man stepped out of the room behind Pop. "Says he's a detective like you; that you worked together along time ago."

"And hated every second of it," Owen said as he moved toward Al Gunderson,

"Story—" Gunderson began a grin on his face.

Owen didn't let him finish, "Save it and get the fuck out."

Gunderson, a large man going to fat and doing nothing about it let the grin slide off to be replaced by a mask of intense dislike, "I just wanted to have a friendly chat, give you the chance to come clean; I thought it's the least I could do. I'll even escort you down to the station and put it out like I convinced you to come saving you from the humiliation of being dragged in like some piece of shit off the street."

"That's your friendly chat?" Owen moved up into Gunderson's face making him jerk back. "I've had enough of those for a lifetime; the next one can be with my lawyer. Get out. Now."

"There you go, Story," Gunderson raised his arms and let them flop back to his sides, "Acting just like I knew you would, goddamn unreasonable."

"Yeah?" Owen moved fast behind Gunderson and grabbed the back of his jacket and the seat of his pants before the man knew what was happening jerking him up on his toes. "I'll show you how goddamn unreasonable I can be."

"Hey, let me go," Gunderson yelled digging his heels into the floor as he tried to grab hold of anywhere on Owen who, strong on anger, frog marched him toward the front door.

"I bet you didn't expect this did you," Owen questioned through clenched teeth his grip on Gunderson steel. "You came alone you prick without a warrant, with nothing but your big fat mouth leading the way. Pop, open the door."

Grunting and twisting to get away, "You're crazy," Gunderson shouted. "I tried to make it easy on you out of respect for the badge but you had to go and act fucking nuts."

Scrambling forward the old man opened the door wide as Owen picked Gunderson up and tossed him through out on to the porch. The man went down hard on the floor, a grunt of pain flying from his lips. Hauling himself up he whirled on Owen, his face a heart attack red with fury, "I should shoot your crazy ass," he screamed as he stumbled backwards down the stairs, "I'll be back with a warrant and the entire department and get you, you son-of-a-bitch."

Pop slammed the door on the cursing, retreating figure before he looked at Owen who stood with his head down taking deep breaths before his gaze caught on the concerned look on the old man's face, "They're coming out the wood work aren't they?"

"Why don't you go upstairs and get some rest, you've obviously had a busy day."

Owen shook his head, "I got things to do."

"A few hours sleep is what you need. "

"You win," Owen forced a tired smile. "I have to make a call first."

At the hall table he picked up the phone and dialed a private number only a handful of people in the city knew. As he listened to the ringing line he looked at his father-in-law in the mirror above the table; he looked graver than usual, sicker as he stood in his threadbare green sweater and stained jeans that hung off his withered hips. They looked like father and son the sad realization settling on Owen like a brick; connected by their grief, loss and utter disappointment in a world gone haywire.

"No one understands that's all," Pop said, "how much you two loved each other."

Owen glanced away from their images as the party on the other end picked up, "Can I see you in an hour?" he asked listening then, "All right." He hung up and looked at Pop, "I'll go up now." He gave the old man's shoulder an affectionate squeeze, "Don't worry this all will get straightened out I promise."

"You hungry?" Pop asked watching him up the stairs.

Owen stopped, "I should be asking you; some care taker I'm turning out to be. No, thanks."

"Get some rest I'll make sure no one bothers you."

The old man waited until he heard the bedroom door close before moving into the dining room and over to the sideboard where he took the lid off a soup tureen sitting beside a vase of dying white roses. Reaching inside he pulled out P220 Sig Sauer pistol.

Slipping out the cartridge he confirmed it was fully loaded before snapping it back in place, "I'll make damn sure."

CHAPTER 24

It was fifteen minutes to three when Owen hurried into the lobby of Johnson and Ayres Ltd. on Liberty, a block over from Wall Street. He paid no attention to the black sport utility vehicle cruising pass; it was just one of the numerous vehicles headed toward traffic-heavy Nassau Street.

With his eyes on the disappearing detective Berniak clicked open his cell phone, punched a button and with the phone at his ear pressed down on his horn as he eased out of traffic and over to the other side of Liberty into a parking space just vacated by a black Hummer the size of a small bus.

The other end of the line was picked up by his boss, "Go," Riviera gave his usual greeting. Berniak could hear car horns and other traffic noises in the background.

"The cop just went into the offices owned by Richard Giordano."

"Repeat," Riviera said, Berniak heard a faint click and knew he was on a speaker.

"The cop just went into the offices belonging to Giordano."

"Story's file says they haven't seen each other in a year and a half," Williams' voice came over clear.

"Right," Riviera said. "And now he visits his old friend a known mafia hood days after his wife is murdered. There's too many things wrong with this picture."

"Former mafia hood," Williams added.

"Bullshit," Riviera snapped, "there's no such thing."

"What could be their connection now?" Carter asked.

"I don't know but I'm going to find out. We're a block over, Berniak. I'm going to make an unannounced visit to Mr. Giordano; put a scare into his day. Let me know if anything

123

changes," Riviera hung up. Berniak clicked off having heard the ready-to-battle glee in his boss's voice.

Owen crossed a marble floor to a set of double glass doors and pressed a button situated on the wall. A thin middle-aged woman sitting behind a desk looked up and stared at him deadpan before the door's latch clicked and he entered.

"Owen Story to see Mr. Giordano."

She smiled then her face going alive, "I'll call your escort."

Seconds later a recessed door to the left of the desk opened and a man with cautious eyes and the lean physique of a sprinter stood there. He looked Owen over before stepping back and pushing the door wide. He led him down a thickly padded red-carpeted hall to a gleaming gold gated elevator. Holding the gate open he waited for Owen to precede him before stepping inside and pulling it closed. He pushed the only button in sight. The elevator rose smooth and soundless stopping with only a slight jerk.

He led Owen down a long hall to a set of brass double doors pushing open the one on the right allowing Owen into a large beautifully appointed reception room with burgundy leather couches and black marble tables. At the end of the room was another set of doors made of black obsidian glass, stylish and bulletproof Owen knew. Another man, this one large and muscular moved up to the escort and whispered in his ear.

The Sprinter looked at Owen, "Come with me," he said walked up to the nearest wall. He pressed it and to Owen's amazement though not surprise the wall slid open. He motioned Owen forward into a room the size of an office kitchen where sat a small table and one chair. On the table was a pair of handcuffs. A window the size of a sheet of notebook paper was cut in a sidewall. The Sprinter disappeared back behind the wall without another word.

Moments later the wall slid open again and a man walked in, a grin on his face as he took Owen in a bear hug. This was Richard Giordano, entrepreneur and chief-executive-officer of Johnson and Ayres which manufactured custom made bottles; Harvard educated, alumni of Columbia Business School, a quiet philanthropist and the only son of Don Joseph Giordano of Long Island; a small family, but a mafia crime family nevertheless.

Richard Giordano, a so-called "made man" before he turned his back on his family and for the most part gone his own way. More importantly to Owen, Giordano was his most trusted friend and had been since their teen years, young bucks together starting off knowing nothing about each other's lives and not caring until they had no choice.

"It's good to see you," Giordano stood back and patted Owen's cheek as he took in the lines of weariness and strain on his face crisscrossed with the cuts and bruises that made him look years older. "You've looked better."

Giordano looked his opposite. He stood tall, healthy and perfectly groomed in his expensively wrinkled black shirt and black and white striped silk tie. His shoes and slacks telegraphed wealth making him look as a very successful businessman should.

"Come on I want to show you something," Giordano motioned him to the cut in the wall. "One way glass."

Owen watched a man he knew was a cop by the way the guy nosed around the room his nostrils flaring as if he smelled something bad. The guy was sharp all the way around Owen could tell; definitely on the make for someone.

"FBI agent-in-charge Dennis Rivera," Giordano said. "I've deducted he's here because you're here."

"Shit, what did he say?"

"You know his kind," Giordano grinned. "He hasn't said anything outright; just asking a lot of questions he knows I'm not going to answer. He's trying to rile me up, trying to scare me," they looked at each other and laughed. "You can listen while I get rid of him then we'll have a sit down." He pushed at the glass and it shifted back a few inches.

A few seconds later Owen watched the muscled guy push the door open in the other room as Giordano entered talking, "I have a business to run so I'll have my friend here look after you so that you don't fall down and hurt yourself on the way out; I wouldn't want to be blamed because you're accident prone."

"You'll be more than blamed Mr. Giordano," Rivera flashed a smile of pure white menace. The guy was slick Owen thought, not one to be intimidated, "Since you're being uncooperative I won't keep you though I'm positive we'll be seeing each other again real soon and maybe in not so nice a setting."

125

"Do I have to call my lawyer and sue you for harassment just to get you out of my building?"

"Your cop friend doesn't have long either."

"Bye bye," Giordano said.

With a cosmopolitan nod of his head Rivera moved to the door, pushed muscle man aside and walked out.

"Make sure he leaves and doesn't detour," Giordano told his guy who disappeared the way Rivera had gone.

Owen was escorted into Giordano's lavish office where his friend led him over to a glass table and chairs positioned in front of the expansive floor-to-ceiling window overlooking the city.

Along the other walls were paintings and photographs upon first glance seemed to be erotic images of nude women but on closer inspection were glass bottles of various shapes and sizes crafted so artistically and brilliantly they looked like women who had been well loved; these were only some of the examples of the glass products Giordano's company sold to the rich and famous all over the world.

At his desk Giordano hit a computer key then spoke out loud, "Paula some coffee and those little German chocolate Danish."

"You don't have to I'm not hungry."

"You need to eat you look terrible," Giordano said as he moved to sit across from Owen.

Taking care of me again Owen accepted as he flashed on the sad long ago when Giordano had fought side-by-side with him when he could've walked away or joined in. Their relationship had begun with an encounter with neighborhood bullies full of stolen beer who'd seen him walking down a dark street and thought he would be easy prey.

He'd been a thin, narrow kid who looked no problem but he'd surprised the hell out of the three and fought hard; yet it was still one against three making his chance of coming out the winner slim to none but with courage and the ignorance of youth he hadn't run off or yelled for help even when he was getting his brains beat out of him.

His assailants were on the verge of kicking him into bloody ruin when through his pain he'd heard the screech of tires and seconds later a heavy body had hurled itself into the fray changing the odds and saving his life.

Giordano had laughed as he threw punches and bodies seeming to enjoy every second of the brawl. The hoods had taken a look at their new adversary and fled. In the silence that had followed, filled only with heavy phlegm filled breathing and pained coughs he had stared at Giordano who had grinned at him through a blood soaked mouth and nose. Giordano had stuck out a hand and after a heartbeat he'd taken it and been helped to his feet. Giordano had asked if he needed a ride to where he was going and he'd accepted.

As he'd gotten out of the mint condition steel blue '57 Corvette at his destination, Giordano had asked only one other question, "You think you could've handled those assholes yourself?"

He'd begun to feel the bruising pain the thugs had left him in but had said, "Maybe."

Giordano had laughed shaking his head, "See you around." He'd roared off his car moving swift and sleekly beautiful through the dark night.

Afterwards he'd seen Giordano at a football game, a dance, a party and they'd nodded in passing then had asked around about the other. He'd been surprised when told who Giordano's family was or at least his father and at the time he'd been impressed. Giordano had been different from what he knew of the "mafia" he'd garnered from the movies.

He'd finally understood why those jerks had taken one look at his rescuer and taken off. Giordano still insisted it had nothing to do with his being the son-of-a-mob-boss that had made those assholes run scared but because of his prowess with his fists. Back then Giordano had seldom mentioned his family and never once had he apologized for them and Owen had never expected him to; he hadn't come from a prize-winning set of parents either.

As the years passed they'd come to each others rescue a few times and ended up close friends, no, more like brothers. They'd finally put it down to chemistry or fate for the reason they'd taken one look at each other and totally accepted who and what the other was and had yet to regret it.

There was a brief knock at the door before it opened; the Sprinter stepping aside to allow a beautiful young woman with brilliant black eyes in a creamy skinned face to enter. She carried a silver tray covered with a platter of Danishes, demitasse cups and a silver carafe of fragrant coffee she poured for them before exiting.

"That Paula beautiful ha? Last year at Smith and straight A's all the way through. I'm going to make sure she marries a banker; who doesn't need a banker in the family?" Giordano said.

"Thank you for the fruit, the flowers and the catered from Luna's."

"I was worried about you. I know her death was a blow."

For the first time in what seemed like ages, Owen relaxed back in his chair feeling safe, "I still can't get my mind around it."

"Understandable," Giordano stirred his coffee.

"How's your father? I have to go by and see him one of these days."

"Healthy and as complicated as ever; he drives me crazy. The old man?"

"We're getting along. How's the bottling business?"

"Thriving. There's always something to put into fancy one-of-a-kind bottles. You know why things from designer jellybeans to toilet water are so expensive? It's the packaging, the goddamn packaging," Giordano grinned in gleeful satisfaction. "Those consumers are out there paying sixty-five percent for the packaging and thirty-five for whatever they get in the damn thing."

Owen listened enjoying himself. He wasn't ready to get into his problems; the reasons why he was here, he'd put it off for a while and let himself indulge in a little home town gossip, "You hear about Sammy Mancuso? Somebody ran him over with a loader until his insides came out his mouth." He watched Giordano wince; a bark of laughter escaped him, "Oh come on, it isn't as if you haven't heard about it?"

"I didn't say I hadn't," Giordano sat the cup in the saucer with a decisive thud. "It's just that I'm here now a long way from our Long Island roots. You know Johnson and Ayres did three hundred million dollars worth of business last year? In a couple of years I'm going to be on the big board, go public like the real players," he winked. "Make out like a bandit."

"Meaning, you haven't gone back to the dark side unless it's necessary."

"I can't get away from it—family—entirely. Who can?" Resentment tainted the words, "I have obligations I was born to you know that as well as I do."

"So you knew."

"I still get news from home; most of it I pass on to you anyway." Giordano looked at him ruefully, "Why are you busting my balls here?"

"It makes me feel good and I haven't felt that way for a while. Tell me what happened."

Giordano leaned forward and lowered his voice, "The story goes; Sammy was stealing from Bobo Well's crew out on Passaic Avenue."

"No," Owen said this news heightening his interest. "You're kidding? I remember Bobo being so tight with money he probably keeps the first dime he ever made taped to his ass. No one's ever seen an extra cent he's taken in, not his relatives, his associates and definitely not the IRS."

"It's downright psychotic his obsession to hold on to a dollar and for some reason Sammy, knowing Bobo as long as we have, misjudged that sociopathic part of the man's personality. Bobo owns—at least his wife does on paper—all those junkyards with attached chop shops over on Reynolds. Sammy got promoted taking down stolen cars for Bobo and after the car's are cannibalized the leftovers are nothing but junk that's tossed out back with the rest of the junk."

"Bobo never let's anything go."

"Right. So all these useless parts, trash, are in the yards lying around getting rained, snowed and pissed on by junkyard dogs turning into rust, landfill refuse of use to no one; that's what Sammy is thinking and anyone in their right mind would think the same. But rule number six; you never assume a fucking thing with these guys."

"The way I heard it: when they went into Sammy's house it was like going into a parts factory. He had sixty, seventy thousand dollars worth of thought-to-be-useless shit he'd managed to fix up—something those other assholes didn't have the brains to do—and he was selling it and making a nice profit for himself."

"Selling fixed up trash," Owen nodded. "Okay, but what was such a big deal it got him killed?"

"That wasn't the problem. It was okay he took the junk, fixed it up and sold it. What wasn't okay—what got him popped—was not giving Bobo his cut. A definite no, no, no."

Owen understood and the fact he did made him frown, "Meaning the Giordano's didn't get their cut either."

Giordano sipped his coffee thinking it over, "What was it? Ten, fifteen maybe twenty percent of seventy thousand? Pennies. Chump change. He shook his head, "It makes no sense to me; a man killed over pennies. That's why I can't be part of my father's world where you get what you believe is your due or take it by blood."

There was silence between them as this truth weighed heavily on their minds.

"Who killed him?" Owen asked.

Giordano pushed at finger out at Owen, "You," he grinned shaking his head at Owen who smiled. "A loader ha." He put down his cup and stared at his friend his gaze serious, "So we're done with the social graces and catching up. Tell me why you needed to see me today and why the FBI's head guy came calling."

Owen felt the tension tampered down rise up through him again like a surfacing shark. He wanted to say the right thing but decided to give up the bald-faced truth instead his friend deserved it especially in light of the fact he badly needed his help.

"There's only a few people I can truly trust; Pop, Cush and then there's you, though I know I've backed off over the years and its something I've regretted. We've been through a lot together from the moment you first saved my ass."

"Yeah and you've resented it; it's more like a nasty little secret between us than anything else."

"Not true, I—"

"You've always been honest about us Owen," Giordano cut in, "don't disappoint me now. To you I reflect badly on that good cop image you have of yourself my being the son of a so-called crime boss though you won't admit it, even to yourself. I've understood and accepted it because you're more than a friend to me."

"I've never taken our friendship lightly. Never will."

"Good," Giordano nodded. "So you're in real trouble."

"People believe I killed them; killed Lorna; the Feds, the cops, members of my own squad think I did it." Owen stood and moved to stare out the window before turning to face his friend, his own face open and bleak.

"Did you do?" Giordano asked without a hint of accusation just slight curiosity.

"I didn't kill anyone especially not her," Owen answered as Giordano waited for the punch line he knew was coming or his friend wouldn't be here. "But I wanted to," Owen's face had turned paper pale as his words stumbled out. "I wanted to smash her face in, crack her skull into tiny pieces, bury her alive." Guilt flooded his eyes, "God for give me it was only for an insane instant and I'll never forgive myself because of what happened to her."

"What did you find out?"

"I didn't find out anything; I didn't have to; she told me the morning of the ball she'd been having an affair."

"Ah," Giordano said without any surprise. "More than one person has killed for that one. I would've felt the same."

"But you would've done something about it; all I did was punch a hole in the kitchen wall. She told me it was over between them and I believed her. She said I had nothing to worry about and I believed that too."

"She give you names, times, places?"

"Names? Who do you think she was?" Giordano didn't answer, just looked at him. Owen said, "I didn't ask. I couldn't. He was in love with her she said and I don't doubt it. She was going to make him understand it was over between them."

Owen turned back to the window and really looked at the city for the first time in a long time and was as taken back as always at its well-earned beauty and the way it could make him feel as if the world was at his feet and he could do anything, including turn back time.

"She said she still loved me and the thing is I still love her," he glanced at the listening Giordano then back to the receding world. "We'd decided to try and work it out and were doing our best to have a good time though I was still pretty crazed when we arrived...."

...They faced each other in an alcove near the ballroom's main hallway unaware of the people taking notice of them as they passed by; they had eyes only for each other. Owen grabbed her right arm, "I told you it was over," she tried snatching her arm back. "Stop it Owen, you're—"

Two men stopped behind Owen who didn't turn around though he felt their presence and it heightened his annoyance to a fevered burn, his eyes never left Lorna's even though her gaze left his.

"You all right?" one of them asked.

"My wife's fine," Owen didn't turn around, "Go away."

"Let's go back to the party," the other man said. Owen felt him move off, the other remained behind him like a menacing shadow; he started around to confront him but Lorna put a hand to his chest intercepting him, he gripped her hand in turn as she said quickly, "Please go."

Owen felt the man reluctantly move off as Lorna tugged her hand free of his dispelling his anger, "God I'm sorry," he raised his hands as if giving up his face ashen. "Did I hurt you? I didn't mean to hurt you. This whole thing has made me crazy, Lorna; we should leave."

She didn't move, "Not until you calm down, you're scaring me." She reached out and caressed his right cheek and he closed his eyes at the feel of her. She whispered, "We can work through this, Owen. I love you."

"I can't lose you."

"It'll never happen. Trust me now." She put her lips close to his, "Let's go back inside I want to dance with you."

The other couples at the table watched as Lorna Story, the most beautiful woman in the room as she'd been told numerous times that night, danced with her husband before leading him back to the table.

Owen dropped into his chair and took a napkin to the perspiration on his brow, "You can hardly move on that floor."

Lorna sat beside him sipping her champagne.

"Meaning there's a lot of belly rubbing among other things rubbing going on out there," Cush said.

Everyone laughed as the song ended and the band started up another popular love ballad.

Lorna sat down her empty glass and threw a smile around the table, "I love that song it's wonderful to dance to." She put a hand on Owen's arm, "You can't be worn out?" He dropped his head to the table groaning as the others laughed. Lorna swatted him playfully, "All right, all right I get your point poor baby."

"I'm just kidding," he started up.

Lorna pushed him back, "It seems I've danced my husband out." The other men started to their feet but she waved them down, "You guys keep him company while I find another partner." With a sway of hips she glided off seemingly to take the light and energy with her.

Cush leaned around his wife and said to Owen in a loud whisper, "You're a lucky man, a very lucky man."

Connie smacked Cush on the head; he ducked away grinning. She leaned over to Owen, "So you two are doing fine now?" He looked at her surprised, "Lorna mentioned you two were having problems. We've all had them at one time or another; it's not easy making a marriage work when one of the partners a cop." Her eyes slid from his and widened, "I don't believe it."

"What ho?" Cush pointed. "Look who Lorna has managed to get off his butt."

Heads turned to stare as Lorna wove her way through the dancers; behind her, his hand clutched in hers, Chandler. In the center of the floor with the eyes of everyone in the room on them, Lorna opened her arms wide and with a sensuous drift of her body to the music beckoned him. Chandler stepped into her embrace, his face sliding toward hers as she turned her smile toward their audience.

"I've never seen him dance at one of these things," said a large brunette who could've been Roseanne Barr's twin. "And we've been coming for ten years."

Her husband as equally large and brunette said, "He rarely leaves that platform let alone getting down here on the dance floor with us street meat."

As Owen watched them one question chased itself through his mind: is he the man sleeping with my wife?

A small diamond encrusted hand slid around his shoulders and down his chest like a dazzling snake. He jumped and looked up into the flawlessly made up face of Jocelyn Chandler, a woman in her late forties with an expensively maintained beauty whose svelte figure, coiffured black-bobbed hair and large dark eyes were emphasized by a stunning red designer gown that gave her dark mature looks an air of smooth, calculating brilliance.

"She is sweet," she whispered close to his ear before moving off on a cloud of expensive perfume. Owen's eyes helplessly followed her until his gaze was pulled back to the couple who danced as if they were the only two people in the world...

"She was having a great time with everyone watching them; her," he turned from the city, from that night and looked at Giordano. "It had been a long time since I'd seen her so happy. I have to find the guy."

"Why? Because you want him dead."

"He could've killed her because she broke it off."

"But she wasn't the only one hit. What about the cop and Chandler's old lady? Maybe there was a hit put out on her to get back at him. He's the big-dick-cop right? Meaning he's made a lot of enemies getting there."

"I can't see it and anyway I have another take on the Commish. I believe he was involved in the murders."

"He's always struck me as slicker than duck shit and if anyone has criminal appeal it's him; but getting his hands bloody," Giordano shook his head. "No; getting someone else to do it while he watches? Absolutely."

"The only other scenario I come up with is: cop. Cop murdered. The wives of two cops murdered."

"You got your connection then."

"A kind of terrorist attack targeting the police," Owen frowned. "Maybe a war-on-cops and those we love are the prime targets. It did happen at the Policeman's Ball even with all those cops around." Agitated by his thoughts and imagined scenarios he paced. "Anything could be possible but what if it's something simpler? What if the cop just happened to stumble into a situation gone bad, a robbery or rape and the guy panics and just kills them all; I don't know," he rubbed hard at the center of his forehead. "I'm still left at square one: find the killer because if I don't I'm gone."

Giordano's face darkened, "It's a damn shame." Owen opened his mouth to interrupt but his friend held up a hand, "I know what you're going to say: 'None of this has anything to do with my being a cop.' Bull shit, Owen. Look where your love of being 'cop' has gotten you for chrissakes; fucking wanted."

He stood and pointed at Owen, "You get over here, work hard, follow their rules and still—still—they find a way to royally fuck you over; the sons-of-bitches. We've known each other a long time Owen but for the life of me, I will never—ever—get why being a civil servant, putting your life on the line for strangers who could give a shit, means so much to you."

Owen understood Giordano's anger and had learned not to take offense at it. Giordano's old confusion and more than a little contempt at his career choice had not smoothed out over the years. He still remembered when he'd told him he was going to become a cop and the horrified look that had come over his friend's face, as if he'd said he was going to rob graves for a living.

Giordano had grown-up with total disdain for the police and any other civil, state or federal authority. In his opinion these so called protectors of the public based their right to exist on the power to suppress everyone else. The supposed guardians of peace, security and justice meant nothing in his world; they were nuisances believed insidiously corrupt and were far worse than the hoods and criminals that populated the world he'd been born into. The so called "law" was an annoying pain-in-the-ass fact of life that must be circumvented at all costs.

In Giordano's world view he, his family and those he was close to were subservient to no one and anyone who flashed a badge had no redeeming value except to deal with the human trash of a society who didn't understand true justice; it wasn't a pretty picture yet it was the way it was. He was Giordano's one exception and only because he knew that deep down Giordano believed they were just the same.

"A damn shame," Giordano said again, "What can I do? Anything."

"Will you use your connections, your people out there on the street and underground to come up with a name, address or even this so-called-witness who keeps appearing then disappearing?" Owen paused, "I can pay."

Giordano angrily waved the offer aside, "Don't insult me. Of course I'll do it; I'll have people out around the clock. I'll get it moving right now." He pressed a button on the computer and in seconds the Sprinter appeared. Giordano spoke to him in lowered tones before sending him away.

"Thanks," Owen said it was heartfelt. "One last thing." He took out the red book and tossed it to Giordano. "Ever heard of it? Her?"

Giordano opened to the first page, "Lily is Lily's." He raised his eyes to Owen and tossed it back, "And it's off limits to the police; never been infiltrated."

"No place is off limits to the police."

"There you go again being naïve. What about Lily?"

"I found the book among Lorna's things."

"Lorna," Giordano expelled the name on a weary sigh before scribbling something on a notepad and handing the paper to Owen. "It's time you finally knew what the bitch had been up to."

"What are you talking about?"

Giordano ignored the question, "I'll tell Lily you're coming. Take a box of pricey white chocolate truffles with you; guests never arrive without a gift. We finished here?"

At Owen's nod Giordano grinned with boyish charm as he put an arm around Owen's shoulders and walked him toward the door, "So how about some rigatoni with clam sauce from Degrazia's down the street? You look half starved. This coffee business is good for show to impress the clients but when you're used to doing a favor for an old friend it can't be done better than over a glass or two of wine and a plate of rigatoni with clams."

"Sounds good," Owen said then, "Tell me about the handcuffs."

CHAPTER 25

O wen bounded up the stairs of the beautifully kept Tribeca townhouse and felt as if he was finally getting some where. At the gleaming blond-wood door he pressed the bell as he stared at the row of windows up and down; it had to be fifteen rooms or more. The place spelled money, he realized and lots of it.

The door was opened by a small, brown-skinned Latina wearing a black and white maid's uniform complete with white frilly cap and apron. She smiled shyly as she addressed him formally, "Mr. Story, Miss Lily is expecting you."

She stepped back allowing Owen into a spacious black and white tiled foyer. On his left was a pristine white wall hung with a large gilt framed mirror its glass spotless as it reflected his image back to him. Underneath the mirror sat a slight white and gold claw footed entry table even he recognized as antique; on top of it sat an expensive, simple Tiffany vase holding a few, fragile, white chrysanthemums. Beside the table was an archway he assumed led into a living or family room. To his right was a wide white staircase to the next floor; he could see a number of closed doors at its top.

The maid had stopped as he looked around and assuming he'd concluded his perusal led him under the archway into a large living room decorated with two large sofas printed with delicate spring flowers that were repeated in the carpet at their feet. Between the sofas sat a wide, Italian, glass topped table holding a large vase of blooming yellow tulips and several large artfully designed decorative boxes filled with chocolates

The room was softly lit by antique lamps and though evening was taking over the day the room still managed to have a light and airy feel that brought to mind flower shows and spring luncheons. The woman who sat on the sofa on his right reading a novel fit perfectly into the setting.

Owen estimated her age between forty-five and fifty-five. She reminded him of a show he'd once watched on the Learning Channel profiling society women of Palm Beach, Florida. The women had been beautifully coiffured and stylishly clothed in thousand dollar dresses complete with thousands of dollars worth of jewelry; they had reeked of large disposable incomes. But to him, despite the luxurious trappings and seemingly enviable lifestyle they had all been on the verge of losing the race with time. The best make-up and cosmetic surgery in the world couldn't win forever against inevitable harsh lines, deep visible age spots, sagging skin and the other marks of deterioration; this woman was the New York version of the Palm Beach matron.

She was well dressed in a cashmere winter white suit, a smooth gold necklace encircled her neck which was beginning to bag. Gold earrings with large diamond centers adorned her ears and around her wrist winked a cascading diamond bracelet. She had upswept blond hair fighting gray held in place by a diamond hairpin and on the woman's straight patrician nose sat half-glasses; behind these were deep-set appraising green eyes ringed with lines of experience and worldliness. She removed the glasses and sat them along side the book Owen noticed was the poetry of Robert Frost.

"Mr. Story or should I say Detective Story," she gave him a tight smile. Her voice was deep and perfectly modulated, "It's nice to finally meet you."

He registered her last words first and didn't know what to make of them, "Nice to meet you too, Lily," he offered her the box of candy.

Her smile relaxed a bit, "How kind of you." She took the box without glancing at it and sat it beside the others before patting the seat next to her, "Please sit down." Owen sat as she turned toward him putting a little space between them, "Something to drink?"

"No, I'm fine," he easily pictured her younger version, the lines gone and her hair gloriously blond. She must've stopped traffic he thought, recognizing her appeal; a very sexy appeal time couldn't easily diminish.

How did Lorna know her? Was she a major real estate broker Lorna had apprenticed with? Or was she a client Lorna had sold an expensive home to maybe this townhouse?

She glanced at the silent maid, "Thank you Helen I'll call if I need you." When the woman had gone she looked at him the smile absent, her face taunt and aged brittle in the glow from the lamps, "You're a friend of Richard's who's a business acquaintance of mine so I assume at the very least you aren't here to harass, accuse or bribe me, detective." Surprised at her speech Owen didn't respond waited for her to continue. "Let me inform you those tactics have been tried and I'm still here doing what I do."

"And what's that, Lily?"

"You have no idea what we do here?" surprise registered in her eyes. "I thought Richard would've told...." She trailed off as Owen shook his head.

"No, he didn't say but my wife seemed to have an idea. I found your name a number of times in one of her date books."

Owen's leg twitched as she laid a hand on his thigh, "I was so sorry to hear about her death. I cried all night. She will be missed here."

Owen moved and Lily's hand slipped off his thigh, "Where is here?"

She stood smoothing down her skirt, "Let me introduce you to Lily; the reason why your wife enjoyed coming here." She led him out the room and up the wide staircase. Over her shoulder she spoke with enthusiasm like a well-trained tour guide, "Lily's the place a woman of exceptional talent and ambition comes to learn everything there is to learn about being the best she can be in the pursuit of getting and having it all."

At the top she opened the first door on her right and nodded to Owen who stepped forward into a room decorated like an English drawing room. Two attractive women sat talking over a china tea set. A tea party, okay; he looked at them puzzled as they smiled at him; he didn't smile back. He retreated as Lily closed the door.

Some kind of women-only club he decided; an expensive finishing or charm school. Yes, he could picture Lorna being interested in a place like this the way she had been so relentless about saying the right thing and looking the right way; she would've fit in easily here. Relief flowed through him; so this was all there was to it. Thank God.

Lily pushed open the second door and Owen stepped inside without hesitation. The room was lit by candlelight, black shades covered the windows and a small fire glowed in the fireplace. The room smelled of perfume and heat. A young woman and an older man their features almost indistinguishable in the semi-darkness sat at a table, a candle flickered between them as they held hands and whispered. On the table were plates of half-eaten fruit, a decorated box of white chocolates, two champagne glasses and an open bottle of wine.

Mesmerized by the scene, an intimate meal for two taking place while it was still light outside Owen felt a rush of shameful voyeurism roll through him even as he was startled by a shadow that moved in the far corner. Someone else was watching; he couldn't make out if it was a man or woman only that the person ignored him and Lily just as the couple did.

The clink of silverware drew Owen back to the couple and as he watched, the young woman took the man's hand and led him over to a grouping of pillows in front of the fire pushing him down on them. She then moved back to the table and picking up a glass of wine handed it to her companion.

"You can reverse your rolls Allison," the person in the corner said. Owen's head swung around toward the shadowed speaker, a woman. "There're no rules here. Nothing distinguishes the male from the female except the obvious," she laughed a throaty throbbing sound. "He can fetch you some wine," the man rose and went to the table doing as he was told.

"Pose for him Allison," the woman's voice was sexy and instructive. "Tantalize him with your beautiful body."

Owen's eyes widened as Allison unbuttoned her blouse and slid it open to reveal plump firm breasts with nipples the color of strawberries.

"Yes," the woman said. "Beautiful."

Lily tapped Owen's shoulder as she opened the door. He ignored her and continued to stare at the couple lying against the pillows fondling each other. The man moaned with pleasure, Owen's stomach twisted; he recognized the sound as his reeling brain tossed up the idea: this was some kind of sex therapy place, not a charm school and he was watching a session between clients there was no other explanation. Why hadn't Giordano warned him what he'd find? More importantly what had his wife been doing here? It damn well wasn't discussing the housing market. Had she been seeing a therapist and having these sessions? With who? Had he killed her? Lily clutched his arm forcing him into the hall.

"What was that?" his voice strained with suppressed anger.

"A learning experience."

"Are you serious?"

"Oh, yes," a malice edged smile slid onto her face. "You can't be shocked. The world's all about sex isn't it? In one form or another. It's what you—men—believe. What is a woman to do if she wants to grab a hand full for herself? She has to know all about the Big Motivator and how to use it."

Owen stared at her as if her head had just popped off, "That's nuts and you're old enough to know better."

Her face reddened. Turning to the last door at the end of the hall, she pushed it open before beckoning him forward with a crooked finger. Owen didn't move; he couldn't. He was afraid to look behind door number three because the scariest question grinding itself into his head still hadn't been answered: What does any of this weird shit have to do with Lorna? Was the answer behind that door? Only one way to find out. A bolt of fear stabbed through him even as he moved toward Lily who put that crooked finger to his chest and whispered, "Who's in control?"

He ignored her, stepped inside and stopped short. The smell and the sound of sex hit him first. A couple lay naked and entwined on a canopied bed. A gorgeous woman stood beside them, the fingers of her left hand resting on the sheet next to their thrashing bodies. She was tall with waist-length black hair, almond shaped dark eyes and wide red lips in a face of sharp angles that came together in a bewitching combination of features.

She looked dressed for a board meeting in a ankle length black skirt and high-necked white blouse but as his gaze sharpened in the dimness Owen saw the skirt was split up to her navel revealing marble white thighs and the blouse was unbuttoned to her waist so that a long swath of pale skin shown. Draped over this skin was a long strand of white pearls she stroked with her right hand as her avid gaze ran over the gyrating couple.

"Yes, Michael she's all you want," she spoke in a raspy accented voice. "Show her so. Harder. Uhm, that's good." She put a knee up on the bed causing the skirt to slide open and display pubic hair as dark as that on her head. "Put your hand right there and pull it Caitlin it won't hurt him and you'll both enjoy the sensation. Yes, bite there he'll love it." The couple did as instructed and moaned causing the woman to smile.

Owen charged up to the bed, "What the hell are you doing?" He knew the question was ridiculous yet was unable to come up with anything rational to yell. The motion on the bed ceased as the couple, Lily and the woman stared at him.

"You—" the woman came around the bed and stopped a breath away from him. Her blouse fell open spilling out a heavy dark-nippled breast she seemed to either not notice or care, "can watch but not speak; not speak; no."

"Don't tell me what to do, I'll have your ass arrested."

"Out, Mr. Story," Lily grabbed his arm. "Get out of here right now."

Pulling out of her grasp, Owen stormed out the room and down the stairs, "You're running prostitutes, Lily."

"What we do here is based on—"

Owen jerked around on her, "I don't want to hear another spiel about men running the world with their dicks and women having to eat it; this place is nothing but a new take on the old whorehouse."

She threw a fist toward his face; he caught it against his palm before it collided with his nose and shoved it aside. Her face was the color of a cooked lobster the comb having slipped from her hair leaving it to swing messy around her face, "Don't you dare use that word in my house."

"Then what do you call what those people were doing? Knitting sweaters?"

"They were being instructed on the art of sex, pleasure, pleasing their partner in turn you saw it for yourself. The instructor—who's paid very well I might add—can—"

"Instructor?" he turned and went the rest of the way down to the main floor. "You're out of your mind; what you got here is sexual deviance."

"Its therapy," she shot back following. "Somewhat unorthodox maybe but it—"

"That's it," Owen headed for the front door. "I'm not listening to anymore of your crap, lady. You're delusional. You don't need to be arrested but taken over to Bellevue for a psych evaluation."

"Really," her tone was deadly, "then your wife would have needed to go along with me."

Owen's fingers froze on the doorknob as his mind tilted, a sheen of cold sweat breaking over his body as he looked at her, "You don't know what you're talking about; Lorna would never—"

"Oh, yes she would," Lily countered, "What do you think she was doing here? Knitting sweaters?"

"She wasn't up there screwing strangers," Owen denied closing off the truth roaring in his head.

"She went way beyond that; she was extraordinary. She could promise with a look it was her power. Picture her upstairs," Lily advanced on him as he backed away from her and the horrifying pictures of Lorna her words conjured up. "Sitting in a dark corner; her legs crossed all prim and proper, she's wearing those little glasses she needed for reading and that gorgeous hair of hers is loose about her shoulders settling on a meek, white, secretary's blouse buttoned up to her throat but reaching down to crotch less pants as she tells them to do whatever she wants just on the implied promise they could do it to her next."

"Shut up," Owen shouted though it came out a tortured whispered. "You lying bitch."

"She was one of my best. She came here looking for something different, something new, more, and oh, didn't she find it. And she learned fast, exceptionally so until she was regularly requested. It was that voice of hers sometimes so sweet and pleading and at others so commanding and demanding her clients loved that contradiction in her, they couldn't get enough."

Unable to take his eyes off her, his fingers fumbled at the doorknob, horror on his face as he finally got the door open almost falling down the stairs in his haste he just managed to keep from smashing into the sidewalk. Lily laughed at him from the top of the stairs.

"Lorna was special wasn't she, detective," she called after him as he fled.

Rocketing down the street on squealing tires followed by the angry blare of horns from the vehicles he almost destroyed; Owen held the wheel with one hand as he pounded the roof and dashboard with the fist of the other while shouting obscenities at his dead wife, "Goddamn you Lorna, you secretive, unfaithful bitch. What else? What else did you do?"

He rounded the corner of Hudson Street doing sixty; the car shuttered and dropped him back into the world with the realization he was driving dangerous; crazy. He slowed trying to do the same to his racing heart and mind. How could she have done those things? Why? He looked through the rearview mirror for cops alerted to his furious dash and was jolted by the fact someone was following him.

He reduced speed around the next corner his eyes on the mirror as he joined the traffic. A Ford Taurus of a color he couldn't make out in the darkness completed the turn two cars behind him. He followed close behind a red Saturn his gaze shifting from the road to the Taurus. You've caught me on a very bad day you shit heads the thought roared through his head as he whipped around the Saturn ignoring the driver who stood on her brakes as he pulled in front and kept going.

He sped up to a four way intersection his hands tight on the wheel; he didn't bother checking his rearview he knew they were there. Pressing on the gas as the light turned red he honked his horn one long blare as he careened through the intersection into oncoming traffic the other drivers stopping in all directions managing only by a hairs breath to avoid a multi-car pile-up.

"Jeezus, he's gonna kill somebody," James Lee Carter stomped on his breaks just missing the rear end of a stopped car.

"Come on, come on," Williams urged. "Just go around these people."

Owen switched from lane to lane and sped around corners once on two wheels before spotting a tri-level garage up ahead and bulleting toward it. The electronic arm was up, he shot pass the empty attendants booth and up the first ramp his eyes on the mirror. Reaching the second level his intent gaze swung back and forth between the up ramp in the mirror and the darkened parking spaces as he listened to the tail car coming fast.

"Shit," he twisted the wheel and the car lurched to the right missing by inches the bed of a Ford pickup backing out.

"Goddamn Fords," he shot up onto the third level and heard the Taurus coming. Pulling tight into a darkened parking space between a hospital transport van and a large sport utility vehicle he got out of the car taking the jack he kept under the seat with him.

The Taurus appeared and slowed as the men inside looked out their perspective windows. "I don't hear him anymore," Carter said. "I hope we haven't lost the sneaky bastard; he had to've stopped on this level there's nowhere else to go and he sure as shitten didn't pass us going down."

"He's here," Williams scanned the empty vehicles. "Slow down so I can see."

The rear window exploded and Carter screamed as he pressed reflexively on the breaks jerking the car to a jarring halt. His hands flew to his face as blood flew from his glass encrusted cheek. Williams' forehead struck the dashboard with a thick thud as the skin above his right eye popped open and spilled blood.

With the jack in both hands Owen held it over his head a moment, a look of resigned calm on his face as he brought it down with a decisive chop through the driver's side window sending glass shards flying.

With the same calm he reached through the ragged hole, pulled the keys out of the ignition and tossed them across the garage, "The object is to follow and not be seen; you assholes were obviously seen. Have a nice day," with a wink he jogged away off into the darkened recesses of the garage.

CHAPTER 26

Owen flipped to the last page of the notebook and checked the only address he'd found in the entire book against the number on the front of the house. It was a small house painted a sun-dried red with an attached garage. He rang the bell his heart beating a painfully rhythm until he felt like a man stranded out at sea during a typhoon.

The door was opened by a white-haired Asian man. They stared at each other, "Say m^e?" he said in Vietnamese. "Say m^e?"

"Yes," Owen said not understanding but getting the gist of the words."

The man stepped aside allowing Owen to cross the threshold. Without a word he led him up a narrow stairs and down a short hall that ended at a door painted sunshine yellow. Owen glanced at the man who retreated down the stairs as he put his finger against the door and pushed. He stepped inside.

The room was austere, a gray cell with a single bed, a dresser and a vanity the only furniture. An opened door on the right led into small spotless bathroom as impersonal as one in a second rate motel. The only other door opened to a closet holding clothes he'd never seen. A tiny window in front of the vanity overlooked the quiet street. The bed, the only other furniture was covered by a black quilt, no pillow. A white silk robe with Japanese script printed on it lay across the bed.

Off the dresser Owen picked up a framed photo of Lorna. She wore the robe as she stared into the camera unsmiling, her face pale and naked of make-up, hair unkempt. On the vanity was another picture, she again wore the robe but this time it had slipped down her shoulders; she looked over the right one again unsmiling. Who took them he wondered as he put it face down, struck by them both and their similarity to those of rape victims taken during evidence gathering.

He opened a plain white box the only thing on the vanity and wasn't surprised to find it filled with expensive bracelets, rings and watches. Moving to the bed he lay down. He picked up the robe he put it to his face inhaling as he closed his eyes. Tea Rose. Lorna. Had she met him—them—here? Another weird tutorial in the art of sex?

Crumpling the silk he got off the bed and searched the room for some kind of explanation to the why of all this. He plowed through the clothes in the closet and did the same to the contents of the vanity and dresser drawers until the room looked as if a tornado had hit it. Tossing the robe and bed clothes from the bed he pushed the mattress to the floor before dropping to his knees and looking under the box spring. Taped to the underside was a brown envelope; his hands shook as he pulled it out.

Printed on the left hand corner were the words: Gifford Brooklyn Womankind Center. He opened the envelope, two pieces of paper fluttered out to the floor. The first was a mental evaluation conducted by a Ms. Karen Winter, PHD. The patient: Mrs. Lorna Story. It was a typed conversation. Winter: You believe this is the right thing to do? Lorna: It's the only thing to do. Ms. Winter: You don't have to be alone in this, we'll call anyone for you, anyone you want. Lorna: There's no one. Winter: Will you like to list the father? Lorna: No, it doesn't matter. I don't… Winter had then written: Interview ended. The client upset and refusing to answer any further inquiries.

Owen picked up the second sheaf of paper and read it, then read it again before he realized it was a set of instructions, directives for care of self after a termination of pregnancy. "Oh, God," he said. "An abortion," his body went to stone. Was it mine? Mine? He tore at the papers, ripped them into pieces before he grabbed them up in search of a date. He found it; it was over a year ago, he let them fall to the floor. She'd kept her monstrous secret for a year, had smiled and laughed with this sitting inside her in the place where a child—maybe his child— had lain. The terribleness of it all struck him like a punch in the mid-section, he ran from it, out of the room and down the stairs.

The man stood at the bottom, "Spellbound is no more," he said in English. "She will not be coming back?"

Needing to get free of the house, of Lorna and the devastation she'd left behind, Owen pulled open the door and lurched out onto the doorstep before turning back with the only answer, "She's dead. Burn everything."

CHAPTER 27

Owen walked into the East Street Pier warehouse barely noticing the workers moving around him filling crates with originally shaped bottles ready for shipment. He didn't look left or right, he felt hollow inside with everything turned off. Stopping at a large crate he crawled atop it like a wounded animal crawling away to die. The workers watched him as they went about their duties. He lay with his back to them rolled into a ball. Exhausted physically and mentally he sank into a fitful sleep of retreat and forgetfulness. One of the workers found a blanket she laid across him as he twitched and muttered in his nightmares.

They heard footsteps and looked down the aisle as their boss approached carrying a brown paper bag. Giordano nodded and they disappeared. He stopped next to his friend who slept uneasy. He'd known it would be devastating for him, learning the woman he'd loved had been more than unique and clever but so manipulative and secretive he may never recover from the knowledge. Worse, his old friend had known and been a party to it keeping that secret in his own dark place. Had it been more than a year since he'd found out he and Lorna were partners?

He'd been sipping a glass a champagne after he and Lily had enjoyed a bit of voyeuristic entertainment featuring a client with a fetish involving used tea bags, when Lily informed him she'd found someone to enhance their business and bring in new ideas. A brief knock had sounded before the door opened and Lorna walked in; he spilt his drink at the sight of her.

She sat down across from him wearing a black leather coat and high black boots her hair a flame against all that black, "Hello, Richard. Surprised to see me?"

149

"Nothing you do surprises me, Lorna. How's my friend Owen?"

"Trying to scare me??"

"A bazooka pointed at you wouldn't scare you."

"He's doing well, catching bad guys and girls as usual. Do you have any objections to my joining the team?"

"You mean besides the fact you're the wife of my best friend the cop? A few."

"That's what makes it so delicious don't you think?" she laughed. "No one would ever suspect and definitely not Owen," she flipped her long hair over a shoulder before staring directly at him. "He trusts me. I can help Lily's expand its clientele; I can bring in new faces willing to pay well for their pleasures and I can promise some unforgettable experiences."

"Don't you sale houses?"

"On the side," she grinned perfectly.

"To expand the clientele; that's your only reason for partnering with Lily—with us?"

"And the opportunity to meet very important people I may be able to persuade to see my point of view on a few issues. You know as well as I do some of our clients are premiere movers and shakers in their sphere so shouldn't they give favors in return for the ones they get?"

Fascinated by her despite the shudder of revulsion rippling down his spine he watched as she pulled tight the black belt at her waist the leather squeaking. He wondered if she was naked underneath. He glanced at her face, her eyes were lowered but she was smiling, the smile aware. He understood then she'd done it deliberately, she'd known he couldn't help wondering if she wore only the leather. She had manipulated his thoughts, knew exactly how his mind would work and had enjoyed making it happen. There was no doubt the woman amazed and terrified him.

"I'm doing this mostly for Owen."

He laughed, "Now, you're going too far."

"Imagine what I can do to secure his future. Owen's good at his job, the best and he should be given the opportunity to go as far as we can in the department. But his being good isn't enough, Richard; he needs an edge and I'll do whatever I can to get it for him. You're his closest friend; don't you want him to be a success; to have what he deserves?"

"Including the wonderful you?"

"Always."

"But at what price? I believe he'll think it way too high."

"Don't you worry Richard," she stood and walked over to him. Putting her hands on his shoulders she placed one black stocking knee on the chair between his legs. She smelled of roses, "I'm willing to pay that price; I'll do anything for him."

"Lorna, you give a new definition to the phrase wifely duties."

"And so would you Richard, do anything for Owen." She gave him a chaste kiss on the forehead before sliding out her knee and stepping back, "We'll be seeing each other around."

"Not if I see you first," he meant it.

"You've always had some balls, Richard."

"I can say the same for you."

Laughing, she'd walked out her hair leaping fire against the blackness of the long leather.

Giordano shook his friend, Owen sat up and ran a shaky hand down his gray face, "I was having a nightmare."

"Lorna was featured right?" he took in Owen's new injuries. " What happened to you?" he asked as Owen got down from his wooden bed.

Owen glanced at the meaty side of his palm that was covered with blood smeared Band-Aids. He had been so pumped with adrenaline he hadn't realized he had been cut until he was a block away from the garage, "Flying glass. I ran into some jerks who got too close. I hope there's liquor in that bag; I could use a shot or ten."

"No," Giordano sat the bag on top of the crate, "Real nourishment. You recognize them?"

"Feds, though I was too busy to ask for proof."

"They could've shot you."

"They didn't look like they could spell gun let alone fire one. I didn't leave them on a positive note so I suspect they'll be looking for me with Riviera leading the charge."

"Jeezus, Owen."

"Why the hell didn't you warn me about Lily?"

"What was I supposed to say," Giordano spread his hands. 'Hey, my long time buddy, friend, pal, guess what? I have a stake in this bizarre—but very profitable mind you—venture involving sex and domination with a touch of positive reinforcement thrown in and I've seen your wife there, regularly. How do you think that would have played with you, Owen?"

"A lot better than hearing it from that woman," distress filled Owen's face. "I went in there expecting—I don't know—but what I got was off the chart. I still can't fucking believe it and to find out Lorna—" He turned and kicked the crate again and again until his foot went through the wood. "Goddammit," he wrestled it out before slumping against its side defeated.

"I'm a silent partner in Lily's; it's one of the business interests I inherited; you know how it works, Owen. I don't partake in any of the offered services though a lot of men do; some of them you've met. They need that kind of stimulation—humiliation—whatever you want to call it badly enough to pay top dollar for it."

"So you condone it because of the money; always the fucking money."

"Fuck you Owen I don't condone it; people's livelihoods are involved here whether I like it or not."

Owen stared at him, "Is it the world that's fucked up or just me? No matter how you try and spin it Richard it isn't right."

"It's not what's going on in Lily's that's messing up your head but the fact your wife was a relevant part of it."

"You think I'm not hurt by that? Destroyed."

"Get over it; she's the one who betrayed you not the other way around and she's still putting you through it."

"You can't help who you love."

"Then there should be a shot for it."

Owen scrunched his eyes closed as if it hurt to see, to be alive, "How could I have been so wrapped up in my own life I didn't know my wife was some kind of insane-sex-freak-dominatrix?"

"It didn't have a thing to do with sex; that was a tool like her beauty. Lorna was in it for the power."

"Oh, that makes me feel better."

Giordano smiled for a heartbeat, "Don't forget the control, she loved the control. I knew what she was the first time I laid eyes on her." Giordano caught the question that flashed in Owen's eyes, "You wonder if she ever tried to work herself on me? She wasn't the kind to let a little friendship get in the way was she?" Owen felt his muscles clench in anticipation of an answer he didn't want to hear but had to.

"No, I was your friend so she respected the line. She loved you; possibly more than she loved herself."

Owen doubted it but felt the tightness in his chest loosen, "How many people you think knew who she was? Knew about her?"

Giordano stepped close to him, his voice sure, "It doesn't matter does it? Those who might have known aren't in any position to point fingers. And any secrets she knew she took with her I hope."

"You think she was killed because she may have known something or someone who didn't want her talking?"

"Anything's possible."

"Did you think I killed her?"

"For a second," Giordano's gaze frosted, "if you ask me; you had good reason. But I know you, you could've never done it; you wouldn't be able to justify the need."

Owen took a breath, "All right that's it then. Okay. There's a lot of things—bad things—terrible things I've seen; my God, we've done together so this will just be another thing between us; another secret safe with us."

"Safe."

"Safe, safe, safe" Owen repeated the mantra as he turned away.

"You're a mess," Giordano called, "you need to go home and take a couple of pain killers. Hey" he called and as Owen turned back he tossed him the bag, "You forgot the meatballs with provolone."

CHAPTER 28

Outside, Owen walked. It started to rain, he paid no attention to it or to his route, the neighborhoods he passed through or the people who hurried by him. He walked because he understood that if he got in his car and took off he'd be dangerous; as it was he was having trouble making the connection he needed to put one foot in front of the other to keep going. He couldn't think; his head was full of warring thunderclouds, lightning and tornado winds and didn't clear even when the first bullet struck the sidewalk in front of his right shoe. He froze as the second shot whizzed past his left ear; he felt its speed and heat and heard its passage even in the rain.

Life exploded back on in brilliant Technicolor as he took in the blackish rain slashed street and smelled the cold heart of it as it hammered his bare head and body; oh, what a bullet close to the brain can do for you he thought as he dove behind a mailbox his shoulder striking the blue steel as the third bullet slammed into the trunk of the tree next to the box.

A man with a scraggly beard cradling a tattered garbage bag peered out from the recessed doorway of an apartment building, "Somebody's shoot'in at you," he shouted. "You'd better call the cops."

Owen looked around both sides of the mailbox; it was hard to make out anything in the blinding rain. He wiped at his eyes but caught only washed shadows. The shooter could be anywhere. Anyone. Why was someone trying to kill him today of all days? Or was the question who wasn't trying to kill him? Should he risk trying to shoot back? How, when he couldn't see a damn thing.

"I'll take my chances," Owen called back. "You see him?" The man shook his head. They watched the street as the rain fell harder, sheets of it obscuring everything.

"A hellish down pour," the man said and Owen agreed with the hell.

"There," the man's hand flew up a finger pointed down the block." Right there," a figure materialized as it ran from behind a parked car dressed in black from head to toe almost coalescing with the wet gloom of the night.

Owen took off after him yelling, "Thanks," to the man who'd stepped from his hide away to watch the chase.

The specter was half a block in front of him moving very fast. Owen picked up speed trying to at least close the distance and slipped on the slick pavement. His back collided with the sidewalk as the wind whooshed out of him in a bone shattering rush. He lay stunned unable to catch his breath; wide open to the icy drops assaulting his visible skin in stinging bites. He rolled over and sat up the movement causing a bolt of pain to shoot from one end of his spine to the other.

His clothes were soaked and weighed him down. He staggered to his feet and tried to pull his body inwards to conserve the little warmth he had left. He looked up and saw he was in front of a set of stone stairs leading up to large double doors. Quaking from the cold within as well as without as he moved slowly up the stairs and through the entrance where he turned his back to the interior to study the street. The shooter had long disappeared into the night.

Turning toward the interior he saw he was in a church. It was empty and candle lit the light reflecting warmly off the polished pews and stained glass windows. The interior lights were turned low giving it the cozy safe feel of a haven. The rain tapping on the high windows was now a smooth unhurried sound.

It had been a couple of years since he'd been in any house of worship the last had been a synagogue and it was of course because a crime, murder had been committed on its property. He hadn't gone to church of his own free will in years. His mother Miriam had been Catholic, lapsed but forever a Catholic. His father Harlan had no religion, no beliefs; he'd been nothing.

Owen stepped out of the narthex into the nave and sat down in the first pew on his right. The silence buffeted him as he stared at the body of the beatific Jeezus Christ hanging before the altar; the church's quiet welcoming atmosphere seeming to give the Savior's carved skin the glowing patina of life and the blood that flowed down his lithe body a richness and hue he could almost taste.

He stared and wondered how he could have not known; the questioned bludgeoned him over and over; he'd talked to her every day, made love to her countless times, slept next to her, watched her dress, eat; so many intimacies never imaging there was another world living inside her where he didn't exist.

God forgive me, he closed his eyes, but I hate you Lorna the words whispered through him like a prayer. He hated her not just because of what she'd been, what she'd done but because even now at the bottom of this, deep in darkest heart of him he loved her still and knew no matter what he did he'd never be able to rid himself of that love; never be able to force it out, cut it out or crush it and the surety of this caused a burning pain to inflame the back of his throat and sear his eyes.

He gripped the pew in front of him with both hands for its solidness, the reality of it kept him from exploding from the maelstrom that churned inside him because he was at blame too. He'd seen the signs she was someone else but had consciously or unconsciously decided not to see, he hadn't the heart to figure out which one he'd deliberately chosen to do. How fucking ironic her rising-star-detective-husband had been afraid to confront her, afraid he couldn't be who she wanted him to be or give her what she needed and now he lived the terrible truth of both realizations.

A priest stepped out of a room off the side of the altar. He was in his early fifties the look on his weathered face of studied reflection. He started toward Owen just as Owen opened his eyes; the look in them of such glaring pain it slowed the priest but didn't stop him, "For some it takes a long time to find the peace we seek. It won't come quick or easy," he said stopping a few feet away from Owen who stood.

"Especially when you don't deserve it."

"Most of us search for it anyway no matter what the cost and grab hold of it as if we mean never to let it go," the priest smiled. "Its life my friend."

"Then life's not good enough for me anymore, Father." Moving out of the pew Owen nodded to the priest before walking out into wet night.

The priest watched him go before closing his eyes and crossing himself as he said a prayer for the man so lost he didn't want to be found.

CHAPTER 29

After driving around most of the night afraid to go to Pop's in case the shooter or anyone else was waiting to finally take him down, Owen found an off the map motel in the Bronx, the Red Roof Lodge its roof the color of sand and as flat as a pancake Owen noticed. Paying for a room in the back he was thankful the attendant was the I-don't-know-and-don't-want-to-know type who barely looked at him as he handed over the cash and was given genuine steel key to the room instead of an electronic plastic card.

He took a tepid shower then soaped and rinsed his dirty clothes hanging them on the shower rod to dry. Before lying down he flipped off the lights and stood a long vigil at the side of the window looking out. No one will find me easily he thought as his eyes ran over the parking lot below.

One other vehicle, a green Dodge Ram with a stack of plywood in the back was his car's only company in the hour he watched. Dropping down on the bed he put his gun on the flat pillow next to him before settling into the thin coverlet and into a dream filled sleep.

The next morning before he stepped out the room he again looked out and saw only his car and the pick-up no additional guests having arrived during the night. Feeling confident he'd gained some time for himself though unsure of how much; he was at his car pulling the door open when a black SUV came out of no where, moving fast and braked in the center of the lot it's engine firing.

Owen stared rapidly clicking it into place: Lorna's office and possibly Giordano's, "Shit," he quickly pulled his Glock and aimed at the smoked front window.

As if his action was a switch from behind and in front of him cars roared in and surrounded him. Doors flew open and men rolled out their guns drawn on him; his finger tightened on the trigger.

"Drop the gun," said one of the men who wore a thick bandage above his right eye.

"I'm a—"

"We know who you are. We're the FBI. Drop your weapon."

"The hell I will," Owen stared hard at him. "You think I'm going to let you take me like some punk?"

"We need to talk to you."

"Good way of going about it. Show me some ID."

The man flashed him a look of intense irritation as he pulled out an identification card and held it up. Owen hadn't needed to see it, he'd recognized him from the encounter in the garage; he'd obviously done the guy some damage.

"All you had to do was ask nicely, Williams," Owen slowly put his gun away.

"We need you to ride with us," Williams holstered his weapon as the other agents followed suit though their eyes never left the detective.

"And if I don't give a shit what "we need" and say no?"

"Why are you being uncooperative and hampering the investigation into your wife's murder?" Williams stared at him his irritation having slid into impatience." But it's up to you, detective; we can do this as long as you can." he opened the back door on his car and waited.

"Yeah and I'm Santa Claus," Owen let it hang a moment then, "All right but I'm calling my lawyer. You guys could be more circumspect don't you think?"

As he bent into the car Williams punched him in the stomach, he sagged into the seat as the agents looked on without expression.

Williams raised the bandage and displayed an open red gash, "For this and the cuts to my partner's face; he can't see out of his left eye you asshole."

"Fucking with you," Owen managed despite the pain flaring in his belly, "was the highlight of my day."

Williams slammed the door in his face.

CHAPTER 30

A boom sounded in Owens's empty apartment rattling the windows and the china in the display case it made the small antique clock topple from its perch off the mantelpiece. It was followed by another and another as the front door bowed then splintered down the center. The final blow sent wood peeling back like the skin of a banana.

A black gloved hand appeared threw the hole and tore out pieces of wood until it was large enough for a man to step through. A foot appeared, then the rest of a body as Gunderson stepped into the hall followed by Harwood then a flak-jacked cop dressed all in black and holding a black battering ram.

Gunderson tossed a folded piece of paper on top of the hall table, "Take the upstairs," he turned to look at the cop as Harwood walked away. "Stay outside in case of nosey neighbors," he said before opening the drawer on the hall table and rooting through its contents of useless mailings, flyers and discarded keys before shutting it with a bang.

Walking into the living room, "Look at this place," he said with jealous outrage as he flipped over couch cushions and looked behind books and picture frames on the shelves. Not finding what he was after he then rifled through the cupboard in the small entertainment unit which housed the television and DVD player before checking behind the logs in the fireplace then up the chimney cursing as his hand came away with only black soot as his reward. He grew angrier by the minute at not finding what he was positive was hidden someplace in the apartment.

Stalking into the dining room and over to the china cabinet filled with delicate dishware he searched through the fine boned plates and teacups knocking over the prettily etched pieces which

160

broke apart, "The prick's living like a rich bitch."

In the kitchen he opened the oven door and peered inside and like before found nothing; he slammed it shut hoping Harwood was having better luck though if he had he would've called out. Gunderson's eyes gleamed as he fantasized over how sweet—how damn sweet—it was going to be to find right there in the jerk's house the weapon he used to wax his wife. And they could take their time looking for it too because Story was by now in the hands of the Feebs and he hoped they kicked his ass around until he confessed.

He picked the plastic bag out of the trashcan and glanced inside before dropping it back in place. At the freezer he removed foiled packages he opened then tossed to the floor as if they were frozen pieces of garbage; he did the same to the refrigerator's insides dumping out containers and their contents; tossing out boxes of Chinese food, packages of cheese even a carton of eggs until it looked as if the refrigerator had thrown-up its innards onto the floor.

Harwood appeared empty-handed, "Shit," Berniak said. "You sure you checked everywhere? Maybe I should take a look in case you missed it."

Harwood looked at him, a turning down of his lips the only sign of his irritation, "Help yourself but there's no gun upstairs."

"The sneaky son-of-a-bitch," Gunderson's face tightened like a dried prune. "He thinks he's so goddamn smart but that's all right he'll get stomped on. We'll worry about the gun later we've got enough anyway to make sure he's headed for death row. Let's go."

They left the apartment and not as they found it.

Berniak watched the cops come out of Story's house and made the call, "They're gone."

"Good," Williams answered as he watched Owen and a shorter man he assumed was Story's lawyer head into one of several buildings where the Bureau held some of their interviews, "I'll call Riviera and tell him Story's on his way."

Riviera stood alone in the men's room as his cell phone rang. He dried his hands on a towel before unclipping it from his belt, "Yes?"

"They're getting ready to run the ball on the pick-up," Williams said. "The cops just left Story's place and he's on his way to you."

"Good," Riviera looked at himself in the mirror. "I'll wind it up pretty quickly though I am looking forward to meeting this bad cop. Make sure you don't leave anything out of your reports; they're going to be needed for the record. Be on him when he leaves this building and if he tries to run you have my permission to give chase and use force."

He clicked off and stared into his eyes as he asked himself the one question he'd avoided since the phone call from the commissioner and all he'd learned up until now. Did he believe Story had murdered those people—his wife? He was unsure of the answer and the fact he was still undecided gave him pause. Story was connected with Giordano which was enough to make him suspected of some crime yet until they were face-to-face only then would he know if the man was capable of murder or not.

Smoothing out his hair and straightening his perfect shirt cuffs, he gave a mental shrug settling his curiosity about Story aside, it didn't matter one iota what he felt or believed about the cop because in the end it wasn't up to him but a jury of Story's peers to decide if he was innocent or would get a date for death.

CHAPTER 31

Owen sat in a large room on the fifth floor of a decaying building staring from the scarred wooden desk in front of him to the walls with their sky blue peeling paint. A man sat across the room typing on an ancient personal computer ignoring them. He wondered how far these people were going to take him. Was this the end result of Harwood's warnings, of Cush' pronouncements or just the beginning of the end?

This place needs to be condemned he decided as a cold draft whistled across his ankles. "Can't the government afford better accommodations? This place is halfway between a dump and a dump," he said to Manny Felder his lawyer.

"Federal money must be tight. Listen," Manny, a small spare man with thinning brown hair and a full mustache lowered his voice. "From all indications this is a basic Q and A and part of their routine in being called in to assist in this type of thing."

"Fine, I have no problem cooperating." Manny laughed as Owen frowned at him, "I don't. They're the ones who came after me remember?

But I'm overlooking that because I'm eager to go along as far as they need me to; I want my wife's murder solved more than anything else in the world."

A tall athletic looking man with sharp handsome features entered and stopped behind the desk. He laid a pile of folders on its top then reached a hand toward Owen who reached back, "I'm Paul Riviera. A-I-C of the Manhattan bureau."

As the man shook Manny's hand, Owen got a better look at him than he had at Giordano's place studying his eyes with their intense direct stare. He had been right, this guy didn't miss a trick. Manny thinks this is going to be your everyday ordinary Q

163

and A but with this one it was going to be more like a Nazi interrogation.

"I hope we didn't inconvenience you," Riviera settled into his chair. "Nor you Mr. Felder." His gaze hit Owen, "Though you didn't need to bring council Mr. Story."

"It's Detective Story and when they say don't bring a lawyer is when you should."

"If you say so," an un-offended smile showed off white teeth, "Detective Story. Not to take up much more of your time let's get down to details." He pulled forward a yellow legal pad and a pen, "First of all we don't expect this investigation to be any longer or more arduous that it has to be."

Owens's brows shot up, "Is that because you know something I don't?"

"These were horrendous crimes of course and if you haven't heard a reward of ten thousand dollars is on offer for the capture of the perpetrator with an increase of ten thousand more on the table. Money like that floating around can cause people to give up their mother's if they have to."

"So you do have something or someone you're hooked on to?"

Again Riviera smiled as if he enjoyed being the only one who knew a delicious secret, "Unfortunately I can't discuss any details at this time."

"Why not? It's not as if I'm a civilian."

"But you're involved in the case," Riviera scribbled on the pad before he looked up at Owen. "You have no idea why someone would kill your wife?"

Owen blinked, surprised at the first question though he recovered quickly, "No idea."

"You weren't involved in any way?"

"I don't like where you're heading," Owen's gaze sealed to Riviera's. "If you're trying to accuse me of murdering my wife in some slickly underhand don't, just say it, get it straight out," Owen stood. "Go ahead."

Manny put a hand on Owens's arm, "Sit down and let me handle this." Owen sat his eyes still on Riviera, "You're accusing my client of murder."

"Of course not," Riviera's sharp gaze was placid. "I understand your client is upset, jumping at bogeymen; I'm just gathering information not accusing him of anything." He slanted a speculative gaze toward Owen then leaned forward, "But if you'd like to confess I'm all ears."

"Forget it."

Riviera looked at Manny, "I think Detective Story may know more than he's telling."

"I don't have to tell you a thing though I'm willing to help if you don't continue to piss me off."

Riviera flipped to the next page in the pad, "How much you have to drink that night?"

"Some champagne. A whiskey at home."

"Were you intoxicated? Drunk?"

"I was not drunk and I certainly wasn't intoxicated."

Riviera ignored the wry comment, "Were you involved in any questionable incidents that involved your wife or any of the other victims?"

Damn, Owen thought as frustration dented his belly as the so-called 'fight' again reared its ugly head. "No," he said as Riviera's laser like gaze sliced across his face.

"One last question: were you two having marital problems?"

"All roads lead to no, Riviera."

"Agent Riviera," he twirled the pen between his fingers. "I have it here," he pointed to the pad, "you two were having difficulties."

Owen shrugged, "You know rumors; there's always a hand full going around and everybody gets their turn at being the subject of one whether true or not."

"You're right; I've been the subject of quite a few my self," he smiled, "so I should know better. Okay," Riviera closed the pad, "that's it then. Thanks for—"

"That's it?" Owen asked surprised; he felt duped and didn't like it one bit. "Have you interviewed anyone else?"

Riviera stood, "Such as?"

"Such as police commissioner Chandler or because he's the commissioner he doesn't get one of these cute little tête-à-têtes."

"You're the only one on my interview list," Riviera said. "One other thing: we believed there was a witness but it turned out we were off base on that one which usually doesn't happen to the FBI," he smiled at his attempt at humor before he reached over and shook Manny's hand again. "Thank you for coming; we'll be in touch if there's any need to talk to your client again."

He turned to Owen the smile gone, "Off the record Detective Story; if you fuck with any of my agents again you'll answer to me."

"Is that right?" it was Owens's turn to smile.

Riviera's dark eyes did a dangerous twist, "Oh, yes. You can take the elevator down though the stairs are quicker. Good-bye."

Dismissed they left, Riviera watching them out. In the hall Owen nudged Manny over into an alcove beneath the stairs, "So what was that all about?"

"Besides the threat and barely concealed accusations," Manny said dryly, "he asked you some questions."

Owen shook his head, "That was somewhere between getting dumped into a tank of piranhas and standing in front of a speeding bullet train."

"You're nuts you know that?" Manny said exasperated humor flashing across his face. "Are you talking some conspiracy theory here?"

"Weren't you listening?" Owen whispered his voice and eyes hot, "He was telling me in not so many words but in just the right ones I'm being set up. He's playing his part like everyone else, hell even I'm in on it by coming down here and talking to the guy. They're reeling me in Manny I can feel it; closing me off and God only knows how little time I've got left."

"You're paranoid, Owen; there's nothing going on here," Manny insisted, "especially not between the Feds and the police."

"Is that so? Then tell me why no one from the department or the union showed up for me? You know as well as I do if a cop's in court for spitting on the sidewalk there's a crew sitting in back supporting him from his boss to the union lawyer."

"I guess nobody got wind of this."

"No way, you know there're no secrets in the department. Everyone knew yet not one guy showed for me. I'm here conversing with the FBI—the guy in charge no less—and other than you my naked ass is hanging out there alone and wiggling in the wind."

Manny checked his watch, "I gotta go I have a meeting in twenty minutes," His gaze serious on Owen, "Look, I don't know what's going on or what you think is going on but please don't go off half-cocked Owen; but in case you can't help yourself call me right away if anything happens." He turned toward the stairs and glanced back at Owen whose face wore a hunted expression, "Stop worrying. What can they do? Kill you?"

CHAPTER 32

Outside Owen felt hollow and bought a hot dog and a can of orange soda from a vendor. He sat in a bus shelter to eat though his mind wasn't on food as he tried sorting out his jumbled thoughts. How much time do I have? An hour? Four? What do I do? His stomach twisted and he tossed the half eaten hotdog and unopened soda in the nearest trashcan his hunger crowded out by fear.

I've been accused of murder not officially but there's no doubt in my mind the machine is running full force with IAD and the Feds joining in ready to eat me alive. All that's left is the official arrest where I'm picked up by flak-jacketed heavily armed men and the only thing positive about that picture is that I'm armed too.

Leaving the shelter he stood at the curb considering what to do before it was too late. I need the person responsible for the crimes—Chandler—and proof he's up to his neck in our wives' blood if I'm going to extract myself out of this insane situation before I'm dead.

He turned back into the building and took the stairs. On the third floor he pulled on closed doors at random until one opened. Entering the vacant office he walked down its hallway where he found in its center the freight elevator. He pushed the button and heard the whine as it rose up to meet him. He took it down to the basement where he exited into a short hallway leading up to a loading dock where two men were stacking empty water jugs in back of a Distillata Bottling truck. He passed by them and walked out onto a side street next to the building. He didn't look back as he crossed into a parking lot. Weaving around cars until he was out on Mercy Street where he hailed a passing cab and got in giving the drivers Pop's address.

He didn't glance out the back window as the cob took off though he was sure he was still being trailed by the FBI; two guys sitting in a car waiting for him to again come out the building and because they had no imagination, it would take them a while to realize he was on foot and give chase but by then he would've seen Pop and told him it was worst than they had imagined but he was innocent of murdering his daughter, only after would he run.

He got out of the cab a block over from Pop's place. As he made his way over to the house he watched the street for signs of a trap and registered nothing. As he stepped onto the walkway the front door flew open, Pop, his face red and twisted yelled, "Run Owen. They're here."

He turned in an instant and was hit by a truck. He went down his face smacking into the cement walk, his bottom lip splitting and gushing blood as two large muscled arms wrapped around him pressing his body into the ground before his arms were wrenched behind his back. He grunted in agony even as he heard the jangle of handcuffs before he felt the cold steel snap around his wrists.

Pop clambered down the stairs, "Let him go you bastard."

Pulled to his feet Owens's teeth snapped into his tongue as more pain bolted across his shoulders as he was bent forward and a hand tugged out his Glock. Jerked upright he stared as patrol cars—it had to be ten of them—their sirens screaming ran up on the sidewalks, front lawns and in the middle of the street braking hard with cops jumping out at the ready.

The front door of one of the lead cars was thrown open and a grinning Gunderson got out, "You can step back, Brody."

The hold on Owen disappeared. He looked around at his truck a young cop wearing body armor who looked like a steroid induced monolith.

"You're under arrest for the murders of Lorna Story, Jocelyn Chandler and Bobby Tynon," Gunderson held two folded pieces of paper up. "A court order to search here for the gun," with a sharp twist of his wrist he flicked the paper into Owens's dazed face, "We've already searched your house." He tossed the second piece of paper at him, "The warrant to arrest your sorry ass."

Owen spat a wad of blood on the warrants and on Gunderson's shoes, "That was fast; blowing the judge Al? Pop?" he called as Gunderson glared from him to his stained shoes. "Call Manny and tell him I'm in trouble."

The old man hurried into the house.

His lips cornered with ferocious spittle, Gunderson's eyes blazed with triumphant, "You son of a bitch," he smacked a fist into Owens's chest forcing him back a step even as he strained against the cuffs. "Didn't I tell you I'd get you? I knew the minute you stepped into the squad room you were trash thinking you were better than everybody else when you're nothing but a goddamn killer."

Owen smiled the gesture causing his split lip to widen fleshy red and grotesque, "Does that mean we'll never be friends you fat lazy shithead."

Gunderson grabbed Owen around the throat and dug his nails into his flesh as he brought their faces close. His breath smelled of bad meat and temper, "You need to save your smart mouth for that bull queen whose little bitch you're going to be in prison."

"Take your hands off me now."

Wrapped up in each other as the patrol cops stared on no one paid attention to the unmarked that stopped hard behind the patrol cars. The driver's door opened and Harwood bolted out. Behind him pulled up a black Taurus a smiling Williams stepping out to watch.

Harwood rushed up to them just as Owens's head shot back then forward and crashed into Gunderson's face; blood jettisoned from his nose over them as he screamed. Enraged, he squeezed tighter even as Harwood wrestled his partner's fingers from around Owens's neck. Owen stumbled back coughing and gulping air.

"Al, stop this shit," Harwood looked into his partner's bloody face, his cool control strained, "You're setting a bad example for the new hire."

Brody stood with his mouth open along with the other cops in the street. They had been called to witness and reluctantly participate in the arrest of one-of-their-own only to watch it escalate to a cop-on-cop killing.

"Take these things off me," Owen rasped. "I don't need to be cuffed; I'll go willingly."

"No," Gunderson roared as he wiped blood off his face with a sleeve. "Don't trust him; he just busted my fucking nose."

"Come on," Hardwood coaxed, "he's still a cop."

"I won't touch you again, Al."

"You won't get the chance," Gunderson's voice was nasal as he pinched the bridge of his nose with two fingers. "We got your gun but try any more shit and I'll shoot you myself. All right," he glanced at Brody, "Tak'em off."

The cop removed the cuffs and backed away as the front door opened. Pop hurried down the stairs toward them and a few steps away from Gunderson he raised his right arm.

"Gun," Brody screamed as Pop crammed the muzzle into Gunderson's right ear and cocked the trigger. Everyone froze.

Owen was the first to find his voice, "Oh shit, Pop."

"Old man, what the hell do you think you're doing?" Harwood's control had finally disappeared.

"Any of you go for your guns and I'll blow this greasy bum to the back of beyond," Pop shouted his gun hand steady. "They can give me the chair if they want I'm not long for this world anyway."

"You don't have to do this," Owen said astounded by Pop's actions on his behalf.

"Yes I do or they'll put you in prison for something you didn't do, I know you didn't hurt Lorna. Go Owen, through the house and out the back. Go," he pressed the muzzle deeper into Gunderson's head causing the man to whimper.

"This is crazy," Owen managed feeling his heart beat on the verge of imploding in shocked disbelief even as he stepped back toward the house.

"No, it isn't; you felt more for me than my own daughter did and I'm just paying you back."

Owen backed up the stairs to the front door and stopped torn between Pop's safety and his unbelievable chance at escape.

"Put the fucking gun down," Gunderson croaked through lips bloodless with fear.

"Shut up," Pop raised his voice toward the cops in the street who stood on the balls of their feet hands on their guns, "Stay back or I'll give this asshole a new one. Run Owen."

"Don't take another step Story," Harwood yelled.

"Thanks, Pop," Owen said and ran.

CHAPTER 33

Owen sprinted out the back door and through the bushes that bisected their backyard from the next; flashes of Pop holding the gun keeping pace with him.

Sirens filled the air as he darted down the neighbors' driveway and across the street between two houses. He moved fast, sweat coating his skin as he crossed from yard to yard. A Doberman barking and chomping in frenzy jumped on him and almost knocked him down as he broke through a hedge; startled he crashed threw the fence between the properties getting away from the dog and tripped over a broken fence post. He righted himself only to dive back to the ground and crawl underneath a porch. Breathing hard, covered in cobwebs and dead leaves he watched a line of cruisers speed past him down the street.

He had to get out of the neighborhood before he was trapped inside where they'd get him. Crawling from underneath the porch he ran across a side street into a small wooded area backing the courtyard of a rundown apartment complex. Moving down the rocky weed choked pathway separating it from the building next door he stood back against the side of the other building and looked out letting out his breath as he recognized here he was, Brewster Avenue, a busy four lane street lined on both sides with apartment houses, beauty salons and variety stores.

He waited watching for patrol cars before brushing at the dirt on his face and clothes and walking toward the nearest walkway. No one looked at him as he joined the few pedestrians waiting for the 'to walk' signal and when it appeared he moved along with the rest.

He watched an MTA express bus, its sign flashing Midtown Manhattan slow at the next corner without stopping. A woman

173

with a grocery bag on each arm ran up to it just as it pulled off with a roar of exhaust; another was a less than half a block behind coming up fast. He ran toward the stop; he had to get on that bus and get out. "Tell it to wait," he yelled at the woman as the bus halted in front of her the doors opening. She stepped up inside and the doors began closing. He put on a burst of speed but caught only the bus's tail end as it pulled away. Banging on its side he almost collided with it as it stopped.

Hurrying inside before the front doors pneumatically closed, he searched both pockets and came up with a handful of change he tossed into the fare box. As the bus merged with traffic he headed down the aisle and chose a seat beside a black teenage girl wearing headphones and reading "A Midsummer Night's Dream". Het he closed his eyes almost sick with relief; he was headed back to Manhattan, a fugitive but safe, safe; for now thank God.

The driver swerved and braked to a hard stop at the curb. Owen's eyes flew open as a row of police cruisers, their emergency lights on frantic whir, their sirens blasting rushed by right beside them.

"Uh oh," the girl said, "somebody is about to get jacked."

CHAPTER 34

Owen stood in the back room of a bodega the phone's receiver at his ear; his head pounding with pained shot reaction as he waited for the line to be picked up. He turned as the door opened and Roque Kwan, the owner of the store stepped inside carrying a handful of aspirin and a bottle of water both Owen gratefully downed.

"There's a policeman outside," Roque said in accented English as Owen hung up.

"He ask you anything?"

Roque shook his head his eyes calm, "I've never seen him before. He asked Sherry for a ham-and-cheese; she's setting him up now."

Owen hurried over to a wall calendar dated nineteen sixty-five depicting Martin Luther King and Ghandi shaking hands and moved it

aside uncovering a peephole positioned to take in the entire store; it complimented the cameras stationed all around the property inside and out. Roque was from East Timor in Southeast Asia and had survived its tumultuous fight for independence due to equal parts vigilance and suspicion.

The cop was leaving and as Owen caught the back of his head he felt a tickle of recognition slide down his spine. He squinted as he watched the cop stand outside the store looking up and down the street before he crossed to the other side and was out of sight. Owen let the calendar drop back in place as his mind ticked over frightening possibilities: had the cop just happened to walk in hungry for a ham and cheese? Or had someone seen him come in and had called the police who were now surrounding the building for the rush in to take him down?

175

"Anything else happening out there, Roque? Anything changed in the last hour?"

"Nothing unusual, I've been checking the cameras since you arrived."

Owen nodded, picked up the phone's receiver and dialed again as Roque left. He listened through several rings before the line was picked up, "How's Pop? They'd better not have hurt him."

"He's okay," Cush said. "They roughed him up so Manny had them take him to St. Mary's; he won't let anybody near him again; he has a round-the-clock guard though. What about you?"

"I don't know. I'm in deep shit here, Cush."

"Listen, go to the apartment and stay out of sight, I'll meet you there after I go home to Connie; she's worried sick about you. You and I can come up with something and if we can't we'll find a way to get you out of the city."

"I'm not ready to try and escape like some-most-wanted; not until I have no other choice."

"Don't do anything crazy, Owen," Cush warned. "Go to the apartment you'll be safe there for a while; I'll show up—"

"No, don't get caught up in anymore of this; you got a family to think about."

"Nobody's gonna touch my family," Cush's voice was hard and sure. "You worry about yourself."

"I will. Leave me your extra gun."

"What're you gonna do?"

"Go to Chandler's—"

"Owen, didn't I just say don't do anything crazy? Why'd you wanna go and get yourself killed on sight?"

"He's up to his neck in this," Owens's hand tightened on the receiver. "And it's the only thing I can do that makes any sense to me; I'm just playing it by fear here, Cush."

"It's suicidal. Hold on a sec." The line went dead then Cush said, "I gotta go, I've been called down to the Plaza no doubt to be grilled over about you. I'll get away soon as I can."

"You're a good friend."

"And you're a pain in the ass."

"I know. Don't forget the gun," he hung up as Roque stepped back into the room. "You carry mini-tape recorders?"

CHAPTER 35

Pacing out of sight in the backroom until the sun set, Owen left and took the Number Five bus up Riverside Drive. He'd thought about taking a taxi but suspected the drivers had already been alerted and his picture posted around, he couldn't take the chance he'd meet the one-in-a-million cabby who looked at the circular and wanted to be citizen hero. Exiting the bus half a block from the Chandler's house in the Rosedale Community; a gated and exclusive enclave of expensive condominiums with designer gardens and armed security; he kept in the shadows as he approached the complex alert to patrol and undercover cars as he stopped beneath a thickly branched bare willow tree not far from the community's black-gated entrance.

Parked nose to nose in front of the gate were two police cars; the officers stood outside the cars talking to each other. With his eyes on them and as quiet as possible, Owen backed up before turning back the way he'd come.

The gate was cemented into a sand colored brick wall about seven feet tall that ran around the property. He moved down it until he came to a tree he thought sturdy enough to hold his weight and climbed. Swinging from it onto the wall he almost tumbled over to the ground, he only just managed to grab hold a limb and save him self before dropping carefully to the other side. He felt like a low rate sneak thief as he stood still until satisfied he hadn't been seen or heard.

Slipping across manicured lawns avoiding areas with security lighting he stared through open windows and un-curtained patio doors anxious to find the man. Stepping near a flagstone patio he heard the blare of a television set and glanced through glass doors opened to take in the winter breeze at the Commish, who sat

177

behind a desk watching television, a child's party hat cocked on his head.

As Owen watched he picked up a large tumbler of dark liquid and saluted the set, "Run fast as you can Mr. Policeman," he laughed.

Owen looked from him to the television where his own face took up most of the screen; dismayed though not surprised he just managed to click on the hidden recorder before moving across the patio into the room.

Chandler grinned seeming not at all taken back at his sudden appearance, "Glad you could make it," he said with jolly good humor. "Come to join the party." He tapped the colorful cone-shaped hat perched on his head, "Want one?" Underneath his desk his hand shied away from the alarm button planted in the wood and moved instead on to the of the desk where he picked up the remote control.

Owen stared at him; Chandler was drunk. He moved toward the desk before halting a few feet away as caution hit his brain. He didn't have a gun but Chandler might, underneath the desk and pointed right at him.

"I guess you don't need to hear all the terrible things being said about you," Chandler clicked the remote and the television blackened. "You're the top story on all networks and not just the major ones," he took off the hat and smoothed his silvery hair. "I'm jealous."

"I don't care what they're saying, it's all lies."

"I can assume then you didn't come here to celebrate the fact my wife, the Wicked Witch of Manhattan is dead."

Chandler stood and came around the desk to stand tall and stalwart in the center of the room as if he was readying to give a speech and every eye in the place was on him. He tries to take up all the oxygen in the room Owen thought, even when drunk out of his mind and face to face with a so called killer.

"Did you know that brainless Blume asked if I wanted to see her? Her lifeless, torn, bullet-riddled blood splattered body lying right there in that dirty, piss filled alley?" His brows rose in calm inquiry as if he'd been asked to view new patrol uniforms. "I had to push the idiot away to keep from howling in his face because I knew if I'd gone out there and taken a nice long look at her I would've not only kept laughing I would've..." Chandler spun around and Owen's mouth dropped open as the man did an old soft shoe routine, "started dancing. This would've caused people to look at me funny don't you think?" He threw back his head and roared with such delightful glee Owen felt horror rush threw him like cold sickness. "Though," Chandler sobered, "it was too bad your wife was involved. Too bad she got to know the late Mrs. Chandler a little too well."

"Lorna didn't know you wife."

"Not true or you wouldn't be here. They knew each other," he winked. "In more ways than one."

"I don't believe you."

Chandler strolled over to the fireplace mantle and took off a gold framed photo of his wife who was smiling benignly at the camera. His grey eyes formed ice flows as he held the picture toward Owen, "Let me enlighten you about wifey here; she was a first-class-bitch in heat. She would boast about her conquests from the petty affairs lasting an afternoon to the ones that went on for months. To look at her you'd think butter wouldn't melt in her mouth when God only knows the kinds of things she let into that hole."

"None of it has to do with my wife."

Chandler smacked the picture down on the mantelpiece hard enough to cause its glass front to shatter, "I told you she loved to brag about her relationships. She told me they had the same world view—whatever that meant—they enjoyed the same things and each other; literally."

"No," Owen blurted shocked he could still be shocked by any revelation regarding Lorna. He flashed to the only words Mrs. Chandler had ever spoken to him 'she is sweet'. What her words may have implied made his stomach roil, "You're lying."

At his desk Chandler opened a drawer and pulled out a hand full of photographs, "Pictures," he cackled, "I have pictures. Of them." He tossed the photos face down onto the desk blotter, "Want to see?"

"You sick bastard," Owen said unable to move.

"No, a cautious one," Chandler tapped a picture his face as rigid as flat stone. "These were my insurance policies. Don't blame me Detective she made me do this because she was doing it to me. My wife was a jealous manipulative woman who wanted it all for herself; you don't have to take my word for it ask anybody who crossed her path and lived to tell about it. We were holding each other by the balls and I'm glad she got hers chopped off first."

Reaching inside a drawer he produced a half empty bottle of Black Label whiskey and refilled his glass before taking a healthy swallow, "It was an absolute nightmare living with that woman," his words were layered with disappointment. "When we first got married I believed we were the same kind of people, allies in all things, in every endeavor. I thought we knew each other better than we knew anyone else. She was smart and ambitious and I saw us working together to become a major power house in this city then the state, then the country; to get real things done."

His eyes darkened to the color of storm clouds, "But somewhere down the line she fooled me, detective. I don't know when it happened but one day I realized she wasn't who she pretended to be; that she didn't want what I wanted but wanted everything I had and would've done her worst to get it. Here I was, on the cusp of becoming the mayor of the greatest city in the world and that bitch was trying to ruin me."

"Did you kill her?" Owen asked barely able to breathe, the air in there was stifling, poisonous, he had to get out soon.

"No," Chandler's face sagged with regret, "Though I wish I'd had the guts to do it."

"I didn't kill them."

Chandler gave him a narrowed eyed stare as if he were a new species of bug he'd never seen. He lowered his voice as he leaned against the side of his desk, "I'll let you in on a little secret," he glanced left and right as if to make sure they were alone. "If you haven't figured this out already; I don't care who killed her; dead is a good look for her. My problem was that the constituents demanded someone pay for it and I needed to give them what they wanted so in return they'd give me what I wanted. So I took a look around and lo and behold..." he held his arms out toward Owen, "there you were, so conveniently dropped in my lap like a goddamn Christmas present. I could've asked for a better lamb to the slaughter."

"Convenient? You fucked up my life because it was convenient?"

"And it was easier to do than you could imagine. Someone had to be fingered for the murders to make the citizens feel safe and in the bargain I got rid of a wife I despised." Chandler grinned, "A win-win for me all around."

Owens's fury pushed him nose-to nose with the man. "You'll never get control of this city once people know what you are—"

"What if they find out instead how your wife and mine were lovers," Chandler cut him off. "Turn over the pictures and see for yourself. No? Because you're afraid right detective? Too bad. You want to know another thing? They were blackmailing me into almost giving them the run of the police department, using me." Ferocious menace snapped Chandler's eyes to slits, "And nobody uses me and gets away with it."

"And I wasn't the only cop my wife was fucking over some of her other bed partners were cops, young ones; oh yes, she loved a big gun. So who do you think people are going to believe? The police commissioner wronged by an immoral unfaithful wife? Or you a triple murderer?"

"I didn't kill anyone."

Chandler rolled his eyes, "Have I at anytime given you the impression I give a shit? You've heard it all detective, now get out of my house." He made a dismissive wave at him then held up a finger, "Wait, one last thing

I need to tell you; I would've loved a slow taste of your beautiful Lorna." He licked his lips, "Yum, yum."

Owen's fist connected with the man's face and Chandler staggered back, an "oomph" shooting out his mouth as he tumbled into his chair and almost out of it onto the floor. Grabbing the edge of his desk he pulled himself to his feet. Wiping at the blood on his lips he looked at it then at Owen, "I've just tapped the emergency button; my security team is now right outside the door." He licked the blood off his fingers, his gaze merciless, "I should've called them the minute I stopped enjoying your company."

Owen turned as the library doors flew open and ran out on to the patio seconds ahead of the bullet that shattered the glass pane. Bent low in anticipation of another round he looked up in time to see Blume running toward him; tucking low like a defensive end he threw a shoulder into Blume's middle slamming them both to the ground. He was up first, rolling away as another bullet struck the flagstone inches from him sending sparks and knife sharp pieces of stone into his face. Fleeing across the yard he disappeared into the darkness expecting at each step to feel a hot bullet sheer through his terrified flesh.

CHAPTER 36

He just managed to escape the rush of police cars and helicopters that surrounded Chandler's house. He scaled the wall fast as he could not daring to breathe or look back until he found himself at a construction site of new condominiums. Slowing to a jog Owen made his way through the skeletal partially built structures until he came out on to an unpaved road. He walked unmolested along the wooded side of the road disappearing in the bushes whenever a lone car passed by.

Finally coming to a bus stop he took the first one that came along and was deposited at the end of the line near Central Park where he vanished inside to huddle on a bench beneath a tree, out of sight of patrols until exhausted, hungry and bone cold he left unsure of what to do or where to go next. Cursing himself for forgetting to carry his cell phone he searched for a pay one which was almost obsolete in the city and spotted what looked like a working one beside a CVS Drug Store. He moved toward it only to melt back in the shadow of a closed coffee shop as a white van with the words: New York Post written on its side halted at the curb. The driver stuck out his head out and tossed a bundled set of newspapers to the sidewalk before driving off.

Owen grabbed up a paper before he dug for leftover change in his pocket to make the call. His hand froze, "Goddammit." The tape recorder was gone. He must've lost it either during the altercation with Blume or when he ran. Chandler probably had it by now and was laughing with dirty amusement under his party hat.

Huddling around the phone his back against the wintry cold and any possible recognition from late night strollers he dialed then scanned the front as he waited, the headline read: One of

183

New York's Finest Wanted For Triple Murder. "It's me," he said as his party came on the line. "I knew you'd be there."

"Jezzus about time," Giordano turned away from staring out at the city. "I was worried. You're everywhere."

"I know," Owen tossed the paper in the trashcan.

"Are you safe?"

"No, I'm—"

"Don't tell me," Giordano cut in. "In case they try and beat it out of me. I have some good news; I have the witness."

Owen whooped, "Thank you, God."

"You're welcome," Giordano laughed.

"Where is he?"

"He's over at the Connors on 49th. Room 402. I told them if they let anybody in other than you or me they'll be wearing cement overcoats by morning."

"Thanks Giordano. I owe you."

"Don't; because you know someday I might have to collect. Take care Owen I mean it."

Giordano hung up and looked at the Sprinter who stood by the office door, "Call Lou and tell him our friend is on his way." He waited until the man left before he turned back to the view. His friend was out there and he prayed he would make it because if he didn't there would be hell to pay.

CHAPTER 37

Though the night was frigid Owen took a sweaty bus ride to Times Square his eyes never leaving the window. He was all beat up nerves seeing bogeymen on every corner—just like Riviera had said—carrying handcuffs and sharp needles. He was surprised he wasn't worse, pulling at his hair and balling like a baby at how trapped and on the suicidal edge e he felt. The guy in room 405 was his last chance to prove his innocence and the fact his life hung on a stranger's willingness to tell the truth, sent his heart into such convulsive fits it made the walk to the hotel feel like the one down death row.

Stepping inside the lighted doorway of a Radio Shack he took from his breast pocket the picture he'd managed to grab from Chandler's desk before fleeing the room. He took a long look only to sag back against the door in relief as he stared at Lorna, alone, sitting at an outdoor cafe.

She was dressed in a blue fall sweater, long black skirt and black boots. Sunglasses covered her eyes though a pensive mournfulness had settled around her mouth. Who had taken the picture he wondered. One of Chandler's spies or Jocelyn's? Had she been meeting someone? Who? Had she been thinking at that moment about the child? Questions, endless questions that would forever run through his soul never to be answered.

The Connors sat on the corner of West 49th between Broadway and Fifth. It was a not-yet-seedy-hotel managing to retain a semblance of its grander days. The two columns decorating its front gleamed clean and white from the streetlamps and as he walked up the stairs he noticed the wine red carpet leading into the hotel was threadbare but of good quality.

A man stood behind the registration desk, Owen nodded to him before taking the stairs to the fourth floor. He knocked at door number 405; it opened a fraction of an inch to reveal a sliver of a face staring back.

"You look like your mug shot on TV," a gravel tossed voice spoke out of the partial mouth.

It was opened a few inches more and Owen slipped inside before it closed after him. He stood in a sitting room featuring a couch covered in green plaid, two green plaid armchairs, a coffee table and a big screen television playing football on ESPN; two closed doors led off his left. He looked at the man who'd let him in. The sliver-of-face was just about the guy's entire face; blue eyes were bisected by a ski jump of a nose that hung over ruler thin lips.

"It's not a mug shot but my police ID photo," Owen said.

Sliver Face looked him over. A smirk formed on those non-existent lips as he leaned against the wall beside the door, "I still think the cops look more like the criminals these days don't they Jerry?"

Jerry, a compact man with blunt features didn't answer. He sat on the couch looking from the game on the screen to a thin black man who paced and smoked in front of the open window, "That's him," Jerry said.

The man glanced at Owen before blowing smoke into the air. He was in his mid-thirties, angular, with black pompadour hair and a caramel colored complexion highlighting a perfect nose and mouth below dark, soulful eyes. He wore a light blue silk shirt and pencil slim black pants. He reminded Owen of those fifties album covers his mother used to collect featuring the young and smoothly handsome Johnny Mathis.

Without being invited Owen sat in one of the armchairs he angled toward the witness, his possible savior who was staring out the window. "You want to sit?" he asked. "What's your name?"

The man walked over to the coffee table and stabbed out the cigarette in an ashtray overflowing with dead butts as he looked at Owen, "What's my name got to do with this?" his voice the deep and damaged one of the perfect balladeer.

"Everybody's got a name and it's more polite than saying, 'Hey you,' "

The man took a Kool King from the pack on the table and lighted it with the flicker of a match pulling the smoke deep into his lungs he released on a sigh. He's scared, all beat up like I am Owen realized as he watched the man's lips shake around the cigarette.

"Bell. Carlton Bell. My mother named me after her hometown, Carlton, Mississippi; some tiny desperate place from what she told me. She got here a month after turning nineteen and met my old man almost the minute she got off the bus." Carlton's eyes squinted through the smoke at Owen, "And no he wasn't a pimp and she wasn't a whore. He sold life insurance."

"You saw what happened outside the International?"

"Shit yeah," Carlton said seeming not offended by Owen getting to the point of his visit, "But I don't think I saw it all."

Jerry stood and stretched his muscles popping loud enough to make them glance at him. Crossing in front of Owen over to a small refrigerator in the corner he opened up the door and stared sullenly in at its contents.

"What do you mean you didn't see everything?"

"Man, I was trying to get away from the place; there were cops everywhere. I thought I had been tossed into a cop convention for my sins."

"What were you in the joint for?" Owen wanted what he felt about Mr. Bell confirmed.

The damaged look in Carlton's eyes was enough to bring tears to any teeny bopper, "Petty shit I regret being a party to; burglary and a few other minor offenses, it was a long time ago and I paid for it"

"What were you doing near the hotel?"

"Minding my own business," Carlton puffed harder, the smoke thick until it almost concealed him. "I was going to meet my girl when I stepped into the alley to take a leak and saw these people laid out there and this guy standing over them. Man," his voice cracked. "When I saw them I got out of there quick."

"Where you on anything, drugs, drinking?"

"I don't remember, I mighta had a joint," Carlton's eyes narrowed, offended, "a small one—earlier—but that scene straightened me right out."

"You recognize the guy still standing?"

187

The man's smooth features twisted in sudden, angry confusion, "Recognize him? Man, how was I supposed to recognize him?"

"Had you seen him before by any chancel?"

Carlton bent over the table and stabbed out the cigarette, "Listen, how was I supposed to know him?" He straightened and looked at Owen, "I just told you there were cops everywhere and they all look alike to me."

A click sounded in Owens's head so loud he expected everyone in the room to have heard it as the pieces slammed together. He leaned eagerly toward the man, "Can you describe him?"

Carlton opened his mouth as an explosion ripped through the room taking Carlton's throat with it. Owen dove to the floor between the couch and the coffee table his hands over his head as blood and bullets flew through the air pulverizing everything.

Screams and the earsplitting sounds of deadly destruction were deafening, the cacophony of the world coming to an end. Owen tightened his hands over his head as the television exploded and caught fire, the smoke released the smoke detector's shriek as the sprinkler system unleashed rain, the bullets tearing through the drops and flesh. The window was shot out to a ragged frame; the walls cracked with holes sent plaster dust into the wet air, the furniture was hammered to bullet riddled pieces. Carlton's torn body crashed into the table that collapsed from his weight his corpse tumbling on top of Owen as the barraged stopped.

"Oh God, oh God," Owen moaned his senses overwhelmed by the smell of cordite and blood as he stared at Carlton. The bullets had ripped across his neck leaving strips of flesh the only thing keeping his head from falling off. Owen closed his eyes and careful of the destruction done to him, gently laid him to the floor.

Getting unsteadily to his feet, he stared at the rest of the carnage. Sliver Face had been shot through the wall, dark holes stitched his belly and back as he slumped on the floor. Jerry had been struck repeatedly as he stood opening a can of soda; his body hung blood soaked over the open refrigerator.

Owen backed toward the door with a last look at Carlton, his last hope gone and pulled it open; it fell apart in his hands as he began yelling, "Call 9-1-1-1." Running down the stairs and through the lobby where a group of terrified looking people wearing their nightclothes stood huddled around the front deskman who was on the phone, he bolted out on the street looking left and right and saw only a couple walking toward him led by a French poodle on a leash. Shit, he pounded his legs with his fists, the shooter had disappeared. How could the bastard have gotten away so fast?

The couple and the dog passed by giving him a wide berth the woman clutching at her companion's arm. Owen barred his teeth at them before rounding the corner on the other side of the hotel only to stop and back track down a dimly lit set of stairs to the doorway of a darkened basement apartment.

A police cruiser moved slowly toward him its emergency lights flashed though the siren was silent. He watched it pass by waiting a minute, then two, before he left the stairway to hurry in the opposite direction of the prowl car.

CHAPTER 38

Stepping into the darkened house Owen closed the door and fell back against it sliding to the floor. Three people killed in front of him and he'd barely survived; almost losing his life as he lost his last chance at salvation. Getting to his feet he moved to the phone dreading making the call. A hand came out of the darkness and gripped his arm; he swung around fist cocked ready to fight for what remained of his life with the little energy and self-preservation he had left.

"Whoa," a familiar voice halted his attack, "you're gonna punch my eye out?"

"You scared the crap out of me," Owen said flipping on the cheap lamp.

Cush glared at him, "Who else were you expecting?" he held out a .38 caliber revolver. "It's loaded up."

"Thanks," Owen pocketed it. "You sure you weren't followed?"

"If I was they're in Hoboken by now." Cush stared at Owen, his clothes, the cuts on his face, his dead eyes, "There's blood all over you—"

"It went bad," Owen picked up the phone with a hand that shook and dialed as the carnage imprinted on his eye lids revealed it self again, the bullets, the blood, the bodies. "All of them are dead," he said as Giordano picked up.

"Tell me."

"One minute I'm asking the witness," he closed his eyes. "Carlton; his name was Carlton; some questions and the next bullets are flying and I'm down and your men are cut to pieces—"

"Owen, take it easy," Giordano said. "Go slow."

"He didn't want Carlton to talk to me and killed him. The police might—"

"Don't worry about the police, I'll send some people over and if something can be done they'll do it and if they can't because the cops are there then there's still nothing to worry about. Those guys weren't local and have no records far as I know. Owen, there will be no connection to trace back to you or me okay. You just be careful and lay low. I'll be in touch."

Owen hung up and looked at his partner, "The shots took out everybody; everything." His voice was dazed, "Except for me," he smiled something terrible. "Like I don't deserve a bullet right? I got out of there yelling for the police like some idiot; reflex, I guess."

"Sit down before you fall down," Cush took hold Owens's arm and sat him on the couch they had salvaged from a street dump.

"Ironically enough," Owen crouched on the edge of the cushion as if his body was made of glass ready to shatter. "A radio car was coming around the corner while I was looking for the shooter. I didn't stay to see if he was headed for the hotel..." his words drained off as Carlton's words hit home. Carlton had said he'd seen nothing other than cops that night; had a cop witnessed the murders? Someone from the ball who hadn't spoken up? Had one of those cops been the killer? They were accusing him of the crime so why couldn't it have been another cop?

"Carlton said he saw a cop in the alley that night."

"So what?" shrugged Cush who sat across from him in a discount store picnic chair. "There were a hundred cops crawling over the place after the discovery, he—"

Owen shook his head, "He saw a cop_standing over the bodies before they were found."

Cush thought it over, "So one of us got there first; got scared and took off afraid to step up," he shrugged again. "It happens."

Owen rubbed feverishly at a spot on the back of his neck, "No that's not what he meant. He saw a cop, the one who killed Lorna and the others."

Cush stared at him, "That's loaded as hell, Owen. You're accusing one of us of—"

"I know, I know," Owen stood and moved to the tiny window that looked out on the street. "I've hit a wall looking for the guy which makes since against the fact everyone believes the guy is me." He turned toward Cush, his hands held out in a gesture of appeal. "There's no where to go from here, Cush, I'm trapped." His face was waxy pale his eyes bleak and accepting, "I'm not going to jail; not for something I didn't do and if I have to play it out in the streets with them I will. I won't let them take me down easy, take me alive and if I have to eat the 38 to keep it from happening I will."

"Hey," Cush got to his feet and pointed a finger at Owen's pale face. "Stop that shit right now. This ain't the O.K. Corral and it this ain't over yet. Let me meditate on it while you don't say another damn stupid thing, not one and just let me think." He closed his eyes for a lifetime of seconds then, "What ho," his eyes opened. "You ever meet David Murphy?"

"Who? What does—"

"Bobby Tynon's partner," Cush said impatient.

Owen remembered, "Once, at Lorna's funeral." The young dead cop. He'd been so caught up in his own earth-shattering-life-altering-Lorna-centered-universe he hadn't thought about Tynon, the third victim, "Tynon hasn't been my main focus."

"You've gotta talk to Murphy then because Tynon is the only angle you've got left. He could be the central figure here, not Lorna or Jocelyn. He coulda had a beef with the killer who came after him and they got in the way. And who would know more about what was going on with Tynon than his own partner? You saw for yourself how torn up Murphy was over his death. I talked to the kid; he seemed a good guy through all the tears and Owen you have nothing else to lose."

Owen let Cush's word sink in, "Of course I wouldn't of focused on Tynon; I was told he was a good cop; you don't question that so I never imagined him being the key to all this."

"Your imagination leaves a lot to be desired," Cush grinned.

Owen laughed, excited now, "Dammit, I overlooked him. What if he had been the target and we've been looking at this thing the wrong way from the beginning. I need to talk to Murphy, right now."

"We can't, he's on first shift so he won't be home for a couple of hours. We'll wait then pay him a visit. It'll give you the chance to clean-up and get some sleep—if you can. I'll get us some food. I told Connie don't wait up and if anyone comes looking for me to tell'em I'm visiting my mother."

Owen grinned, it felt new, "This is it, Cush." Hope bloomed in his chest, "This really could be it."

CHAPTER 39

The next morning Owen lay down in the backseat to avoid the slightest chance of being seen as Cush drove to a modest apartment house off Bowery Street near Chinatown. There was a chill in the air, only a mention of the sun which made it difficult to tell what the day would bring. They stood at the end of a walkway that led around back of the building speaking low and brief so as not to cause attention to themselves.

"He's in number 1099," Cush said quietly. "I'll meet you up there after I park. You're going to have to find your way in."

Owen waited until Cush had disappeared before he walked around to the back of the building keeping away from the small back yard area set with patio furniture in case someone glanced out a window, wondered why he was skulking around back there and called the police. He tested the metal back door and found it locked.

He tried the ground level windows and at the last one found it cracked open half an inch. He thought about putting his legs through and just dropping inside into the unknown but didn't want to take the chance he'd tumble into the place one of the tenants kept his urban-raised pet tiger. Managing to push the window up enough to get his head and upper body underneath he looked inside and found he was he was in a tiny storage room filled with old suitcases, boxes and old furniture. Sliding the rest of his body through he landed on a stack of boxes that rang with tiny explosions at his weight. Righting himself he opened one of them and found he'd crushed a batch of crystal Christmas tree ornaments.

Opening the door he peered into a long empty corridor. Stepping out he walked pass a row of closed doors and an empty laundry room up a set of metal stairs to a door at the top. He glanced out a window cut in the door onto an empty lobby before starting up the next set of stairs. Murphy lived in apartment 1022, nine more flights to go.

On the tenth floor winded and hot Owen stepped out into the hall and was glancing at the numbers on the apartment doors when a man exited the last apartment on the right keys in hand. Owen recognized him immediately from the funeral. Murphy was thinner than he remembered with basic brown hair and eyes, the rest of his features unremarkable against pale skin marred by a light coat of red acne. Just a young boy Owen realized. one of the hundreds he'd seen over the years eager to become cops .

"Murphy," he said walking toward him.

The cop looked around, his features flattening with sudden panic before a small tight smile of recognition settled onto his face giving its ordinary countenance a specialness, "My God Detective Story how are you? I'm surprised to see you, I mean with what's happening and all ..." he trailed off blushing. "I was going to get something to eat; I work the first shift and when I get off I'm starving."

"I promise not to take up much of your time," Owen glanced over his shoulder then. "You mind if we talk inside? It's a little too open for me out here."

"Oh," Murphy reddened even more, "sure, I'm sorry," he keyed open the door allowing Owen in first.

Owen looked around at the simply furnished apartment as Murphy led him over to a small kitchenette. On top of the table sat a Glock pistol, a fresh magazine and gun cleaning tools. Murphy picked up the gun and a piece of oilcloth and resumed cleaning the weapon.

He flashed a shy smile his eyes downcast, "If you don't mind I'll just finish up. You know what they say—"

"A clean gun makes a clean way of life," they said together then laughed until Owen sobered and hit it home, "You know what I'm up against don't you?"

Murphy nodded and slid the cloth over the gun barrel, "I know all about you. And I meant what I said at the funeral; I was really sorry about your wife."

"I appreciate it. Let's talk about Bobby. I know you two were close, good friends as well as partners; sometimes you don't get that lucky but when you do it's half the battle in our line of work."

Murphy nodded but remained silent his eyes on his task. Owen glanced from him to the gun as it seeped through that not once since they'd sat down had Murphy looked him in the eyes. Was the kid that shy? Maybe, with all that blushing he did or did he have information not too easy to talk about?

"Because you two were close I thought you might be able to tell me something about him no one else knows; something that might explain why Tynon was in that alley in the first place. Why someone may have wanted to kill him."

"Why?" Murphy fingered the magazine. Owen watched him pick it up and slide it home in the gun's butt with a satisfying snap. He then mumbled something so low Owen frowned and had to lean forward, "Excuse me?" Murphy looked up at him then his eyes terrifying as he simply said, "Because the fucker wouldn't share." Owen reared back not just because of the fury filled curse or the insane look roiling in his eyes but because Murphy pointed the loaded gun at him. He stood knocking his chair over, "Get up and raise your hands. Do anything I don't like and I'll shoot you through the face."

Owen rose slowly taking the time to get over the tilt-a-world feeling of disbelief at what was happening to him. His luck had obviously soured again.

"The son-of-a-bitch just wouldn't do it and even then I didn't hate him for it; I even kinda understood; but you would think as my partner—my so called fucking friend," his voice rose on a spike of outrage, "he would let me of all people in on his good thing."

"Come on David, "Owen managed through a lump of fear as large as the moon. Where the hell was Cush? "Please put down the gun David and tell me what this is about."

"You don't know?" Murphy stepped back from the table, his eyes pits of rage, his face sweat coated and as red as an open wound. "Much of it I can't figure out either because it was fast, so damn fast I don't think God could've stopped it. It was just like that guy said: there were fucking cops everywhere."

"Jezzus, you killed them," Owen said knowing he wouldn't be less stunned if Murphy suddenly pulled the trigger. "At the hotel."

"Which hotel?"

Owen read the confusion in his eyes, "Both. You were following me too; kept trying to kill me."

"No, not—" Murphy shook his head a look of bewilderment sliding across his face. "No," he said again before abruptly nodding. "You're right; but you have it all wrong; I wasn't even sure I could get him but I had to do something about your witness; what else could I do?" this came out a boyish whine. "When I heard there was somebody who might've seen me I panicked, I couldn't help it. I knew you were on the trail to find me so I turned it around and followed you instead. The first time though it wasn't my fault you have to believe me."

"All right, but you have to put down the gun," Owen said though he believed in only one thing at that instant; this young clean-cut cop had murdered six people and was readying to kill him. Where was Cush? Parking in the Bronx? He was on his own and needed to do something now or the last thing he'd see in this world would be a bullet coming at him out of a spotless gun barrel.

He carefully shifted his weight from one foot to the other Murphy caught the movement and raised the gun, "Do it again and I'll shoot; it's your last warning. You know what I was doing the night of the ball? I was on duty while Bobby got to go and you know why?" He jerked the gun at Owen's nose, "Ask me why?"

"Why did Bobby get to go to the ball and you didn't?" he was willing to ask this insane-stoked Cinderella anything to buy time.

"Because he was fucking the Commish's wife," Murphy laughed the sound jagged. "Can you believe that shit? He was screwing Chandler's wife and she rewarded him by getting him the best details and the most lucrative assignments and if he got reprimanded she'd get it written off just like that. Once he was going to get suspended for busting up some innocent citizen and she took care of it; she even got him a key to the evidence room at the stationhouse."

Through her sick and terrible hold over Chandler Owen realized, "And nobody knew?" he asked playing it for Murphy's benefit, his heart racing. He wanted Murphy to let down his guard so he could try and go for the gun in his pocket before he got a bullet through the face. He lowered his hands a fraction.

197

"He never told anyone except me. He took money and jewels not a lot at a time just enough to keep his pockets full. He was smart enough not to get anybody suspicious and he could be generous when he wanted, even so I kept thinking, why him? Why should he have it all? Why shouldn't I get a bigger share? I had never told another soul what was going on so I deserved more."

"What happened that night?" Owen asked trying to keep Murphy talking.

"It wasn't like I hated him or anything, he was my partner okay? I asked him to meet me so we could straighten it out. That was all I wanted..." Murphy's eyes shaded over as his sight turned inward though Owen saw that his gun hand remained steady, the barrel looking as wide as the Holland Tunnel.

But as Murphy began to speak Owen found himself drawn into each scene as if he'd been there a dark and indistinct shadow unable to do anything except witness.

"...I walk into the alley and there's Bobby. He has this woman humped up against the wall; his mouth is all over her, his hands up her dress," Murphy's eyes flared, "I wanted to kill him then. I'd told him to meet me alone but there he is practically screwing in front of me. I'm almost on them when a door off the hotel flies open and the Commish's wife bursts out. She jumps on Bobby cursing and hitting him until he pushes her off."

Owen swallowed, "Who was the other woman?" he asked though he already knew. He closed his eyes shutting out the image of her—them.

"Her," Murphy giggled the sound so sly and dark it caused Owen to stare at him for once instead of the gun. "Your wife, detective. I was surprised to see a classy looking woman like her letting Bobby practically fuck her in a rat infested alley."

"My, God," in his anguish Owen's arms had dropped to his sides; neither one of them noticed.

"Don't get too upset," Murphy soothed; the sly grin still in place madness around its edges. "She puts in some effort trying to get away from him as he says over and over how much he loves her. She tells him to let her go because they were finished and it was his fault he couldn't accept it. I thought it was pretty brave of her because Bobby wasn't good at listening, he heard and did what he wanted."

"The Commish's wife is listening and turns on yours. She say's something terrible—I couldn't hear it over Bobby's yelling and the music coming from the ballroom—but whatever it was it didn't seem to upset your wife too much she smiled and made these kissing motions at her."

"And that's when I move up next to Bobby and he tells me it's a bad time and to go the fuck away just like that." Desperate hurt rang through Murphy's words and even though he didn't want it Owen felt a stab of sympathy for the man. "As if he was talking to an idiot, a nobody. Go away you fuck up he tells me."

"Why didn't you, David? Just leave before it was too late?"

"Hey?" Murphy's touched the gun barrel to Owen's nose causing his hands to shoot up reflexively. "Haven't you been listening? It was my show; I was the one in control. We weren't on patrol so Bobby wasn't going to order me around anymore. He and Ms. Chandler are still yelling at each other while your wife stands there laughing like crazy and the music is getting louder and louder and all of it's driving me nuts. I scream shut up, just shut up for chrissakes. They ignore me; ignore me; so I pull the gun."

"You shot them in cold blood."

Murphy slapped a hand hard to his greased forehead leaving a vicious white print in the red of his sweaty face, "No, it was just to scare them. I tell Bobby to give me the key to the evidence room and he tells me to go fuck myself; just said it to me like I was nothing," his face twisted, " and I'm the one holding the gun."

"Mrs. Chandler says: 'Give him the key Bobby you won't need it anymore.' She starts screaming and hitting at him again. He raises a fist to hit her back and that's when I step between them and even now I don't know why I did it." Tears mixed with the fear and pain on his face until he looked like an unhinged toddler, "I forget about the gun until Bobby grabs it. I still can't figure out if he was trying to use it or take it away from me. We struggle—the trigger and the gun fires—"

"No," Owen saw it in his mind's eye. The muzzle flash. The bullet hitting flesh, "Lorna."

"So you see it wasn't my fault. If Bobby hadn't grabbed the gun...but he did," Murphy's tears flowed faster as if from a bottomless well of sadness and regret. "And the bullet hit her.

We all screamed then. It became a line of blurs. I think I let go of the gun into Bobby's hand; Mrs. Chandler is beyond hysterical and flings herself on him and like an endless nightmare the gun fires again and she drops. Dead."

"Still holding the gun Bobby falls to his knees and crawls moaning over to your wife. I'm frozen, can't move, even when he puts the gun to his own head and fires. There I am: blood all over me surrounded by three dead bodies and all—" Murphy raised the gun half an inch, "shot by this gun."

Owen stiffened as Murphy blinked his eyes focusing again and what Owen saw in them, a despair so huge it scared him enough to try for his own weapon and take his chances because Murphy had come to the end of his rope which meant the end for him.

"All I could think to do was pick up the gun and leave the scene. I came home, changed clothes and went on patrol and when the call came in I showed up like everybody else."

"You were the one crying on the curb."

"I was still pretty upset, not thinking straight. I only got it together after I heard later it was you they were after instead of me. I hadn't thought they'd go after another cop; I'm sorry."

"It's all right," Owen tried to sound reassuring instead of scared out of his mind. "Everything's going to be fine. You've told me what happened so now we can tell—"

"Stop the bullshit," a small bitter smile crossed Murphy's lips, "it's not fine and it's not all right. I knew it was going to come to this, knew you'd figure it out and come for me." He stepped around the table even as Owen stepped back, jamming the muzzle into his chest, "Then I would have to kill you."

Owen did the only thing he could, he grabbed the gun's barrel and forced it into the air as Murphy pulled the trigger. The shot exploded through the ceiling as Murphy snatched the gun back Owen feeling the solid oiled barrel slip through his fingers as the apartment door flew open and Cush rushed inside, "Put it down, Murphy," his gun pointed at him.

Murphy fired driving them to the floor as he ran past them out of the apartment.

Rolling to their feet Cush shouted, "You hit? You hit?"

"No, you?" as Cush shook his head, "Then where the hell were you?" Owen retrieved the gun from his pocket. "Parking in

Jersey?" He didn't wait for an answer but followed Murphy yelling over his shoulder, "Get back up."

He heard a solid bang to his left and ran to the still swinging exit door at the end of the hall. He paused before pushing it open to peer inside and caught a glimpse of feet going up a concrete stairway. "Stop Murphy," he shouted then ducked back as a bullet punched through the wood. Hearing the bang of a heavy door being thrown open, Owen waited before he tossed himself into the stairwell landing up against a wall. He came up on bended knee his gun pointed up the stairs at an open door framing harsh blue sky. Lowering his weapon he breathed.

God knows he didn't want to hurt Murphy, a tormented kid caught up in a disastrous mix of envy, theft and adultery which had led to the accidental and suicidal death of three then metastasized from there to attempted murder and finally the actual murder of three others. It was beyond tragic.

"David listen to me, we can work something out," he called up. He waited. No response. "Answer me. Let me help you." Nothing. "Dammit."

He turned as Cush bending low entered and moved up next to him his gun still out, "Everybody in the whole world's on their way; all I had to do was mention your name."

"Good, I'll be glad to see them too. He's on the roof and I'm going out there to him."

"He'll shoot before you step out on the tarmac."

"If I don't get him off they'll try and take him by force and I can't let that happen. You have to keep them back until I can get him down."

"What you're doing is nuts."

"Thanks. See you, Cush."

With his back against the wall Owen mounted the stairs. On the last one he peeked around the right corner of the door's frame but saw no sign of Murphy. With his heart jerking a screeching rhythm that mixed with the wails of oncoming sirens, he stepped out into the open. Walking slowly around the corner to his left he stopped; Murphy stood before him, his face pointed toward the sky as if he were studying it for snow; the barrel of the gun pressed to his right temple.

"Don't do it," Owen lowered his weapon. "David, it was not your fault."

Murphy's eyes dropped from his contemplation of the cold, unfeeling blue and stared at him as he laughed and cried the sound of mourning. "Then whose fault is it? And why do I feel so damn bad? I can't blame any of it on jealousy or fear; it was mostly me, mostly me."

"No, don't think that way we can work it out. Hey," he tried a tentative smile as he held out a hand. "I'm not even mad you tried to kill me. So please David drop the gun and come here to me."

"Because you'll make it better?"

"Yes, I'll do whatever it takes to make it right," Owen moved toward him. He had no idea how he was going to stop Murphy from putting that bullet in his brain but he'd be damned if he wasn't going to move heaven and earth to try, "Let me try, please."

Murphy swiped at his tear stained face with one arm while still holding the gun steady at his head, "It's not okay, fine or all right; I killed my partner and you just don't do that," his voice thin and reedy that of a child whose world had ended.

Owen closed in, "You didn't kill him, believe it David. It was a crazy disastrous mix of circumstances. You said yourself, even God couldn't have stopped it."

"You forgive me then?" Murphy's eyes were pools of misery even as a sad smile floated across his lips.

"Yes, but you need to forgive yourself."

Murphy backed up his heels colliding with the roofs edge. Alarmed, Owen reached for him, "I can't do that," he said and pulled the trigger.

The recoil jerked his head sideways as he went off the roof. Owens's fingers snagged between the two buttons on his uniform shirt as blood and brain matter blew over him. His feet left the ground as he was dragged into space by the momentum of Murphy's falling body. Dead, his mind screamed as his fingers still clutching the shirt were wrenched away and he was snatched, his coat torn almost off his back by strong hands, out of mid-air to fall into thick flesh on top of solid ground. He lay with breath knocked out staring up at the sky instead of down at gray concrete hurdling toward him.

"Christ, I'm alive," he breathed in wonder.

"And heavy as hell," Cush said. "Get off me."

They got to their feet and moved over to the roof's edge where they stared down at the sprawled body of Officer David Murphy surrounded by a crowd of his fellow officers.

"Thanks," Owen said to Cush before he closed his eyes to give thanks to God for his life and to pray that David found a better one.

"No problem," Cush answered easily, "That's what partners are for right?"

CHAPTER 40

EPILOGUE

By
Richard Giordano

Owen survived the roof as you know. Cush ended up bruising his back and was off on disability for two weeks; Owen visited regularly bringing along bottles of Dos Eques. He wasn't charged with any crime because the gun was checked out and the ballistics matched the one that killed Lorna and her companions.

The bodies of Mr. Bell and my men didn't end up in the hands of the police, they were never called; I was. Owen doesn't know this but I'm part owner of the Connors so I went over and took a look. It was like Owen said, that kid had shot those guys to pieces. I took along a couple of people and they cleaned it up pretty well; made the necessary disappear. If you rented that room today you'd never know bullets and blood had bombarded the place.

Owen sold his townhouse and moved in with Pop who spent time in the hospital because of his cancer instead of in a jail cell. I give the old guy total respect for what he did for Owen: you have to protect family no matter what it takes. So now they're living together; cautiously. I told Owen he should get them some girls and have some fun. He declined; the guy just doesn't know what's good for him though I suspect it was because of Lorna. Always Lorna.

He became a hero of sorts and was allowed to keep his badge though he was suspended without pay for two weeks because of his—justifiable in my opinion—altercations with our insane new mayor (you're not surprised) and that prick Gunderson.

I begged him to give the department nothing but the finger; its what they deserve after what they did to him. Wouldn't you? But Owen-being-Owen, he's going to remain a cop. 'To be the best damn cop I can be,' is what he said, 'it's in my blood.' That's when I finally shut-up because I know all about the blood; you can't escape it.

There you have it. I bet you can't wait until the next tale; we'll all be there; well, at least some of us.

THE END

Excerpt from
Begin at the End
The Second in the Owen Story Trilogy

CHAPTER 1

It was a beautiful New York City day for the Eighty-First Annual Macy's Day Thanksgiving Parade, an event that had become a tradition for people around the world. The temperature was a balmy thirty-five degrees, the sky a clear winter wash blue with a touch of sun. All along the route from Seventy-Seventh Street to Seventh Avenue people dressed in their winter warms laughed and shouted as they enjoyed the sheer camaraderie of watching a parade.

The crowd hadn't really come to see the B list celebrity entertainers, the spunky dance numbers, the high school marching bands or even the spectacular floats that sailed overhead, they'd come as strangers to stand together in the cold early morning light to catch a glimpse of the true star of the show; the man who's recognized as the ultimate ubiquitous symbol of commercial getting and giving, the one and only Santa Claus who's arrival would not only signify the end of this year's parade but the official beginning of the race to the finish line of the holiday shopping season.

Thousands watched the show on the street while millions watched it from their homes in front of their television sets or on their computer screens while they listened to the mildly interesting commentary tossed off by the NBC hosts Meredith Viera and Matt Lauer who, in their warm enclosed booth at

Herald Square were trying valiantly to ratchet up the excitement for the arrival of the main attraction.

"We've been so lucky the promised rain has held off," said Ms. Vieira who smiled with perfect teeth at the viewers. "An icy cold shower would've just ruined the parade."

"Yes, we've been lucky so far and luckier still because this is the largest crowd since ninety-seventy-five so there's hundreds of officers out there to keep everyone safe; a phenomenal effort," said Mr. Lauer who flashed his own set of capped pearly whites to the world. "But I predict no matter what happens no one would miss the arrival of the man himself."

"Folks, here he comes approaching Herald Square. Oh, my goodness doesn't he look wonderful," Ms. Vieira bounced in her seat. "He looks exactly like the jolly happy Santa I remember from my childhood."

"He's just stopped in front of the decorated windows of Macy's department store officially ending the parade folks," added Mr. Lauer. "The red nose, the red plush coat fronted by white fur—"

"I hope that's not real fur?" Ms. Vieira cut in her smile losing a couple of wattages as her eyes narrowed on Father Christmas.

"If it is, he's not going to be sliding down any PETA chimneys this year," answered her co-host with a plastic chuckle.

Television screens all over the world were presented with the real time image of a huge red Christmas sleigh filled with wrapped presents and seated among the bounty children of all ages waving at the crowd. High above them on a throne sat Santa Claus, with one hand he held on to white reigns attached to imaginary flying reindeer while he waved with the other. The crowd shouted and waved back as if he were the Second Coming.

He was dressed in the traditional Santa suit complete with jaunty red hat, wide black belt with large gold buckle and black knee-high boots but what hit home to all the viewers in television land as well as those gazing at him from the streets was that he did look like everyone's ideal fairy-tale image of Father Christmas, a white man with a long white beard, rosy cheeks, a round fleshiness to his stout body and wearing a smile of what looked like innocent joy.

He stood atop the magnificent sleigh handing down packages to eager hands. As he picked up a gold wrapped present and straightened, his grin suddenly broke and disappeared. The package dropped from his fingers as the fur lining the front of his coat went from cloud white to crimson red to match the rest of his suit. He fell back onto the throne, shocked surprise on his face as the huge shouting laughing crowd around him went silent.

"What was that?" Mr. Lauer's alarmed voice came over as the image of the slumped Santa was frozen to screens. "What happened? Anyone see what happened?"

"You see that?" Ms. Vieira's voice was heard loud and afraid.

Before the stunned world-wide audience Santa lay slumped until the top of the throne and his head disintegrated in blood and wood that sent him over the side of the sleigh.

"Gun," someone yelled.

Pandemonium in the streets.

CHAPTER 2

A braham 'Pop' Kaplan sat in his Kew Gardens Queen's home watching the Macy's Day Parade from his favorite chair as he tried to take off the top of a jar of nuts. He'd been off chemotherapy for a few weeks, Owen had talked him into getting it after it was found the tumor had grown; it couldn't kill the bastard but could possibly shrink it; all the good that'll do he thought. Owen thought it would help though, might produce a miracle so for his son-in-law's sake he took the treatments which left him weak but determined to do the things he used to without having to ask his son-in-law for help.

Owen did enough as it was: helping him bathe, shave, brush his teeth, get in and out of bed, up and down the stairs; way too much; so he would do this one damn thing himself, get the child proof cap off even if it killed him. And it might, he laughed out loud, something he hadn't felt like doing in a long time.

Twisting hard before his strength gave out he grinned as the vacuum seal gave an audible pop. He took off the top releasing one of his favorite smells of the season: nutty.

He heard a loud bang then curses, "You need any help in there?" he called toward the kitchen as he continued to sit and crush walnuts between his teeth, his eyes on Saint Nick tossing presents to the crowd. Owen appeared holding a raw twenty-pound turkey by one leg just as masticated nuts flew from Pop's mouth as his eyes widened at the television screen.

"Pop, how do you—what's wrong?"

Coughing, unable to speak, Pop jabbed a finger toward the screen.

"Jesus," Owen said the turkey hitting the floor with a meaty thud as the second shot took off the top of the man's head. "Somebody just killed Santa Claus."

Thank you dear readers for taking the time to read You Don't Know Me; I hope you enjoyed it and will look forward to the next in the Owen Story trilogy.

Best Wishes,

Lori A. Mathews